Lauren,

You live life with a lot of enthusiasm, humor and love, and you bring much pride and joy to those around you.

good luck!

your teacher
Dorit.

the gates of the forest

the gates of the b...

the gates of the forest

by Elie Wiesel
Translated from the French
by Frances Frenaye

Schocken Books · New York

For Bernard and Hilda Fishman

Published by arrangement with Henry Holt and Company

Library of Congress Cataloging in Publication Data
Wiesel, Elie, 1928–
The gates of the forest.
Translation of: Les portes de la forêt.
Reprint. Originally published: New York:
Holt, Rinehart, and Winston, 1966.
I. Title.
[PQ 2683.I32P613   1982]   843'.914   81-16547   AACR2

ISBN 0-8052-0896-8

Designed by Ernst Reichl

Manufactured in the United States of America

10   9   8   7   6   5   4   3   2   1

the gates of the forest

When the great Rabbi Israel
Baal Shem-Tov saw misfortune
threatening the Jews it was
his custom to go into a certain
part of the forest to meditate.
There he would light a fire,
say a special prayer, and the
miracle would be accomplished
and the misfortune averted.

Later, when his disciple, the
celebrated Magid of Mezritch,
had occasion, for the same
reason, to intercede with heaven,
he would go to the same
place in the forest and say:
"Master of the Universe, listen!
I do not know how to light the fire,
but I am still able to say the prayer."
And again the miracle would
be accomplished.

Still later, Rabbi Moshe-Leib
of Sasov, in order to save his
people once more, would go into
the forest and say: "I do not know
how to light the fire, I do not
know the prayer, but I know the
place and this must be sufficient."
It was sufficient and the
miracle was accomplished.

Then it fell to Rabbi Israel
of Rizhyn to overcome misfortune.
Sitting in his armchair, his head
in his hands, he spoke to God:
"I am unable to light the fire
and I do not know the prayer;
I cannot even find the place
in the forest. All I can do
is to tell the story, and
this must be sufficient."
And it was sufficient.

God made man because he loves stories.

spring

1

He had no name, so he gave him his own. As a loan, as a gift, what did it matter? In time of war every word is as good as the next. A man possesses only what he gives away.

Gregor loved and hated his laugh, which was like no other, which did not even resemble itself.

Imagine a life-and-death struggle between two angels, the angel of love and the angel of wrath, the angel of promise and the angel of evil. Imagine that they both attain their ends, each one victorious. Imagine the laugh that would rise above their corpses as if to say, your death has given me birth; I am the soul of your conflict, its fulfillment as well.

The laugh of the man who had saved his life.

It was a moonless night. It had rained the day before and, because they felt at ease there, the clouds refused to leave the patch of sky above the houses huddled together in the town below. Later Gregor understood why: they were not clouds, properly speaking, but Jews driven from their homes and transformed into clouds. In this disguise they were able to return to their homes where strangers now lived.

He was about to fall asleep when he heard an unfamiliar sound in the forest. He jumped from his cot and went to the opening of the cave. Tense, he listened. Was it the clouds? They were making no sound, at least not yet. Then what was it? His eyes, wide open, saw into the darkness. Solitude had taught him to use his senses, to let them guide him, to become an animal, ready to jump, ready to run. He stopped thinking, stopped remembering. He no longer lived outside his body.

Where had the sound come from? Now it was gone. A mistake, a false alarm. Back to sleep. A damp wind was whistling among the trees. Nothing more? Nothing more.

Nevertheless he remained on the alert. He loved the night, his ally. He loved the clouds which weighed upon the night. In any case he could no longer fall asleep. He cursed the wind for blowing too loudly. War had taught him to curse.

And so he waited, listening for the slightest murmur of the woods, where behind every tree he could sense a presence in the night.

As a child he had been afraid of the forest, even in daytime. He had been told that it was inhabited by savage wolves that took your life; by bloody creatures that robbed you of your pride; by evil beings sent down to earth to turn men from their way, blinding their vision and draining their passion for life.

Now that he was no longer a child, the forest gave Gregor a sense of security. When he stroked the bark of the pine trees he felt close to the earth; when he listened to the rustling leaves he understood that man's secret outlives man. He had learned that the true forest is the one that drives wolves mad and makes men thirst for blood and compassion. There was no use running away from this forest, it is everywhere, separating man from the image of his destiny and from the death of this destiny. Who opened your eyes, Gregor? *He* did. Did it hurt? Yes and no.

Gregor started. Footsteps! He heard them quite clearly. I wasn't dreaming. Someone is there. Someone is looking for me. He glanced at the luminous dial of his watch: ten past two. He knew the time even though he didn't know what day it was. It could have been Friday or Sunday; what did it matter? He was living in a time of war, outside time.

How long had he been in the cave? He did not remember.

4

His father had promised to come back in three days. Gregor had counted three days, and then three more days. After that he had stopped counting. His father had gone away and taken the numbers with him, forever.

The footsteps were drawing closer; the crackling sound was clearer. Gregor's eyes searched the darkness and found nothing. Only anguish. He tried to chase it away, to beguile it, saying over and over to himself: You're not afraid, no, you are not afraid; a boy, seventeen years old, isn't afraid of night or of the unknown. If you are shivering—just a little—it's because of the cold; if you are stiff, it's because you have no reason to move; if you are holding your breath, it's not for fear of breathing too hard but rather to hear the mysterious sound of night penetrating the forest: two creatures embracing. Sometimes they hurt each other and the earth gives forth a very gentle moan; sometimes they caress, and their song shakes the trees. That is why you are holding your breath, to listen, and also to seize their song and surrender yourself to it. You're not afraid, are you? Gregor isn't afraid of anything, not yet. Gregor is old enough to recognize the exact moment when fear rises, whip in hand, and beats his heart as if to force him to live and to accept himself. Yes, Gregor is also old enough to bar the way, isn't he? I'm not afraid; I hate fear; it's degrading. Gregor talked to himself and trembled. Nights are cold in Transylvania, in the spring.

The footsteps now seemed very close. Since sounds in the forest are deceiving, Gregor did not know where to place them. Could it be father? No, impossible. Father would not come back. Never. He was punctuality itself, incapable of making a mistake or of telling a lie. If he had not come, it was because he had changed; he must be in a world where numbers kill, where promises enclose emptiness.

In the past Gregor had thought his father was all-powerful and unshakeable, clear-headed in a way that both comforted and terrified those who loved him, those who feared him. They all clung to him, to his words, to his vision. In his presence they felt pure, strong, and invincible. He spoke little, but what he said had the ring and conviction of truth. He used to say, "Tomorrow will be a fine day," and the sun obeyed him. He used to say, "Whoever walks toward the spring becomes the spring," and so they walked. But then he had also said, "I'll be back in three days," and he is somewhere else.

Gregor remembered his father's last words: under no circumstances open your mouth or otherwise betray your whereabouts. But the waiting and uncertainty were more than he could bear, and he was tempted to disobey: I am going to scream. You didn't keep your promise: why should I keep mine? Time once more existed.

"Who's there?" he said in Hungarian.

His voice echoed first in the cave and then in the forest, leaping from tree to tree, from cloud to cloud. And yet he had only whispered.

"Who's there?" he repeated.

Silence. Nothing. Night, clouds, the forest. And his pounding heart. Crouching behind the big tree which concealed the opening of the cave, Gregor held his breath. He did not move, nor did the other. They couldn't see each other. Is he also afraid? Is it his fear that makes me tremble and doubt?

The other started walking.

"Stop!" called out Gregor in panic. "Stop there! Don't come closer! I forbid you to take another step."

The other continued to come closer, but Gregor still could not figure out where he was. At times it seemed to him as if the forest were filled with nocturnal hunters, each one of them like the Angel of Death, with a thousand eyes to strangle man's voice and to deform his body. This is my punishment, Gregor thought. I disobeyed my father; I am going to be punished. Words now surged up from his throat, and he could not control them.

"Who are you? What do you want? Who sent you here? Whom are you looking for? Where are you going? Who's calling you and who's with you?"

Carelessly, he stuck his head out of the cave. A thousand thoughts crossed his mind. Was it a policeman making his rounds? A peasant, who would blackmail him? A wanderer? A shepherd out at night? The unknown terrified him. As soon as danger will be there before him, identified, with a face on it, he would lose his fear and recover his freedom. That's why he cried out again angrily, in German this time: "Enough! If it's me you're looking for, come! I'm here, I am waiting for you."

Then for the first time he heard the laughter. Gregor shuddered and his legs became weak. Behind every tree and within every shred of cloud someone was laughing. It was not the laughter of one man but of a hundred, of seven times seven hundreds.

He wanted to stop up his ears: the man wanted to drive him to insanity.

"Stop! Stop laughing!" he shouted, still in German. "I'm alone and the war is still raging. It will go on and on, and I shall be more and more alone. Be quiet, will you? Listen to the war and you won't laugh any longer!"

There was a lengthy silence. Suddenly the clouds seemed thicker—undoubtedly a transport of Jews coming back from far away to light the fires in their homes.

"I'm listening to the war and I'm laughing."

Gregor couldn't believe his ears. The voice, which was now very close, had spoken Yiddish. Not Hungarian or German, but Yiddish.

"I've decided once and for all not to weep," the voice added. "To weep is to play their game. I won't."

Now it was Gregor's turn to feel like laughing. Why hadn't he thought of it? It was all so simple. A Jew! A Jew like himself, fleeing from fate; in search of underground shelter, a place in which to hide himself from the piercing stare of death. A Jew who refused to disguise himself as a cloud!

"What about you?" the other was asking. "Do you like to cry?"

And he laughed again. Gregor paused for a moment before coming out of the cave, not in order to see the stranger but rather to show himself and lead the other toward him. He did not answer the last question, but said in a slightly trembling voice, "Whoever you are, wherever you come from, come here. I have a safe hiding place with room enough for both of us."

Then, realizing that he had spoken German, he quickly added, "Don't be afraid, I'm a friend."

"A friend?"

"Yes, a friend," said Gregor, in Yiddish.

Gregor was standing in the open, a few steps from the tree. Suddenly he turned. The other was there, behind him, his shadow covered the forest.

"So you're a Jew also?" the stranger said.

"Yes. You knew?"

"No, I didn't,"

"Why did you laugh then?"

"Because I didn't know, that's why. I thought I was the only one left, the last survivor. That gave me a right to laugh, didn't it?"

He was taller than Gregor and slightly stooped, as if he were carrying a weight upon his shoulders or trying not to touch the clouds.

"Come," said Gregor. "Let's go in. It's not wise to stay out here."

He took the other's arm and led him into the cave, to the corner where he had put up the cot. They sat down, side by side.

"We can't light anything," said Gregor, to start a conversation. "They'd see it from down below."

"All right."

"But that doesn't prevent you from smoking."

"I don't smoke."

"I do."

"Go ahead, then."

"You're sure it won't bother you?"

"Quite sure."

At home Gregor never smoked; his father didn't allow it. But having found some cigarettes in the knapsack, along with the food, he had begun to smoke, especially at night, concealing the flare of the match in the palm of his hand.

"How old are you?"

Gregor told him.

"You're very young. How long have you been in hiding?"

"I don't really know. Days. Weeks. I've forgotten how to count."

"And before? Did you know how to count, before?"

"I'm not sure."

"I see."

"Sometimes I watch the sun rise and set, but it no longer marks the passage of time. If the sun were to stop, it wouldn't surprise me. It has become a stranger to the earth—it warms out of habit or out of boredom. People don't interest it any longer."

"You talk as if the sun were a wise god, but the gods have chosen madness."

There was a trace of irony in his voice. It seemed to affirm and deny the conclusion: everything is true and everything is a lie; men love and kill one another; God bids them pray and yet their prayers change nothing.

"Where do you come from?" Gregor asked.

"Over there."

"Where exactly is 'over there'?"

" 'Over there,' I tell you. Everywhere. On the other side."

Gregor did not insist. He did not want to upset him. To each his zone of silence. He changed the subject.

"What's your name?"

"I haven't any."

Gregor couldn't help showing surprise. "Everybody has a name."

"True. But I've lost mine."

He laughed, without malice, and went on. "My name left me. You might say that it's dead. It went away one day, without reason, without excuse. It forgot to take me along. That's why I have no name. Of course, I looked for it, but without success. Do you understand?"

"No," said Gregor. He had understood the words but not their meaning. They had a sad and beautiful sound, but they didn't make sense, really.

"You *don't* understand?" said the visitor, half angry, half joking. "You don't see how such a thing can happen? And to anyone? In time of war millions of men live under false names; there is a divorce between man and his name. Sometimes the name has had enough and goes away. Is that so hard to imagine?"

"Yes it is," said Gregor, overcome by a vague uneasiness.

"Then let me explain. Names played an important part in

creation, didn't they? It was by naming things that God made them. True?"

"True," murmured Gregor.

"You admit, then, that a name has a fate of its own, independent of the life and fate of its bearer. Sometimes a name ages, falls ill, and dies much before the man who bears it. Well, my name deserted me. Now do you understand?"

He's making fun of me, Gregor thought with irritation. He talks so that I won't understand him and laughs so that I'll doubt his sanity and my own.

"All right, you've lost your name, is that it?" Gregor exclaimed indignantly. "But before you lost it . . . what was it then?"

"You want to know too much," said the stranger gently. "My name was written and pronounced in different ways. It had an uninhibited imagination and when it took flight nothing could stop it. Men and things weren't enough. It rose above them. It was free. It still is, but I'm not."

A mysterious weight fell upon Gregor. I'm dreaming, he said to himself. Or else he's mad. That voice of his; it must come from another world. The things he's been through must have affected his mind and disconnected him from all reality —past, present, future. What was he to do? What was the right approach? How could he be reassured? Suddenly Gregor felt sad. He thought, some day I'll be like him, surrounded by sadness, some day I'll be someone else.

"Are you hungry?" he asked.

The nameless man was not hungry.

"Thirsty? I can make you some coffee."

He was not thirsty, and coffee did not tempt him.

"Tired, then? Do you want to lie down? To sleep?"

"No."

"Do you feel like talking?"

"Talking? Why? For whom? What for? I have nothing to say."

He lay down on his back and retreated into a meditation from which Gregor was excluded. He set up another cot, stretched out, and pretended to sleep. How could he understand someone whose door is open to delirium, to denial?

Someone who pushed him away, who made fun of him? Much as I admired my father, I didn't understand him either. But that was different. He did everything he could to explain, to make sure that, in the future at least, I would come to understand him. As for my mother, I understood her even at an age when I couldn't recognize my own image in a mirror. Soon the war will be over; will I still be able to understand someone whose life is different from my own?

With his eyes open and his senses aching from awareness, Gregor saw himself in the future—telling a friend, or perhaps his children, of this strange meeting with a man whom he didn't know and would probably never know. I saved the life of a madman who had lost contact with his land and his name. At this thought Gregor couldn't help laughing. What is a madman? Someone who has lost his name. Grandfather, with his beard whiter and his eyes more gleaming than ever, was there listening to him as well; although the old man had died ten years ago, his presence didn't surprise him. In the boy's mind his grandfather was still alive, as was his joy. The night before, in a dream, his grandfather had said angrily, "You're letting yourself go, and I don't like it. You must fight against sadness; it weakens you and paves the way for death. You'll be lost unless you overcome it." His grandfather had been a *hasid* and an enthusiastic follower of the Rebbe of Wizsnitz, for whom song was an instrument of battle. One day the old man had taken his grandson aside and talked to him in a way that was to influence his future: "Later on, when I'm no longer of this world, I want you to remember me and the flame which makes me live. I am a farmer, and so I know the usefulness of a gentle rain that causes wheat and the other fruits of the earth to grow. But the human soul isn't like the earth; the soul needs storm and fire and dizziness. The body has time; it moves slowly and prudently, step by step, in obedience to laws of gravity, but the soul brushes time and laws aside; it wants to push forward, regardless of the cost in pain, or intoxication or even madness. That is the only way it has of raising itself to God. On your way through life you'll meet men who cling to reason, but reason gropes like a blind man with a white cane, stumbling over every pebble, and when it comes up against a wall it stops short and tries to tear it down brick by brick, quite ineffectually, because an invisible hand builds it up again, higher and thicker than ever. We, on the other hand, believe in the power of faith and ecstasy, and no wall can stand against us; with our fists and our songs we bring it crashing down. Gates do not frighten us. Because, my child, listen to this: other people open their eyes wide to see God, but we close them. Yet these others attract darkness while we laugh at it, until it follows rather than precedes us." His grandfather's face lit up and he stroked his beard. "Do you understand?" he went on. "The gleam in the eye of a *Zaddik* is a surer guide than all the science and theories invented by men who have become victims and creators of their own pride."

His grandfather, who had died ten years ago, listened to his story and said nothing. You were right, grandfather. During the war I met a madman who had lost all ties to man and to the meaning of words. You would have liked him, I know it. His grandfather smiled and asked, "Are you so sure he was mad? Perhaps he was a messenger looking for a message, and for that reason he had neither home nor name; he was one of those dreamers, who wander on mountainsides or roads the world over, who have chosen exile in order to detach themselves from time and to exorcise it. Are you sure, my child, that he was mad?"

The stranger was breathing lightly and Gregor thought that he had fallen asleep. In spite of the danger he very nearly struck a match in order to see him, if only for a second, to take in the shape of his face and its features. It may be that we look alike and that the sight of him will frighten me. Something in Gregor already knew that he would meet him again at important moments in his life. He was going to get up quietly, but the stranger wasn't sleeping.

"What's your name?" the stranger asked him.

He hesitated for a moment before replying:

"Gregor. My names's Gregor."

He was lying, and the stranger knew it.

"That's not a Jewish name."

"But I *am* a Jew."

"Your name isn't that of a Jew. You must have another name that is closer to you."

"True. But it's under cover, and that's where it must stay. Your name left you and mine has gone into hiding, like myself. On that score we're even, you and I."

"Are you afraid of me?"

"No, I'm not afraid."

"Are you angry?"

"I don't know what it is to be angry."

"You'll find out."

"Perhaps. I'm not afraid of anger."

They were silent, and Gregor wondered if the other's eyes were open.

"Tell me your name," the visitor said.

"No, I must not. As long as the war lasts I must not say it aloud."

"I can keep silent. That's what I can do best. I can keep my mouth shut, even under torture. Or open my mouth and say nothing. Tell me your name; I'll keep it to myself." He broke off, half smiling, half serious. "You think I'm mad, don't you?" And without waiting for an answer he went on. "I know. I understand your silence. You think I've lost my mind. Suppose it's true; that's all the more reason for telling me your name. I won't give it away. In times like these madmen are our only friends. They don't kill us in the name of beliefs or ideas. They're on our side and they get themselves killed."

Gregor was overcome by emotion. It was as if he had heard this voice before, and what it was saying. In another life, perhaps. This isn't our first meeting, he said to himself. He knows my name, he is questioning me to test me.

"My name is that of an angel," he murmured. "The angel Gavriel."

The stranger gave a sad little laugh.

"Do you know what that means? 'Man of God.' An odd name, isn't it? It teaches us that what we call angels are only men. There are no real angels. And men? Oh, there are men, all right, unfortunately for the angels and for ourselves. And what is worse is that they are real."

Suddenly he fell silent; winner or loser, Gregor didn't know. He could still see his grandfather's lips moving as they said, "Don't be afraid, my child. Madmen are just wandering messengers, and without them the world couldn't endure. Without them there would be no surprise; they surprise even the Creator because they escape from Him and regard Him with pity. Their mission on earth? To persuade us that we don't know how to count, that numbers deceive and trap us. Are you listening?" And heavy-heartedly Gregor answered, "Yes, Grandfather, I'm listening. I think I've lived only for this encounter and for this night." He could hardly hear him whispering, "That, my child, is true of all encounters, of every night."

"Tell me, do you know how to count?" Gregor asked the stranger in anguish.

The other did not answer right away. Finally he said, with a sigh, "Yes, I know how to count. Unfortunately for men; and for angels."

The morning wind slipped into the cave and began to whip the shadows.

2

Dawn was about to break, in a transparent gray. Although he was shivering with cold, Gregor did not dare to get up and fetch a blanket. He was afraid of being knocked down by the wind. He waited. Something was going to happen; he could feel it. The events of the night were just the prelude to some new development whose sequel was lost in the clouds. The silence became crushingly heavy. Gregor cleared his throat and said as casually as possible, "Listen, I have an idea. I don't need my name any more. I'm giving it to you; it's yours. Take it, Gavriel."

The stranger did not find it necessary to thank him and Gregor was pleased with that.

"You like to give, don't you?" asked the stranger.

"Yes," Gregor admitted. "It is easier."

"Not at all. Nothing is more difficult." And he added, as if speaking to himself. "Among Orientals giving is a privilege which has to be earned."

By now it was already light outside and the horizon was preparing to welcome the sun, which was late in rising. The mountain and the forest breathed easily, as if a weight had been lifted from them. Gavriel began to talk, in a voice edged with warmth and melancholy. Gregor, to listen, closed his eyes.

"A dying man takes his soul with him but leaves his name to the survivors. The Germans don't know to what extent they are branded by their supidity: they kill off Jews but they can't find a way of erasing their names. The Talmud teaches us that deliverance will come because Israel has not changed its name. It is not by chance that God is known as the Everlasting; every name has something immortal and eternal about it which defies time. Day follows night and night follows day, men are born and die, but the most fragile things—for what is frailer than a name?—endures. As I walk through this world I find empty cities—empty of Jews, of Jewish tears and hopes and prayers—inhabited by names, by names only. And every orphaned name begs me to adopt it."

I'm lucky, Gregor said to himself. His name was that of his father's father, who had died in the First World War. Jewish tradition requires that a dead man's name be perpetuated, so that the chain may be unbroken. I'm not dead, but I've given someone my name. One is never as lucky as in wartime.

"I've just come from the town at the foot of this mountain," Gavriel was saying. "It's crowded with ghosts, and I certainly know ghosts well. There's no ghetto any more. There was one, I remember, because I know ghettos well, too. Everywhere there are names without bodies, nowhere Jews. The last shipment left a week ago. Big posters—in German and Hungarian (I know German too)—are stuck up on the walls, announcing the good news, that since April twenty-fifth, by the grace of God, the town is at last *Judenrein*: rid of the Jewish poison, of the Jewish plague, of the Jewish vermin. From now on, in an atmosphere as hygienic as that of a hospital, the people can live in brotherly love and happiness and enjoy together the fruits of victory. At least that's what the posters say. It's enough to kill one Jew for things to improve, as if you could eliminate hatred by eliminating the object of hatred. But the good people of the town are fooling themselves. They forgot to deport the *names* of their Jewish neighbors whose homes and furniture and bedclothes they have inherited. The names are still hovering, like memories, overhead, and they will return to haunt their dreams and add blood to their wine. One day, I promise you, these peaceful citizens, these model husbands and fathers, these Christian believers in Christian charity, which is different from charity as such, will be afraid to go to sleep at night."

"Or rather to wake up in the morning," Gregor put in timidly. He would have liked to interrupt him; he was afraid of what would follow. Gavriel's incantation, soothing to the ear, was still terrifying, for it prepared what was to come; and Gregor did not know whether he could endure it without tears.

"Afraid to wake up, did you say? No. The names wait for sleep before going to work. That's their private domain. They invade the brain, the blood, desire: impossible to get rid of them. Finally he calls for death, because death has no name."

Gregor felt himself growing pale. He listened and didn't listen, he was there and far away. A great weight bore down upon him and at the same time he seemed to be float-ing in the air. There was a choking sensation in his throat, his heart pounded. Now he understood the message. His father was not coming back. No one was coming back. His family has gone, leaving no trace, gone with no hope of return.

Gavriel talked on. What he said came from another time, another world. His voice was never the same. Its accent did not change, but its essence was constantly changing. Just as Gavriel had a thousand names, he had a thousand voices. One contained the plenitude of transparent dawn, another the insensate hope of a man condemned to die, another the fearful silences of a child abandoned in the middle of a crowded street.

Gavriel could not be sure whether or not Gregor was listen-ing. He made no sound nor did he move and his breathing was almost inaudible.

Was it Gavriel's intention to teach a lesson, inflict a punishment, convey a recollection, a sorrow? Transmit a message, make some dangerous and terrible confession? De-scribe a long march leading nowhere? It was impossible for

17

Gregor to know. Gavriel spoke in a light, almost detached tone of voice; he told a grotesque, farcical story, a legend to be listened to, a glass in hand, with a light heart. He laughed at it, with neither joy nor cruelty, with the laugh of a man who has known total fear and is no longer afraid of anyone or anything:

A famous medieval cabalist, Joseph di-la-Reina, made up his mind to put an end to the comedy which man is condemned to play against himself and to bring about the advent of the Messiah. At the cost of considerable sacrifice the great sage overcame Satan and threw him into chains. Everywhere —in heaven and upon earth in paradise and in Hell—there was a great commotion: the end was at hand. But the sage made one mistake: he took pity on his captive and succumbed to his tears. Pity is a double-edged weapon, and Satan knows how to use it. He broke his chains, and the Messiah, already on the threshold, was forced to return to his prison, somewhere infinitely far away, in the chaos of time and man's hope. Everything had to start all over, because the poor miracle-maker had a heart which wasn't hard enough.

Gavriel roared with laughter. Gregor surrendered to the anguish which he had felt ever since the first words of the story. He had heard it before, but he couldn't understand why Gavriel had chosen to retell it and to laugh in the retelling. What was so funny about the idea of justice giving birth to its own defeat? Gregor did not dare to question him further or to penetrate this closed world in which things and events must have a secret meaning, a secret bond, impossible to understand, a warped meaning, a warped bond. Gavriel was still laughing, and in order to stop him Gregor said that he liked the story.

"You like it?" said Gavriel angrily. "Is that all you have to say? That you like it?"

"It's a beautiful story," Gregor replied. "Sad and beautiful. I like it."

"And what about the end? What do you say to that?"

"I like that too." He took a deep breath and added: "I

wouldn't have the coming of the Messiah depend upon our lack of generosity and pity, even toward Satan. I don't want salvation to come through fire, through cruelty, and through the sacrifices of others."

The cave was filled with an obsessive sadness, like that which follows upon the departure of an unhappy friend who cannot find consolation. I have hurt and disappointed him, Gregor said to himself, and he thought of his parents and grandfather, particularly his grandfather, who was the embodiment of longing for the Messiah. His mother had told him that when his grandfather was a very young man he had used his first money to buy a beautiful, expensive suit which he never wore. "I'm saving it," he said, with a strange look in his eyes. "I'm saving it for the day when I shake his hand." He raved when he spoke of the Messiah. But he was not a madman.

Gavriel pulled him out of his reverie.

"What are you thinking about?"

"My grandfather."

"Why him?"

"Because he's dead."

"Are you quite sure?"

"Yes."

"And what about the other members of your family? Don't you ever think of them?"

"Very seldom."

"Because they're alive?"

"Exactly."

"Are you sure they're still alive?"

Gregor hesitated before replying:

"Yes. . . . No. . . ."

His heart pounded dully, as on the night when his mother was deathly ill and he had wept and prayed for hours on end until finally he fell asleep, out of sheer exhaustion. When he awakened he ran to the sickbed, his heart filled with fear. Mother is dead. Mother is dead, and it's my fault. I should never have stopped praying. His mother opened her eyes and smiled wanly; he buried his face in his hands and backed slowly out of the room. On the days that followed he came repeatedly to see his mother, his mother's smile, then his heart was finally calmed.

Gavriel's voice became gentle and melancholy. "When I came last night to this town I had no idea that I would meet you. If our paths have crossed, it must be that our meeting conceals some meaning. Let's discover it and study it. If we find nothing, and our meeting seems to have no significance, then we must impose one upon it. Don't you agree?"

"Yes," sighed Gregor.

"Then tell me, do you value your life?"

"Yes, I think I do."

"You only think so? You're not sure?"

"I'm not sure of anything."

Gavriel's voice became harsh. "I want you to value your life. I demand that to win this war. I want you strong and victorious."

Without waiting for an answer Gavriel changed the subject and started to tell him of the roundabout ways in which death had spared him. Contrary to the common idea, death has a sense of humor; it kills for pleasure, to amuse itself, to laugh.

Sometimes Gavriel was so choked with laughter that he had to interrupt himself. His laughter echoed through the cave and mingled with the early morning wind as it blew toward the forest and the mountain, toward all forests and all mountains, as if to shake and uproot them. Gregor told himself that he ought to laugh too, if only out of politeness. But to echo Gavriel would have seemed sacrilegious to him. Madmen won't stand for imitation. To them the outside world is not a mirror or a soundbox. They believe themselves alone in the world, as though they were holding that world in the hollow of their hand and they are right. They live vertically. To drown, one drop of water is enough.

"Are you listening?" Gavriel asked.

"Yes, I'm listening."

"You won't forget?"

"No, I won't forget."

"You won't forget the calls to prayer and the prayers of my

companions when they were face to face with their impassive executioner?"

"I won't forget."

"They looked him straight in the eye, you know, without flinching. They might have thrown themselves at his feet and tried to win his pity. That is what others would have done, but not they. A pride that came down to them from an earlier age prevented them from bowing down even before God, who was there behind the executioner."

"I know, Gavriel, I know."

"And the fragile and heart-rending silence of the children at the hour of their death, you'll remember that?"

"I'll make it mine."

"And that *Zaddik* who sang as he walked to the ditch where the corpses of his townsmen were piled up, will you remember him?"

"I'll remember him always. His song will be my guide; I'll follow it and shall never let it die."

Gavriel's feverish voice was silent. He panted like a man choking to death, then managed to catch his breath and go on: "You mustn't forget laughter either. Do you know what laughter is? I'll tell you. It's God's mistake. When God made man in order to bend him to his wishes he carelessly gave him the gift of laughter. Little did he know that later that earthworm would use it as a weapon of vengeance. When he found out, there was nothing he could do; it was too late to take back the gift. And yet he tried his best. He drove man out of paradise, invented an infinite variety of sins and punishments, and made him conscious of his own nothingness, all in order to prevent him from laughing. But, as I say, it was too late. God made a mistake before man made his. What they have in common is that they are both irreparable."

And as if to illustrate his words he laughed with such passion that Gregor, in order not to scream, refused to hear.

3

In the morning Gregor saw him and was surprised. He had thought of him as older and harder. Barely thirty years old; a sharply defined handsome, tormented face, a pointed chin and a melancholy smile. His eyes, two firebrands, which sear the flesh and pierce the skin of being. They gaze upon you; you will never be the same.

The cave was bathed in a dim, warm light. It was beginning to grow hot. Gregor took off his shirt and advised Gavriel to do the same. Gavriel refused, and Gregor put his own shirt back on.

They spent the whole day talking. Gavriel asked him to talk about his father. Was he kind? Severe? A dreamer? Talkative? A good listener? Gregor found it difficult to reply. His father was all these things, but he was beginning to realize that he hardly knew him.

"Was he a believer?"

"I think so."

"You're not sure?"

"No, I'm no longer sure of anything."

With a look Gavriel invited him to continue, and Gregor could not refuse.

"My father didn't speak often of religion to me; that was my mother's domain. My father was more interested in men; he listened to madmen, beggars, and drunks without ever losing his temper, without denying them either time or money. He never went to the synagogue except when it was time to pray.

"One day a scandal shook the town. Shlomo, the son of a judge in the rabbinic court, rebelled against the law and the traditions of his ancestors: one Sabbath morning, on the square in front of the synagogue, he appeared with a cigarette in his mouth. His father waited for evening to come to sit down on the ground and tear his clothing, for the holiness of the seventh day prohibits mourning. "I no longer have a son," he said to those who came to console him. "I consider him dead."

The next day Gregor went for a walk with his father in their garden. For some time his father strode nervously along without opening his mouth. Then he stopped short and said to his son, "I want to talk to you."

"Yes, father."

"It's about Shlomo."

It was unexpected. Gregor was younger than Shlomo and knew him only by sight.

"Yes, father," he repeated.

"What do you think of him? Of his behavior?"

"Why do you want to know? Are you afraid he has influenced me? Don't worry. He's never spoken to me."

"I didn't ask what you think of yourself but what you think of him."

The boy hesitated for a moment, carefully choosing his words. "He's a renegade."

His father shook his head and showed obvious disappointment.

"I knew that was what you'd say. That's why I wanted to talk to you."

He resumed his walking and there was an expression of such deep humility on his face that Gregor was touched.

"You mustn't judge him, son. Above all when you're not even acquainted. That's like throwing stones at him from an ambush; you risk nothing, he everything. By speaking ill of him you're sure to please everybody. People will say, 'There's a good boy; he's protecting us; he's avenging us!' Too easy!''

Gregor enjoyed these walks, where his father spoke to him as man to man. He could have gone on walking like this to the end of the earth.

"Later on, son, you'll learn how to steer clear of such traps by yourself. Meanwhile you should know this: Never despise, never spit at a man who has broken with the faith of his fathers, who has broken the chain that centuries have forged. You never know where your spit may fall. On yourself perhaps. Not today, but tomorrow. It's man's duty to make a free choice and to push back walls. To a man who is freeing himself from God you owe particular respect, because more than others he is accomplishing his destiny."

Gregor did not argue. They went back into the house. Shlomo left town and, a short time after, the rabbinic judge died.

"Your father was a brave man," said Gavriel. "Braver than Shlomo."

"*Was* a brave man?" Gregor exclaimed. "You speak as if he were dead."

Gavriel stared at him, then slowly lowered his head. "Go on," he said. "As long as you go on he is still alive."

"One day my father fell ill," Gregor continued hoarsely. "We tiptoed into his room as if to avoid waking someone who was waiting for him at his bedside. The doctor came three times a day and several times at night. He whispered questions and my mother whispered the replies. As for me, I stayed away from school to watch over him. Once, at twilight, he opened his eyes and told me to sit on the edge of the bed. 'I want to talk to you,' he said. 'Yes?' 'Yes,' he said, 'about death.' I shuddered, and of course he saw. 'Does it frighten you?' he asked. 'Yes.' 'Whose death frightens you, mine or yours?' 'Yours, and mine too.' His expression grew tender, and I had a guilty thought. I was happy to see him stretched out peacefully, no longer severe. Tears came to my eyes. 'Listen, son,' he said, smiling, 'don't let death take you by surprise. In the second before it snatches you away, try to raise your head and question it. Your victory will outlive you.' ''

24

Gavriel was listening dreamily.

"I like that father of yours," he said.

"He terrified me. I could hardly open my mouth in his presence."

"I like him and he doesn't terrify me. Talk to me about him some more."

Evening came, and shadows again invaded the cave, elongating silently on the ceiling. Gregor looked for his own shadow but could not distinguish it.

"Never mind," Gavriel said, "don't be afraid."

"Afraid?"

"Where I come from they say that if your shadow leaves you, you're going to die within thirty days. Shadows are cowards; they refuse to follow the body into nothingness. That's why in our world there are more shadows than human beings."

"Does that mean that I'm going to die within thirty days?"

"I didn't say that. I said 'don't be afraid.' " And leaning lightly over his younger companion, he added, "I'll be your shadow; I'll protect you."

They were near the entrance to the cave, behind the heavy tree trunk that hid it from view. They looked down at the town, which, like a brothel, undulated among the heavy folds of its curtains and draperies.

Gregor's gaze pierced the forest and retraced the chain of his memories, which led him back to Maria, the old family servant. It was she who had planted in him the fear of the unknown. According to her, the world was full of demons, lying in wait to trip men up at every misstep or slip of the tongue. They were invisible; night is their kingdom, just as it is in a sinner's imagination. So you think you're alone, do you? Wrong; you're not. Solitude is a demon, one among hundreds. You are silent and around you everything is silent. . . . Wrong again! Silence, too, is a demon, stifling its mocking laughter. A man or a woman smiles warmly at you and you smile back. . . . Beware! They are demons, and their smile will bring about your downfall.

Maria was one of the family. They consulted her before reaching any decision: where to go for the holidays, what to have for dinner, what color to paint the bedroom. There was nothing she couldn't do, no trouble she couldn't remedy; she was never caught without an answer or a clever idea. Once a year, around Christmas, she went back to the remote village where she had left a father or a lover, or both, and came back with a bag full of hazelnuts. Even now, whenever Gregor ate a nut he thought of her: a small, plump body, and a sharp tongue which she used to conceal her tenderness. Everyone tried to stay on her good side for fear of provoking her anger.

When Gregor's family was forced to leave home and live in the ghetto, Maria returned to her native village for good. She was distressed, but reluctant to show it. "I'm glad to be leaving," she said; "the man I love is waiting for me, and I'd have left even if you weren't going away." Then, suddenly, she began to sob. She kissed Gregor on the forehead, and he forced a smile. "You were right, Maria," he said; "there are demons, after all, and they parade up and down the streets, visible to the eye. You were right and I was wrong." Maria cried and blew her nose. "Don't worry," she said; "the war won't last forever. We'll see each other again." Before going away she told him the name of her village and described in detail the shack where, in case of need, he would be able to find her. Later, when Gregor had to flee the cave, that is where he took refuge.

"I'll protect you," Gavriel repeated. "I'll be your shadow."

"Just be my friend."

"I'll be your friend. And the shadow will be your friend."

And he proceeded to tell Gregor about the death of a friend who had had his tongue torn out.

"He had the power, by the use of words, to dispel darkness. That's why they cut out his tongue."

"Who was he?"

"I told you. A friend."

"A shadow?"

"No. He was the opposite, he was the enemy of night. Don't ask me any more questions; I'll tell you all you need to know. Not more. He was a friend. And what is a friend? More than a father, more than a brother: a traveling companion, with him, you can conquer the impossible, even if you must lose it later. Friendship marks a life even more deeply than love. Love risks degenerating into obsession, friendship is never

26

anything but sharing. It is to a friend that you communicate the awakening of a desire, the birth of a vision or a terror, the anguish of seeing the sun disappear or of finding that order and justice are no more. That's what you can talk about with a friend. Is the soul immortal, and if so why are we afraid to die? If God exists, how can we lay claim to freedom, since He is its beginning and its end? What is death, when you come down to it? The closing of a parenthesis, and nothing more? And what about life? In the mouth of a philosopher, these questions may have a false ring, but asked during adolescence or friendship, they have the power to change being: a look burns and ordinary gestures tend to transcend themselves. What is a friend? Someone who for the first time makes you aware of your loneliness and his, and helps you to escape so you in turn can help him. Thanks to him you can hold your tongue without shame and talk freely without risk. That's it."

Gregor waited for him to go on, but Gavriel didn't finish his sentence.

"I envy you," Gregor said timidly.

"You envy me?"

"I envy you such a friend."

"How do you know I have one?"

"You said yourself that you had a friend whose tongue was torn out."

"It was afterwards that he became my friend!" Gavriel shouted angrily. "Afterwards, do you hear?"

Gregor had no more questions.

Gregor had never had a friend. He had lost track of the one boy who might have become one when he moved to another part of town. When they saw each other again, years later, it wasn't the same.

He must have been about eight, perhaps a little older.

A dark, narrow street on a day when the town was blanketed with snow. A lowering sky seemed to threaten the earth below. Gregor walked uncertainly toward school, hardly daring to raise his head or even to breathe, because he knew he was on enemy terrain. He was not misled by the apparent peace and quiet, because he knew that the Gang was lying in wait. They would leap on him from the recessed doorway on the corner, where all summer long there had been a gypsy sitting. To beat up a lone Jewish child, to rub his nose in the mud, that was the Gang's idea of amusement. It had gone on for centuries, so that it was more than habit: it had become a tradition, a law. Without this game there would be no organized life. It had to be played for the good of the community; every generation gave birth to a Gang, and every Gang knew how to stalk its prey. Years before, the dead body of a Jewish child had been found in the gutter. The Gang had clubbed him to death and left him in the gutter.

Gregor knew that they were there, that they had gotten up early in the morning in his honor. But he went on, a lamp in his hand to light up his path through the snow. The cold bit his cheeks and brought tears to his eyes; his legs were unsteady and there was fear in his throat. Perhaps he should return to the house and get his father to take him to school. Usually Maria was the one to take him there and bring him back, but she was ill that morning and had stayed in bed. His mother was still asleep, and his father was busy, and he had decided to set forth alone rather than disturb them. Surely he was big enough to face the darkness alone. But now he regretted his decision. It would be wiser to turn back, to knock at his father's door and admit that he was afraid. His father knew all about the Gang; he knew that the leader was Pishta, the son and grandson of notorious Jew-baiters who had passed the Gang leadership on to him. His father would understand, all right, but there remained the fact that he didn't approve of weakness and cowardice.

Gregor continued on his way, but suddenly he stopped almost dropping his lantern, caught by surprise. Someone had called out his name. "Hey, it's you?" asked the voice. "Yes," he whispered back, wondering who it could be. A door opened, and a lantern appeared. "My name is Leib. My father's a coachman. My friends call me Leib the Lion. I know who you are; we're neighbors. I'm also going to *heder*. Come, let's walk together."

He was in a hurry to start out, but Gregor tugged at his sleeve and whispered warningly, "The Gang!"

"I know," said Leib calmly.

"Aren't you afraid?"

"Yes, but it doesn't matter."

They took several steps together, the crunching of the snow filled Gregor with terror. Under their load of snow and ice the houses were silently threatening, like snatchers of children. "Yes, I'm afraid, but it doesn't matter," repeated Leib the Lion. He was the older and taller and the stronger of the two, and even his lantern seemed to be bigger and heavier. He squeezed Gregor's arm and said encouragingly, "Come on; you're not alone." The flames of the lanterns wavered, and Gregor bit his lip in fearful expectation.

There was the door, encircled by shadows. It seemed as if the century-old gypsy was still crouching there, motionless, like a block of darkness. Leib was silent, tense.

Suddenly the earth trembled: it was the attack. The Gang, with Pishta at its head, fell upon the two boys, shouting savagely, "*Büdos zsido, büdos zsido!* Dirty Jews, dirty Jews, go to Palestine! You killed Christ. You'll see what it costs to kill Christ; you're going to pay for his blood." Set phrases picked up at home, in school, at church, in the street, the shouts echoed from house to house and multiplied in number and volume. It seemed as if windows were thrown open and hundreds of heads, distorted by hate, joined the shouting: "*Büdos zsido, büdos zsido!*" Gregor had an urge to run, in any direction, to break through the circle that was closing in around him. But he looked at Leib, who had not lost his calm, his self-assurance, and held his ground. Gregor dropped his lantern, however, and held his hands up, protectively, to his face. Leib's stance was different. He stood still, like a rock, with his legs spread apart, his teeth clenched, and his eyes only half opened, waiting for the attack. Gregor admired him: he seemed to have grown until his head brushed the clouds. Leib remained motionless and straight. When the enemies were within reach, unexpectedly and deliberately he raised his lantern and swung it in circles around his head, bringing it down upon them, without saying a word. He was a fortress surrounded by a wall of fire. For a few seconds Gregor stared at him with stupefaction, unable to believe his eyes. This can't be Leib, the coach-

man's son, he said to himself; it's a hero from another age—
Yehuda Hamakabi or Bar-Kochba, come to chastise the enemies of Israel. But Leib shook him out of his dream. "Look
out for that bastard on your left! Pick up your lantern and
strike; go ahead, I tell you, do what I do!" His voice was
steady and empty of fear. "Hurry," said Judah, the Maccabee.
Pick up your weapon and do what I do!" Gregor obeyed; the
dream pleased him. He bent over, picked up the lantern, and
began to swing it, hesitantly at first, then more rhythmically.
The weapon proved to be effective when it came into contact
with a body and a cry of pain pierced the cold early-morning
air. Gregor felt proud and strong and free; he wanted to dance
and sing with joy. Now he, too, belonged to the kingdom of
legend.

The fight lasted a good quarter of an hour. Pishta ordered a
retreat, and the Gang, many of them bleeding, fell back. The
sun rose over the town and the street returned to its wintry
calm. Gregor and Leib laid down their arms and relaxed. Leib
still looked serious, but Gregor was eager to talk and to com-
pare experiences. Leib looked at him and said, "You're
wounded." "So are you." They took off their fur gloves and
washed their faces with snow. Gregor had never been so
happy.

After that Gregor persuaded Maria to stay home, and he
and Leib walked to school together. The Gang did not
appear again and Gregor was secretly disappointed.

"They cut out his tongue, and he became my friend,"
Gavriel said loudly. "Do you hear me? Every man who has his
tongue cut out becomes a friend of mine."

"Yes, I hear," said Gregor, looking the other way. The idea
that Gavriel was suffering in his presence, as if to underline
his incompetence and lack of fidelity, was unbearable.

Later in the evening Gavriel told another story. He folded
his arms over his chest and spoke in a low voice, barely moving
his lips. Gregor felt close to him, to what he had to say, but
not yet to his suffering.

"The Talmud tells us," said Gavriel, "that the Messiah sits,
waiting to be called, at the gates of Rome, amid beggars and

cripples and other outcasts. The *Kaballah,* on the other hand, says that he conceals himself far from men and near to God, in the most holy and inaccessible of sanctuaries, and from there he sees time unfold—time filled with pity and distress—and beyond time, eternity."

Gregor was sensitive to every tremor of the night. The war's never going to end, he thought to himself. Too bad, for this is where it would meet its defeat.

"For years," Gavriel went on, "I would cry and pray God to renew joy in the heart of Israel and to rebuild the Temple, His dwelling. I spurred my vision to traveling faster and farther into space, seeking to pierce the veil that conceals the future and to penetrate its most profound secrets. I wanted to discover the sanctuary of the Messiah, to grip him by the shoulders and bring him forcibly to earth. One night I stood before the prophet Elijah and demanded his help. Elijah is the prophet of harshness and wrath. When he was alive no one dared approach him for fear of being scarred. Even kings, especially kings, masters sated with power and glory, trembled before him. When it was time for him to die, the Angel of Death drew back and declared himself unable to take him. That is why he is the only one of the elect that rose, alive, to heaven. God sent His chariot of fire to fetch him, and Elijah has never returned it; he needs it for his wanderings. The prophet of the thundering word has become prophet of consolation. He made an agreement with God on Mount Carmel, saying, 'I shall go against my feelings and be angry with your people, who are even more mine than yours, but on one condition only: You will let me return among your unhappy children in a different role, to warm the dwellings of the poor and to lighten their burdens by foretelling their end. Needing Elijah's services, God accepted this condition. And because He likes those who stand up to Him, He gave to Elijah an important mission. 'You shall be the only one to know the hour when the Messiah will go down to earth to mend My creation, to make a link between Myself and man, between the voice and its echo, between the voice and its source. You shall be the announcer.' It is for this reason, too—in order to be ready to appear on the horizon—that Elijah has kept the chariot of fire. And this is why it is to him that I presented the urgency of the situation and the dangers threatening our people. Madmen—unconscious and conscious—I told him, are preparing to kill them in cold blood; indeed, they have already begun. If the Messiah doesn't hurry, he may be too late; there will be no one left to save. I spoke to him of Jewish children, with dreams in their eyes, massacred in front of their speechless parents, who went to join them in the grave. I recalled the phrase from the Talmud: 'Ever since the destruction of the Temple the power of prophecy has been given to children.' 'Soon,' I said, 'there will be none of them left; our only prophets will be dead children.' And I also said to him, 'To you everything is simple because you are an angel. Try being a man among men or a child among men and you will see why to wait any longer would be a crime. Time is no longer abstraction, but a river of blood and death, running into a sea of death and blood.' Elijah smiled at me, and if angels were able to cry, he would have cried. 'I know,' he said, nodding his head, 'I know. I walk across this land; at every step I sink to my knees and pray God to kill me. I get up and walk and fall again and again ask for death. But death evades me. I am condemned to live, to watch, to observe, and to witness the unfolding of the holocaust!' I was sorry for him, and in return he told me a secret. 'The Messiah is not coming. He's not coming because he has already come. This is unknown, but he's neither at the gates of Rome nor in heaven. Everybody is wrong. The Messiah is everywhere. Ever present, he gives each passing moment its taste of drunkenness, desolation, and ashes. He has a name, a face, and a destiny. On the day when his name and face and destiny are one, all masks will fall, time will be freed of its chains, and he will link it to God, as he will link to God drunkenness and desolation and ashes.' 'When will this day be?' But he was sworn to secrecy and could not say. 'God Himself prefers not to know. If He knew, the coming of the Messiah would no longer be an act of freedom.' 'If God chooses to be in the dark,' I said, 'that's his business. But *I* want to know!' 'You're blaspheming, my son,' said Elijah reproachfully. 'If God prefers to wait,' I continued, heedless of his reprimand, 'it's because He can afford to. But I can't; we can't. For us every minute counts, every sacrifice counts.' 'You are blaspheming,' he repeated gently, as if he were envious, as if he would have liked to blaspheme as well. 'God's final victory, my son, lies in man's inability to reject Him. You think you're cursing Him, but your curse is praise; you think you're fighting Him, but all you do is open yourself to Him; you think you're crying out your hatred and rebellion, but all you're doing is telling Him how much you need His support and forgiveness. No, you mustn't blaspheme against someone who shares your suffering. You're asking the impossible. So much the better, but I have no right to tell you any more. Later, you'll understand the importance of the mystery; you'll see the light and perhaps it will pervade you. For the present let it suffice you to know that the Messiah is already among men. The rest, after all, is less important.' "

Gavriel suddenly stopped speaking and did not say another word for the rest of the night. His strange story left Gregor perplexed. Gavriel had seen the prophet Elijah? Where? How? They had spoken of the Messiah? Was it possible to imprison the Messiah with words? The Talmud says of the Messiah that he knows how to sing. To Gregor's father he was something rather than someone. "The Messiah," he used to say, "is that which makes man more human, which takes the element of pride out of generosity, which stretches his soul towards others." Gregor would have liked to talk about this to Gavriel, but Gavriel had wrapped himself in silence, as if he were listening to someone far away, perhaps to the prophet Elijah.

4

Slowly and monotonously the days went by. Gregor didn't like them; he preferred the nights. He wished that the sun would never rise, that darkness would never release the light. This was because Gavriel only talked in the dark. Darkness stimulated him, and he peopled it with images and memories. Gregor never tired of listening. The sadder the stories, the more Gavriel laughed. Sometimes he laughed without saying a word, and Gregor realized that the event was so heavy with horror, experienced or anticipated, that words could really not contain it.

Their provisions were running out; they were nearly at the end of their crackers, jam, and coffee. There were only two boxes of matches and three bags of hazelnuts and almonds. Gregor began to worry, Gavriel was unaffected.

"Don't worry, Gregor. We'll manage. I'm not afraid."

One night Gavriel went out, he said for a breath of air. He came back, panting, three hours later, with his arms full of food.

Gregor questioned him reproachfully: "Where have you been? Where did you get all those things?"

"Down below, in the town," said Gavriel mockingly.

Gregor was about to say, "You must be crazy!" But he held himself back, and Gavriel continued:

"I'll tell you. I knocked at several doors. The people took me for a ghost, a Jewish ghost, and they were terrified. I didn't speak—I don't know their language—but my silence was eloquent. To get rid of me as quickly as possible they gave me everything they had: bread, butter, cheese, fruit, eggs . . . I even turned down two chickens and a bottle of wine. So there! No need to worry."

Gregor didn't know whether to be angry at such foolhardiness or to be amused. He controlled himself and said simply, "Weren't you scared?"

"Scared?"

"Scared they'd report you to the police. That you'd be thrown in jail, deported."

Gavriel looked at him disappointedly.

"I've been wasting my breath," he said. "Don't you understand yet? Death has no hold on me."

He laughed, and Gregor could only shrug his shoulders, without understanding. What was there to understand? Whether Gavriel was mad or exceptionally intelligent made no real difference. If there was a difference, it would come out one day. For the moment, to think of the future seemed futile, even unworthy. He liked this confined existence. He felt as if he were on a desert island, bypassed by history, out of reach of the laws and butchery of men. The war was far away; even its sounds could not reach them.

"Look here, Gavriel; the war could end and we wouldn't know it."

"Don't worry; it's still going on."

Gavriel was not talkative that evening, but Gregor needed to hear his voice and tried to draw him out.

"What if it were to go on forever? That's possible, isn't it? Sometimes I think we'll never again see people walking in the summer sun or running under the autumn rain, stopping to look at shop windows. . . . We won't go to weddings or even to funerals. We'll stay shut up here, while eternity takes our existence for its boundary and the universe has the dimensions of this cave. We'll be new cavemen, that's what we'll be!"

35

"No," said Gavriel, "the war will come to an end, the sword will be sheathed, and blood will cease running. But victors and vanquished alike will be cavemen."

As usual, Gavriel was right. The carnage went on. The clouds hanging over the town grew thicker and thicker, and when the sun came through in the morning, it was surrounded by a violent red halo, as if it were emerging from a bath of blood.

Then came a fateful day. Standing at the entrance to the cave Gregor saw suspicious movements at the foot of the mountain. He stuck his head out, and then exclaimed fearfully, "No!"

"What is it?" asked Gavriel.

"Come here, quickly!"

Gavriel got up from his cot and came to stand behind him. For a long time they were speechless. The game was up and there was nothing more to say. Finally Gavriel broke the silence.

"The bastards. They've reported us. It's my fault; I miscalculated. I never should have gone to the town."

Gregor feebly reassured him. "Don't think about it. We were out of food, and there was no choice."

A gentle breeze played among the treetops, which stirred gracefully under the fragile sky. The two friends avoided looking at each other. The game seemed to be lost, irrevocably.

"There's no hope," whispered Gregor.

"We'll get along without it," said Gavriel, his face darkening.

Gregor tried to make out the uniforms which were moving far away, in the early morning light, but he could not tell whether they were tan or gray, whether the soldiers were Hungarian or German. But what difference did it make? Both were battling on the side of death—however, the Hungarians beat their victims before killing them. And so, what next? Like hunters, the soldiers were advancing slowly, too slowly for Gregor's taste. His nerves were on edge: if the stone had to fall, let it fall quickly. After an hour had gone by he could hear the click of the triggers and the language in which the orders were shouted. The soldiers were Hungarian.

With the help of Gavriel he pulled the rock in front of the

entrance to the cave, leaving no more than a narrow opening. All of a sudden the cave was hot, dark, and dusty. Gregor became more and more nervous, but Gavriel displayed a phlegmatic calm. He lay down, quite casually, on his cot. The trouble intensifying in the bright sunlight outside was only a game in which he refused to participate.

Gregor was irritated, but he contained himself. As long as Gavriel doesn't laugh at the crucial moment . . . he said to himself. But he's just mad enough to laugh. The hours dragged by, but he did not abandon his vigil, although his eyes were tired and his legs numb from not moving. The future was coming, deliberately, to meet him.

Probably the soldiers had orders to make an exhaustive search. Conscientiously they shook the pine trees, clambered up over the rocks and dug holes in the earth in places where they suspected someone might be hiding. From time to time they rested, and an officer shouted, "Hello there, you dirty Jew! We know you're somewhere around here. Come out of your mouse trap! If you wait for us to drag you out by your beard, you'll be sorry." Silence: no reaction. He sent his men back to search.

"What did he say?" Gavriel asked indifferently.

"Nothing of importance. He invited us to surrender rather than waste his time any further."

"Is that all?"

"That's all."

Gavriel returned to his meditation. Suddenly he raised himself up on his elbow and said, "Do they know there are two of us?"

"I don't think so. He addressed himself to one dirty Jew, to me."

Gavriel laughed in a somewhat irritating fashion. "Then everything's all right. Stop torturing yourself. I promise you they'll never enter this cave."

Gregor was amused by his companion's certainty, although he should have been worried. About three o'clock in the afternoon the soldiers were only a few steps away. Gregor could see their helmeted heads, broad chins, and drooping mustaches. If they were to come around the giant tree, all would

37

be lost, for they would inevitably discover the cave. Of course the entrance was covered by a rock, but even a child could see that it had been rolled into position from inside. Gregor held his breath until it seemed as if his lungs would burst. One soldier scanned the ground, displacing branches in his search for footprints; another stuck his bayonet among the branches of a pine tree, which pointed like a spire toward the sky. The first soldier raised his head and cracked a dirty joke. His comrade slapped his hips and laughed. "Yes, those Jews would crawl back into their mothers' wombs to hide." Gregor flushed and bit his lip. But the danger passed. The soldiers were already at the next tree. Relieved, Gregor took a few deep breaths, and turned to Gavriel to signal that all was well. Gavriel was staring at the ceiling. He opened his mouth, doubtless to say that he had foreseen it, but Gregor held up his hand to indicate that they were still dangerously close. Toward evening the soldiers left. They were talking among themselves.

"Where the devil can he be?"

"With these Jews you never know. They're everywhere and nowhere, visible and invisible. If you don't want to see them, they're on every street, in every bank and business office. But if you want to lay your hands on them, they melt into thin air and you can't find them. The devil protects them."

"Words, words! The fellow we're after is right around here, and we'll get him. He won't get away."

Then the soldiers walked off and were lost from sight. Night came out of its hiding place and occupied the earth like a conquering enemy. The sky was without a cloud, thank God, and the silvery stars darted among the trees, distilling a cold light.

"They won't come back," said Gregor without conviction.

Gavriel, lost in thought, did not reply.

"They'll imagine we got across the mountains and into Rumania."

"Is the border so near?" Gavriel asked with interest.

"Quite near. We could reach it in two nights if . . ."

"If what?"

"If we aren't caught."

"I see."

Gregor was depressed and wanted to move on. Every second was precious and might make the difference between life and death. It was dangerous to defy fate too much. Today luck had smiled on them, but tomorrow it might shift its smile elsewhere, or it might just sit back and take it easy.

"Gavriel," he said with anguish.

"Yes?"

"Let's leave."

"What's that?"

"Let's get away from here. Quickly! Don't say no. It's the first time I've asked you a favor. Let's take advantage of this breather and get out of here. We can't expect a miracle every day."

Gavriel did not pause to weigh the pros and cons of this, but said "No," categorically.

"Why not? You don't want us to die, do you?"

"Of course not."

"Well, what do you want, then?" asked Gregor impatiently. "What are you up to? Why did you come in the first place? What did you want from me? What are you trying to prove? I just can't understand."

Gavriel paused before making a reply. His voice was deeper, gentler, and more human than before; it vibrated in the night, and the night vibrated within it.

"I thought you had more endurance. This isn't a reproach, just a statement of fact. It hurts all the same. I can see that if we were shut up here several weeks more—or several months, what difference does it make?—you'd come to hate me. Isn't that so, Gregor?"

"No!" Gregor protested, "No, no, no!"

"Shut your eyes before answering."

Gregor obeyed.

"I hope not," he murmured.

"There, do you see?" said Gavriel, putting a hand on his shoulder. "Now try to understand. It would be a mistake to leave now. They're not that stupid. Probably they're patrolling the mountain. They know how scared we are and they're waiting for us to come out of hiding so they can grab us. Be patient. Trust my judgment and me. It's a matter of patience.

When we're sure they've given up looking for us, then we can come out."

"What if they come back tomorrow?"

"I've thought of that and I have a plan."

"What is it?"

"I can't tell you yet. All I can say is that it will work. You'll see. I'll explain it to you when the time comes. Tomorrow."

"Will there be a tomorrow?"

"Of course, Gregor. Look around you. Your shadow hasn't left you. You'll live, I promise." And after a short pause he repeated, "I promise."

Gavriel's assurance seemed to rise to meet Gregor's anxiety. Every one of his words reflected hope and certainty.

"The future's my domain," he said. "Leave everything to me. I'll keep it under control."

But Gregor stood up for his own logic. "It's no joke, Gavriel," he insisted. "Please, let's go. My father left me some money and we can buy our way to the border. Let's go while there's still time. They'll be back tomorrow, I'm sure, and deep down, you are too. When they come back it will be too late. There won't be any future."

Gregor felt trapped; there was anxiety in every cell of his being. He was afraid, not of death, but of being separated from his companion. If at least he could be assured that they would die together . . . but he had no such assurance, and that's what hurt. Some superior will or widsom had made their footsteps converge; the war itself had broken out simply to create an occasion for their meeting and now for their separation. Never had he felt so sad.

It was their last night together. Gavriel seemed exuberant and in possession of all his powers. Finally, toward morning, he fell asleep. But his good spirits caused Gregor concern. Was Gavriel, after all, crazy? If I live, he said to himself, I'll give the rest of my life to finding out. This will be the aim of my existence. I'll become him in order to understand him better, to understand and love him, or to love him without understanding.

It was six o'clock. Gregor made some coffee and went to stand at the entrance of the cave. He watched the coppery sun rise majestically over the mountain, as if to announce some primordial event. With trembling lips and heart he waited, motionless, for the birth of light, which as far back as he could remember had flooded him with as intense a feeling as if he were witnessing the creation of the world. Night withdraws, dawn advances and that is the moment of choice. A moment of hesitation and all is lost. The new day hovers, indecisive, above the mountain. A giant hand pushes it over the top: go, men are waiting for you! Then the sun, messenger of the gods, finally, appears in all its pride; pines raise their branches, wheat opens its golden blade, and man feels capable of measuring himself against the elements.

If only it lasts, Gregor thought. If only the present would tear itself away from the future and the link be broken. At the foot of the mountain, he saw the commotion he had anticipated. Time was climbing toward him. With a pounding heart he shook Gavriel.

"Wake up! They're coming."

Gavriel stared at him, haggardly, as if he were a stranger. Then he understood and jumped from the cot. He washed his face, said the morning prayer, and gulped down a few mouthfuls of coffee. He was readying himself for a long journey.

Gregor stood at the entrance of the cave, his eyes glued to the narrow opening. The veins in his temples were throbbing and his eyes were heavy. He knew that the soldiers would not abandon their manhunt easily. The Hungarian army, smarting from its defeat on the Russian front, needed a victory, no matter over whom. What was easier or more logical than to capture a hunted man, rejected by the community and living, like an animal, in the wilds? They'll have their victory, these brave Magyar soldiers. Tomorrow they'll get a medal, a three-day pass to go see their wives and tell their story. Here they were, the heroes of the war against two dangerous Jews, their guns loaded and gleaming bayonets pointing to the enemy. When it's a matter of killing, and killing Jews at that, Hungarian soldiers faithful to country and honor, are afraid of nothing and no one.

A few seconds later Gregor started, stifling an outcry. A dog barked, and then another, and then a third, a whole string of police dogs. He did not even turn toward Gavriel but stared at the soldiers and murmured, "It's all over."

Gavriel smiled simply in a kindly, understanding manner.

"Not yet," he said.

"You're like a man burning to death who says, 'As long as my heart beats I'm all right.' But his minutes are numbered."

Gavriel shrugged his shoulders indifferently. "Take it easy, Gregor. Have you lost confidence in me?"

"No. I wonder only if the dogs will be convinced of your power. They'd have to hear you laugh."

"They will."

This time Gregor wheeled around to look at his companion. "You still have some hope? You must be out of your mind."

"I haven't much hope. No. But I'll keep my promise. Let the soldiers play their game and the dogs help them. When the time comes I'll play mine."

"What is your game?" Gregor asked angrily. "Will you tell me that? How much more time do you think we have? Can't you see they're here and that it won't be long before they find us? We're done for, and to you it's still a game. Are you really crazy?"

The smile froze on Gavriel's face. Gregor had never seen him so sad, and he regretted—too late—the words he had just spoken.

"I'm sorry," he said in a choked voice. "I didn't mean to hurt you."

Gavriel continued to look at him, then began to pace, absorbed in his own thoughts.

To break the silence Gregor said, quite inconsequentially, "Our Maria wasn't so stupid. She used to say that dogs are the first to sniff the presence of death; when they bark it means that death has conquered again. She was right. The dogs are barking. We'd better get ready."

Gavriel went over to where Gregor was standing in order to look outside. For a second they peered out together. All of a sudden Gregor turned toward him: he had to cover his mouth with his hand to keep back a cry of fear. Gregor would never have believed that a human face could show so much suffering:

42

Gavriel had no more face. This is the end, Gregor thought, even he admits that the last of the gates is closed. The silence was heavy, weighed down by the passage of time. Silence was everywhere, in the trees, the bushes, and the eyes of the dogs. It even had a smell, the smell of torture, and it spit blood, the odor of a prisoner who has been jeered and beaten and left to die.

"What can we do?" asked Gregor remorsefully. "What can we do?"

Gavriel sighed, and his face hardened.

"What can we do?" asked Gregor for the third time, not expecting an impossible reply but simply to re-establish a contact, any kind of contact, with his friend. "We're powerless before those animals."

And powerless they were. No trick could divert them, no hiding place was secure. They had divine attributes, these Hungarian police dogs; they could see everything, and nothing could stand against them. The clock was turned back four thousand years: a police dog was the animal that now determined the destiny of the world.

Gavriel awakened from his daydream and was once more aware of Gregor's presence. He even smiled.

"Are you still sure you'd never hate me?" he asked, fixing him with such a piercing stare that Gregor could not withdraw his eyes.

"Yes, Gavriel, I'm sure. More sure than ever."

"Then our meeting means something."

He laid a hand on Gregor's shoulder. But Gregor was overcome by a sudden feeling of loneliness. He realized then that their paths were going to separate; they would not die together.

"We still have an hour or two to go," said Gavriel.

"Yes."

"That's enough. Long enough to talk to you, to give you the secret key to a secret door. But promise me you won't get arrested. I want to know that you're alive on the day the war ends. Promise me you'll be careful."

His voice was so insistent that Gregor would have promised anything. He was still young and did not know how to refuse.

"I'll be careful, I promise," he said.

Gavriel gripped his shoulder and went on. "Then listen to me, and don't interrupt. I don't know when we'll see each other again. I may disappear or lose my memory. But before that time I want you to know about the man who had his tongue cut out. It's important for you to know."

"No," said Gregor, "don't tell me. I don't want to know. He was your friend, and that's quite enough. Keep your secret; I don't want it."

"You must learn to listen. Listening gives you a key. You know that the man was my friend, but you don't realize that he's yours as well. Are you listening?"

"I'm listening," said Gregor. And there were tears in his eyes.

After a search that lasted for weeks and months Gavriel finally discovered the one for whom the world was waiting, as the earth waits for rain. He was an eccentric whom children ran after and teased, sometimes kindly, sometimes with cruelty. "Moshe the Mute" he was called, for he said little and let himself be teased. The boys were always at his heels, tugging at his jacket or knocking off his hat. All he did was make friendly gestures and smile. He was fond of them, and in their own way they were fond of him. No one knew where he came from or who were his parents, his age, or what he had dreamed and endured as a child. He appeared one day in the synagogue and asked if they could use a beadle. "What a coincidence," they said. "Avrom, the beadle, died only yesterday. It is as if Heaven had sent you."

And so Moshe took root in the community. By day he taught children the alphabet; by night, alone with the quivering light of the candles, he sang to himself, and his songs came from a broken heart. One evening Gavriel hid behind a desk and at midnight he saw Moshe sprinkle ashes on his forehead and heard him bewail the destruction of the Temple, and the exile of Israel and of the *Shekhinah*. Surely no one had ever wept like this before; his tears were not those of one man but of an entire people; in their source were drowned the beginning and the end of time.

Gavriel went up to him and asked, "Is it you?" And Moshe

the Mute, taken by surprise, stammered, "Yes, it is me." Then, recovering his self-possession, he added angrily, "Who else should it be? I'm the beadle. It's my job to keep watch all night. But you have no business being here. Leave me alone. You're only a nuisance."

This was the only time that Gavriel saw Moshe lose control. "I won't go away," he said impulsively. "I'll stay here with you."

"No, I won't allow you to stay; I don't want you. Go away."

"It's no use arguing, I'm going to stay. From now on I'll always be with you."

"For how long?" Moshe asked despairingly.

"Until the end."

Then Moshe resumed his normal manner and his expression softened. He scrutinized the intruder and was silent, expectantly. "What are you waiting for?" Gavriel asked with impatience. "A sign? What sign? When is it coming, and who will give it? When will you break the chains? With what gesture will you announce your kingdom?"

Moshe merely shrugged his shoulders. With a totally blank and noncommittal expression he plunged himself into the reading of a book. To Gavriel this was confirmation of the words of the prophet Elijah.

Gavriel came regularly to the synagogue; indeed, he spent more hours there than he did at home. Often, when the service was over and the faithful had gone, he lingered to talk to the beadle. Every day he urged him to take action and to precipitate events. But the beadle remained impenetrable and made no reply. He seemed to be saying, "I don't understand what you want," or else, "I understand, but I must be silent."

Gavriel refused to be discouraged. "I know that it's wrong and dangerous to upset the order of creation," he admitted. "There's a risk of delaying the redemption for another thousand centuries. But Jewish blood is flowing in all the cities of Europe; soon the whole continent will be drowned in the flood. Why should you wait, when you can change all this? How can you be so patient?"

He appealed to Moshe's kindness, to his sense of justice and sacrifice. He demonstrated, with passages from the Talmud and the Midrash, that it was his duty to disobey God in order to save the people, the witnesses and martyrs, the people of the covenant, from destruction. No good deed equals in meaning and importance that of saving a human life—any human life. If there is a question of bringing help to the dying, even the laws of the Sabbath may be broken. And in this case the life and death of a whole people are at stake. "Your patience will not be forgiven. Use your fist to strike; strike against Heaven if necessary, and it is necessary."

But the beadle remained intransient. Meanwhile the ghettos were decimated, the streams ran with blood. Gavriel quarreled incessantly with the beadle, reproaching him in more and more disrespectful terms for his passive and submissive spirit and inciting him to anger and revolt. But the beadle remained a beadle.

But not forever. Life went on. Yossel, the moneylender, had a daughter to marry, an old maid who had kept her youthful sweetness and beauty, and quite unbelievably Moshe married her one day. He bought new clothes, began to take an interest in business, and gradually forgot his mission. As he became rich he stopped going to the poor people's synagogue and no longer spent his nights in prayer and weeping. When children saw him on the street they respected his impressive bearing, said good morning and good evening, and received in return small coins. He who had started out to overturn the laws now submitted to them. The earth-shaking had been called off.

Several times Gavriel tried to speak to him and obtain an explanation. But Moshe avoided him and finally said, quite frankly, that he had no more time for the childish nonsense in which he had indulged all too long in the past.

"Incredible, but true," said Gavriel. "I've seen the man who was to incarnate salvation and give it wings. I saw him with my own eyes, I touched his hands. But instead of saving men he had let them contaminate and corrupt him. Because he has waited too long, he who was to bring men their freedom finally resembled them; he has become their equal. Having given up his own destiny he lowered himself to accepting theirs. If a man stays too long in an insane asylum, he loses his mind; if dazzled by false hopes, he loses his reason to hope. Moshe's fall involved the fall of his own generation and of all generations to come. And so, Gregor, I tell you I no longer believe in the coming of the Messiah. The Messiah came, and nothing changed. He lost the path and laid down his arms without fighting; he surrendered himself and voluntarily relinquished his freedom. No, Gregor, there can be no more hope. The Messiah came, and the executioner goes right on executing. The Messiah came and the world is a vast slaughterhouse, as it was before."

But until the last minute Gavriel did not give up hoping. The beadle must have his reasons, he told himself. I'm too blind to see them, too far behind him. I shouldn't accuse him of treason, when I myself live in darkness and cannot bear it. Probably he's waiting for the very dead of night to perform a miracle, to light a spark; he's waiting until pain is so unbearable and absurd to extirpate it, for the beast to have gathered its full strength before he finishes it off with a single stroke of the sword.

Moshe continued to avoid and ignore him; he even stirred up the children against him. But, from a distance, Gavriel kept him in sight. His paths are devious, he said to himself; we cannot tell what deserts they cross and what their final destination may be. We must wait for the end before we cry out that there is no judge and no judgment.

Then came the fatal day, when the Angel of Death appeared in the town. The Jews were rounded up and led to the forest. They were immolated, entire families at a time, and Moshe, the former beadle, looked on and waited for his turn, looked on and did nothing.

"Do you hear?" shouted Gavriel, his face twisted with rage and sorrow. "He looked on and did nothing."

"I hear," said Gregor. "He looked on and did nothing."

Moshe was standing with his wife; he placed his hands tenderly on her shoulders as if to keep them from trembling. Gavriel came and stood directly in front of him. "This is too much," he said. "What are you waiting for? Do something! Haven't you seen enough? Don't you realize that you're betraying the dead and the unborn and condemning yourself as well, unless you stop this massacre? Cursed you will be, and cursed will be he who pronounces your name or prays for you. Aren't you afraid? Have you no shame?"

The wife looked absently at Gavriel, unable to understand what he was trying to obtain from her husband at this hour when neither words nor wrath made any sense. "You've no right to be silent; it's already too late; just look around you!" shouted Gavriel. "For the love of heaven do what you're supposed to do, say what you're supposed to say. A single gesture, a word, an outcry; above all, an outcry from you can change everything."

The other listened with a humble smile and a gesture of impotence and lassitude which seemed to say, "Forgive me, there's nothing I can do; God's will has taken over ours. Before Him we are helpless and panic-stricken."

Gavriel was frantic with rage and indignation. "If this is God's will, then deny it! The time has come for you to impose your will upon His, to pin Him to the wall. You'll have to pay, you say? What of it? You'll be damned? So what?"

The other nodded his head heavily. There was an immense sorrow in his eyes, the eyes that would say to the executioner, "I no longer understand. What game are you playing?"

Meanwhile the massacre went on. Everyone—women, old men, and children—were taken. The beadle did not become a beadle again until one of the killers cut out his tongue; but it was already too late. He took with him his silence, his secret, his shadow.

Gavriel paused to catch his breath. He was gasping and perspiration ran down his face; for a moment it seemed as if he were on the edge of tears.

"I think of him," he said, with the strange laugh of the night that he had uttered when he had first come to the cave. "I think of nothing else. That's the way we're made, I guess, to be blinded by presence and haunted by absence. I think of him all the time, and I laugh. Tomorrow you'll laugh when you think of me."

"I won't laugh," said Gregor.

"I want you to," said Gavriel, his hand weighing heavily on the shoulder of his companion, who wished it even heavier. "Do you understand?"

"No."

"Never mind. Tomorrow, the day after tomorrow you'll repeat my story once, a dozen times, more if necessary: at the end you'll understand."

"And if I'm afraid to understand?"

"At the end you won't be afraid, and then you'll learn to laugh as well."

The sun was high in the sky, and it was growing warmer. All will be well, winter is still far away; the sun gives life and sustains it, all will be well; God sees to it that the harmony may not be destroyed, all will be well; history moves on and men after all weren't created just to slaughter one another.

The soldiers were approaching, the dogs were barking at the sun, and a dull hum, a warning that seemed to have risen from the bowels of the earth, ran through the trees. They'll soon be here, Gregor was thinking. Your story will die with us, Gavriel; your legend will perish between the jaws of a dog. His companion, who was now quite calm, must have guessed his thoughts.

"About twenty minutes to go. They're not far."

"No, they're not far."

"But they won't get here."

"Who's to prevent them?"

"I am."

Gregor had a flash of understanding.

"You?" he exclaimed sorrowfully.

"Yes. I." And before Gregor was over his initial shock he explained his plan. The soldiers had no reason to think there were two of them and as soon as one surrendered they would give up the search. "It's perfectly simple," he went on, casually. "You can be on your way this evening to the Rumanian border."

Under Gregor's legs the earth was reeling, and an iron fist seemed to have struck his breast.

"No! No, no. Gavriel, no, no!"

A rush of words stuck in his throat, but this "No" contained them all.

"I don't like your protest," said Gavriel severely. "It betrays a lack of confidence. In yourself, in me. If we just sit here, we'll both be captured. If you go out alone, they'll kill you on sight. Whereas I can hold them off. They can't do anything to me. How often must I tell you that?"

Gregor wanted to throw himself at his feet and weep, but the tears would not come. One day I'll cry, he said to himself. Gavriel wiped the severe expression off his face and smiled.

"I don't know whether or not we'll meet again, Gregor. I could, with an effort, look into the future, but the time's too short. I'd like you to know only this: separation contains as much of a mystery as meeting. In both cases a door opens: in meeting it opens on the future, in separation on the past. It's the same door."

No more was said. Gavriel searched for something in his pockets. Then he rubbed his hands together and leaned over to move the rock. Gregor stared at him hypnotically through moist eyes for a moment before making up his mind to help. The rock moved just enough to permit the passage of a single body.

Gavriel drew himself up, smiled, and clasped his friend's hand. His eyes wandered over the cave as if he were about to pick something up or put it down; he opened his mouth as if to express pain or joy, then thought better of it, turned around and slipped out.

Mechanically Gregor pushed the rock back in place. His right hand was bleeding and he felt weak and empty, as if he were floating in the air. Through the crack he looked after his friend who was striding down the path. He did not halt until, from every side, the barking dogs surrounded him and threw him to the ground. The soldiers pushed the dogs away and ordered the prisoner to get up, holding his hands above his head. He did not understand their language, and one of the soldiers pushed a rifle butt into his stomach. Gavriel stood up and examined first the soldier and then the loudly panting dogs. Gavriel frowned, his shoulders twitched. Then, in the face of the soldiers and the stupefied dogs, he burst suddenly into overwhelming laughter.

summer

1

"Who's there? Be quiet! People are sleeping here."

The sleepy voice of old Maria. The voice, grown old, of Maria who, in days past, had never been sleepy. She used to rise before the rest of the household and go to bed after everyone was asleep. Now her voice, feeble and resigned: "Who's there?"

Gregor leaned against the door and closed his eyes. I'm dreaming, he thought; I'm dreaming, and nothing can or must surprise me. Nothing can make me any more tired. I've had enough of your dreams and mine; silence your dreams and mine; silence your dreams and mine will follow. Silence dreams, all dreams, and don't speak anymore of surprises; surprises are wearying. Everything leads to weariness and war, dreams too, your dreams even more than mine. And surprises? They are its supreme expression.

I'm dreaming, he thought; now I have a right to dream, because I hear Maria's familiar voice at last. Let nobody wake me ever again. Do you hear, Maria? I want to sleep, sleep, sleep, to sleep until evening, until tomorrow evening, until next year. Let yesterday be erased from my memory and the day before yesterday too. Do you hear me, Maria?

He saw her in her nightgown, with her undone braids hanging down to the floor as she busied herself in the kitchen. Are you fixing that breakfast for me? I don't want it. Don't be angry; I'll go to school without breakfast. I'm not hungry, Maria, I promise. I'm simply tired. Too tired to open my mouth, too tired to dream that I'm talking to you, that it's all a dream. All I want to do is sleep, to throw myself down on a bed, any bed, on a cloud, if you allow me, on the wings of the night if you demand it, and sleep, sleep, sleep.

"Who's there? Go to the devil!"

The voice of Maria. The pretending-to-be-disagreeable voice of the divine old Maria. Gregor felt sorry for himself and for her also. Dear Maria. She wanted to sleep. Everything that remains of the past is in your voice, *is* your voice. It opens up to me like a house, my house, for me to live in and find rest. You don't know it, but your voice is my house, my childhood, my memory: a reddish stream whose rippling waves carry me far away, where the sun is but the head of a Jewish child, killed and thrown to the dogs. Did you know that, Maria? Did you know that the stars are the eyes of Jewish children killed in the transparent light of dawn? No, you don't know. I wish I didn't know either. I wish I could live my life in your voice and sleep a heavy sleep, without echoes, without sun, without awakening. But your voice, it's exhausted: a crumbling house, a house in ruins. And I am only a ghost without the strength to walk or shout.

"It's me," said Gregor. "It's me, Maria."

He was heavy with night and fog, his vitality gone, his legs weak. He had walked for hours through fields and woods, and at every step his body became more shapeless, putting on weight, growing beyond measure, stretching to infinity. It was taller than the pine trees and wider than the valley, as dirty as the swamp waters; his body embarked on an adventure of its own, quite outside Gregor, who stepped and spat upon it, feeling neither pain nor regret but only an immense weariness. He walked, and everything walked with him or against him, while his body, hungry for shadows, kept on getting bigger. There was nothing but himself on earth and in heaven; he was heaven and earth, and then he became God.

From far away, as if out of another dream long denied, long forgotten, Gregor detected the dull sound of bare feet on a wood floor. Good, old Maria . . . she was waiting, she recognized me. She was striking a match, it didn't ignite. She tried again, successfully, and lit a lamp or a candle. How slow she was! She came to the door and slipped back the latch. What a painful sound! Didn't she know that it hurt the ears and burst the brain? At last the door opened cautiously. I must pull myself together and stand up straight, very straight, thought Gregor.

"Do you see, Maria? It's me, only me."

Maria threw the door open wide and he fell into her arms so precipitately that she almost lost her balance. Leaning with her left hand against the door she set the lamp on the floor, crossed herself and murmured, "Dear Lord Jesus, dear Mother of God, have mercy on me!" Then she regained her self-control, pulled the boy inside and sat him down. She went away and came back, insisting that he drink some *tzuika,* which burned his tongue, his throat, his brain. He breathed hard, his head reeled; there were a thousand turbulent heads in his head, which burned without ever being consumed. I have no legs, no arms, no heart; I'm all head. Suddenly he wanted to laugh and sing and dance and shout and forget and sleep, yes, above all, sleep, if only all these heads could lay themselves down and be quiet inside his sleep.

"It's you," said Maria, dear Maria, the only Maria, the most beautiful woman in the world, the sweetest, most generous. It's you. I thought that you had gone away, gone away with the rest of them."

He raised his eyelids. Yes, it was she. He was not dreaming, or else she was dreaming with him. Maria had not changed; she was not a Jew, only Jews change. Only Jews change into clouds. This is no more than justice: they wanted to change the world, and instead the world changed them. But Maria was not a Jew. Fortunately, she was her old self, with the braids hanging down to the floor. She was in a nightgown that came down over her legs, just as it used to do. Have you still got your legs, Maria? Speak to me.

"Last week I went into town, but there was nobody there.

The ghetto was empty, and I thought you had gone away. I asked the passers-by, 'Where are the Jews? I don't see them.' 'They've gone away,' they told me. 'Gone away where? For how long?' No answer. 'When will they be back?' I insisted. 'They won't be back,' they told me. The townspeople always think they know everything, but they know nothing. The proof you're here, you've come back."

"I never went away."

"So much the better," said Maria. "I'm glad you didn't go. You're a bright boy; I've always known that. I'm sure your parents are proud of you. I am."

"Father went. Mother went. They all went. I stayed. Are you sure you're proud of me? They all went away and came back masters of the universe, riding the clouds. But I'm earth-bound."

Gregor spoke and he listened to himself speaking. He was aware of being delirious. Was he shouting? Whispering? Maria's soft voice wrapped him in warmth and well-being. He spoke in order that she should answer in her hoarse and marvelously warm voice.

"You see, Maria, I stayed."

"So much the better, my boy."

"Are you really proud of me?"

"Very proud, my child. As if you were my own son."

"You're glad to see me? Even if I'm alone?"

"Glad to the tips of my fingers, to the roots of my hair. I saw you come into the world, grow up, to become a man; I heard you laugh and cry and sing."

"Are you glad that father and mother have gone away?"

"That's a stupid thing to say."

"You'd have liked them to be here with me, with you?"

"Yes, my child."

"Say it out loud."

"I wish they were here with you and me."

"Who: 'they'?"

"Your father and your mother."

"And the others, too?"

"And the others, too."

Gregor's eyelids were lowered and no power on earth could

have opened them. He was afraid to look up, to see what was happening on the other side of his dream, afraid to find himself in Maria's hut in the fields and not in his room, in his bed. He preferred to listen to her voice and to take refuge in it.

"How did you find my house? Was it difficult? Did you ask someone?"

"No, Maria. I found it right away, even in the darkness. My father described this village to me, and I know it as well as if it were my own. I counted, just as father told me, until I came to the third house on the right after the well."

"So that's why your father came to see me and asked me to show him the village."

"When did he come?"

"I don't remember. Oh! You were already in the ghetto. I don't know how he managed to get out."

"The third door on the right after the well. The third door on the right after the well," Gregor repeated. "It was easy. I counted, I knocked, and here I am."

"I didn't hear you knock."

She was right. He hadn't had the strength to knock, or the courage either. For a brief moment he had feared he was at the wrong door. Then his fear had receded and he had a wild urge to knock with all his might, to wake up the village and all the other villages near and far, to rouse the living from their beds and the dead from their graves and to shout, "Fire! Fire!" But he hadn't knocked at all.

"Why did you open the door?"

"I don't know," she said in a whisper.

"Why did you open the door? Why did you ask: 'Who's there?' Why did you say: 'People are sleeping.'?"

"I don't know why, I tell you."

"Think!"

"Another time. I don't know where to begin thinking. Besides, it doesn't matter. What matters is that you're there."

"You're wrong, Maria. Think. It may be important. Don't you want to know why you got up in the middle of the night, why you spoke out, why you came to open the door?"

"I don't care why."

"But I do."

"Then think it out yourself, and let me alone."

Gregor wanted to get her to talk. In order to sleep he needed to hear the hoarse, soothing sound of her voice. But Maria wasn't in the mood for talking, and her mood wasn't likely to change in a hurry. She was too stubborn for that. He, the fugitive, drunk with fatigue, began to talk at random, about anything and everything, fighting against silence, the way a drowning man fights the force that keeps him conscious. The past became present, everything became confused with everything else: beings lost their identity, objects their proper weight. His own identity merged with that of all mankind, which did whatever it wanted to whomever it wanted in obedience to any law it chose. The human race is drunk and exhausted. It kills and its thirst for blood is without measure; it kills because life weighs too heavily upon it; it creates a lie in order to hate itself; it descends into the sea and fills it with blood in order to drown itself—all this to take revenge on God, that dream of justice, that mountain of injustice.

"Sweet Jesus," murmured Maria in prayer, "sweet Jesus . . ."

"Let him be," said Gregor feverishly. "Let him be. He, too, has been changed into a cloud. He, too, was exhausted; he let himself be killed one day and since then there's been no end to the killing."

"Dear Lord," said Maria frightened, "dear Lord . . ."

"Did you know that Christ was a Jew? That he said he was the son of God? That he took to himself the title of Messiah? Do you know why he was crucified? I'll tell you: because he never learned to laugh. Yes, Maria, that's the truth; I swear it. If from the cross he hadn't appealed to the Father that had forsaken him, if he'd simply laughed, then he would have triumphed over the others and himself as well."

"Be quiet, child, be quiet, for the love of heaven! Why must you talk like this? Whom do you want to insult and why? I hardly know you; you seem like a different boy, a different man, with a strange voice and a strange soul. It's as if someone, a demon I don't know, has taken hold of you—it's that demon who's trying to give me pain and make me angry. It's not your fault, little one. You've suffered too much, little one.

58

You need rest, sleep, food. You need someone to care for you. Don't worry. I'm here; I'll get you back on your feet."

Gregor's head was bursting with words that floated in the air, dismembered and blind. He wanted to drown them in a sleep that would not come, to strangle them, but they eluded him and mingled with sea and sky. And the heads that were in his head . . . old men's heads with gaping mouths, the heads of slaughtered children, heads without eyes or lips, heads with only an enigmatic smile for a face. Where could he run? What door could he open?

"You see, Maria, I'm not the one that knocked at your door. It was the stranger inside me; he knocked and got you out of bed. He is powerful; you must recognize him."

"That's enough, child. You have a fever. You talk like a sick man. A stranger speaks from your lips. I don't want to know who he is."

She made the sign of the cross. "Make him be quiet, and go to sleep."

"Yes, yes, sleep . . ."

"God will watch over your sleep."

"Sleep, sleep . . ."

Maria helped him to lie down on something very soft, a blanket or a sheepskin. Kneeling beside him she stroked his forehead, murmuring something, probably a prayer, whose cottony words he could not grasp. He ran after them, far, very far, leaving his body behind in a stream choked with the heads of assassinated children.

2

When the police dogs and their masters had left the mountain, rejoicing in their victory, the calm which followed was so sudden and severe that Gregor could endure it only by falling humbly to his knees.

Intermission was over. The play began again. The actors were back on the stage and officers in dazzling uniforms stood in front of the firing squads, raising their arms and calling out, "Fire, fire, fire!" And soldiers bored, fired their machine guns, indifferent, thinking of nothing, not even of death. And hundreds of hearts ceased beating, ceased advancing toward a future at the end of which a Messiah—it didn't matter who—was supposed to receive them. "Fire!" called out the officers, and the Messiah himself, a thousand times, a thousand, thousand times multiplied, fell into the ditch.

Spring continued; the war too: they complemented each other perfectly, the one accentuating the other, each prolonging the other's life. Cold weather isn't suitable to murder; it slows it down. As a conscientious artisan the killer prefers to work in the sun: brave and free, knowing no fear, loving hard work and good health, relaxed in his movements and guiltless in the eyes of his fellow men, the killer knows that he is following the right way. "We're doing it for the good of mankind," said the philosophers of murder, waiting for the rest of the world to congratulate them.

Spring warmed the earth of Galicia and the Ukraine. The earth was red, its only becoming color. The streams were red, and the fields and the wheat; the poplars and the apple trees, the days and the nights. It was shining and splendid, the earth of Galicia and the Ukraine under the red sun of the late spring.

For an immeasurable moment, his eye fixed upon the crack in the cave, Gregor felt a strange quiet within him; his sufferings were over. His friend had gone, but the painful laceration he had awaited did not occur. Without knowing how or why he felt in harmony with the visible and invisible forces of nature which run through every inch of the human body. He heard the twitter of birds of whose presence he had not previously been aware; and it seemed to him quite natural that the same segment of eternity should contain the outcry of the tortured prisoner and the song of the forest. Both belonged to the same ancient and secret design and bore witness either for, either against but their testimony was clear: perfect harmony between me and this design, between me and this witness. The events of the last days, from the arrival of Gavriel to his departure, had obeyed a logic whose exact thread escaped him. But he found it normal that Gavriel should be in prison or already dead and that he should be alive and free. What Gavriel had left to him was beyond sorrow, beyond justice.

At twilight an infinitely delicate gray light detached itself from the sky. Mildness and peace. A cool breeze blew, farmers came in from the fields, offices emptied, people went home to love, to hate. Men teased their wives, but their laughter was hollow. Pious souls thanked heaven for the passage of another day of war, but their prayer was empty. The city fought its last fight against the encroaching shadows.

Having decided to leave the cave, Gregor had a choice: either to go back to the city in the hope of being arrested and surprising Gavriel or to make for the Rumanian border, where safety awaited him. At the very last minute, when he was slipping from one tree to another he thrust aside both solutions, judging them to be foolish, and took the road to the obscure village which was the home of the old servant Maria.

"Promise to obey me," she said to him.

"I promise."

"If you want to live—and *I* want you to live, I can tell you, you must do what I ask."

There was a pale smile on her lips.

"How can I disobey you, Maria? At home you always gave the orders."

"Don't speak of the past. Not today. Here's what I've decided to do with you. Listen!"

"I'm listening, Maria."

"First, you are to stay here until the end of the war. Understood?"

"And when will there be an end to the war?"

"That's not your concern; it's up to the soldiers. Your concern is to stay alive. Is that clear?"

"At your service, Maria."

Unaffected by the irony in his voice, Maria went on, "Good. That's settled. Let's go on to the next problem. How are we to keep the village from finding out who you are?"

"How, indeed?"

"To hole up in a hiding place is out of the question. The town's too small. Everyone knows everything here."

"And so?"

"And so we must think of something else."

"What, for instance?"

"You must show yourself."

"In public?"

"In public, yes. On the street, at church, everywhere. People hereabouts are as hospitable as any others. They'll come up to shake hands with you and talk, just as they would anywhere else. That's only natural. They're interested in strangers."

"Yes? I'm listening."

"Here's where the problem becomes complicated. People speak only Rumanian in the village. They haven't accepted the politicians' decision to hand over our spot of ground to the

62

damned Hungarians. And your Rumanian accent—not to mention what you might say—isn't very convincing. The minute you open your mouth they'll know, if not who you are, at least who you're not."

"And so?"

"And so, you mustn't talk, that's all."

Nonplused more than amused, Gregor looked at her uncomprehendingly. With pinched lips Maria spoke the final, inescapable solution: "It's quite simple. From now on and until the end of the war you must be dumb. With yourself, with me, with everybody. You must forget that you ever knew how to talk. Is that clear?"

In her eyes a firmness, a determination which could not be deflected: the old servant had decided, all alone, to struggle. All alone, against the monstrous machine of war.

"You understand, don't you? Yes or no? There's no other way."

Gregor didn't know what to admire most: her courage, her ingenuity, or her goodness. He smiled.

"Yes, I understand, Maria. It's the only way, I know. You're right. You were always right."

She made a movement as if to draw him to her and hug him, and then composed herself. Tears welled in her eyes; she sniffled and wiped her nose with her skirt.

"Good! Everything will be all right. I'm proud of you."

And so, by the grace and will of Maria, Gregor gave up speech. This was no sacrifice at all. Already in the cave he had become used to silence and loved it. Gavriel had told him: "Men talk because they're afraid, they're trying to convince themselves that they're still alive. It's in the silence after the storm that God reveals himself to man. God is silence."

Even today Gregor thinks nostalgically to the peaceful, dreamlike weeks under Maria's protection, when liberty was not law but the absence of law. They allowed him to glimpse a universe which had nothing in common with words. He has kept scraps of this universe and ever since he lost it he has lived for the purpose of putting it together again. Sometimes he fancies he is succeeding and then the sounds of the faraway night become voices and he shuts his eyes in order to hear them.

"You must listen without answering and, if possible, without understanding," Maria continued. "All will be well, you'll see."

Her plans went even further. Gregor must have an identity, a home, a past, a story. She decided to pass him off as her deaf-and-dumb nephew, slow-witted, harmless, a little odd. Thus, from the very beginning, there would be no grounds for suspicion.

"Remember this," she said, "from now on and until the end of the war you are the son of my sister Ileana, of my miserable sister whose sins drew the fire of heaven down upon herself and her children. Clear?"

"Not at all," said Gregor. "I didn't know you had a sister."

"You're too young to know everything."

She made a gesture of irritation, stared vacantly, and hesitated a moment before going on. "Ileana left the village twenty years or more ago, in any event, a year before me, and she's never been heard of since. She's a whore somewhere, in a port or a palace, who knows, married to a shopkeeper or a cabinet minister. It doesn't matter. Perhaps she's not even alive, in which case God have pity on her soul. There's nothing about your 'mother' to boast of. A slut, a real slut, a servant of the devil. Morning, noon, and night, especially night, she ran after the men. She turned their heads and they fell for her. Father used to beat her, but she laughed at him as if to show that he, too, desired her. It may have even been true. She was beautiful; she had the devil in her blood, the slut. Men lost their heads just by looking at her. And she knew it; she flaunted herself in front of them."

Maria struggled to contain her anger or her suffering.

"How do you know she has a son, and one that looks like me?"

"I don't know. I hope she doesn't. A woman like her has no right to be a mother. Shame is carried like disease, you know?"

She shook herself and her voice became normal again.

"But none of that matters. In the eyes of people here you'll be her son, legitimate or not. I don't care, and neither do they. That's it. The rest is nobody's business. If anyone's too nosy he'll have to reckon with me."

A mischievous twinkle lit up her wrinkled face; she liked her scheme: "For years I belonged to your family, now you belong to mine. I hope you like the idea."

"Of course, I'm flattered. The exchange is all to my advantage." And because she didn't seem to understand, he explained, "It's to my advantage to save my life, isn't it?"

Even if he was deaf and dumb and dull-witted, he had to learn the fundamentals of Christianity: to make the sign of the cross, to behave correctly in church, to kneel while kissing the holy images. For there was no necessity to memorize the catechism by rote or go to confession. Being a deaf-mute had some advantages.

Maria left nothing to chance. For one thing she found her nephew's suit too well cut.

"Why not?" asked Gregor, to whom it was a link, indeed the only link with the past. "Your sister is well off, and it's natural that her son should go to the best tailor."

"Ileana may be rich but her money stinks. I'll have none of it."

She took some wool cloth and made him the clothes of a Transylvanian peasant, with a long, collarless shirt, shapeless trousers, and no socks or shoes. A genuine peasant finds shoes useless; he likes to feel the ground under his feet, especially in the spring, when the earth is renewed into life.

The only person she took into the secret was Yonel, a grim, ill-tempered fellow with a sullen glint in his eyes. Gregor could not make out whether he was Maria's husband or a former lover. She spoke of him with a hate that was close to love. "He's a woman-chaser, a gambler, a grumbler, an idler, and a liar," she said. "The devil can take him, for all I care, but even the devil doesn't want him nearby."

"You loved him, admit it," said Gregor, "You still love him."

Maria became violent and raised her fist as if she were about to strike him. "Love! Love! You young people can't talk or think about anything else. You're crazy, I tell you. As if love were the most important thing in life!"

"Well, what *is* more important, Maria?"

"How should I know? I'm no longer what you'd call young. And then, you're the one who ought to know. You're the one who goes to school. And its your nose, not mine, that was always in books—where there are only words and lies. What have your books taught you, tell me that!"

Yonel had built his yellow cabin with the corn-stalk roof in an isolated place at the far end of the village, but at night he was rarely home. Sometimes he appeared at Maria's dead-drunk and barely able to keep his balance, and she took care of him as if he were a child, tenderly, but cursing him the whole time. "You'd have better died in your mother's womb!" she told him.

Gregor made Yonel's acquaintance the first morning after his arrival. Loud voices had awakened him. Maria was arguing with someone who was threatening and insulting her. Gregor listened.

"He must go away! He'll be too much trouble."

"No, Yonel; he's going to stay. And he won't be any trouble at all. The amount of time that you're here . . ."

"If you keep him, I won't ever come back."

"I'm keeping him."

Gregor held his tongue. The sun must have risen, the light was burning his eyelids.

"The war may last twenty years. Are you going to keep him that long?"

"Fifty, if necessary."

"And if I say no?"

"Too bad, that's all."

"You've never spoken to me that way."

"That's too bad. I should have."

"And if I throw him out?"

"I wouldn't advise it."

"What if I were to report him to the police? What would happen then, can you tell me? I'd get a reward and they'd arrest him. Good riddance, I'd call it."

When Maria said nothing, he cleared his throat and went on: "I don't like the Jews, and I don't understand how you can deal with them. They don't know how to drink or curse. They're not real men. If you love them the way you do, it means there's something wrong with you, something rotten inside, a screw loose. Ask the priest, and he'll tell you it's a sin

66

to be a Jew-lover; it's not normal. But I'm normal, and the police, they're normal, too. I really think I ought to report him. What do you say?"

A long silence followed. Gregor felt it echo through his body. He wanted to raise his head and look at the two adversaries, especially Maria, to see if she was capable of violence, whether she would turn white with rage or cry, whether she would fight or give in. But all he could do was to bite his lips, clench his fists, and wait. Finally Maria came out with an answer, and her voice was as cold and cutting as a knife.

"If you do that, Yonel, I'll kill you," she said, emphasizing every word. "And I mean it. I'm warning you. If anything happens to this boy, I'll take the axe there in the corner near the stove, and kill you. You know I don't waste words. I'll do just what I say I'll do. I'll wait for a night when you've had too much to drink, when you're in a drunken sleep. Even if I have to wait for years, I'll do it. I'll have no pity."

There was another but shorter silence.

"You're crazy," he said with a nervous laugh.

"Do you really think so?"

"Yes. That's crazy talk. You sound like the widow of Mihai, the one who wanted to dig her dead husband out of the grave and murder him a second time. If I didn't know you, I'd say you were crazy. What does this boy matter to you? A little beggar Jew, with the police after him. . . . Are you going to take in the whole lot of them? Have you decided to open an orphan asylum?"

Maria whistled between her teeth, and Gregor was sorry that he couldn't see her face.

"You're a bastard, that's what you are, Yonel, the biggest bastard in the world and the world's dirty for your being in it. You're worse than a snake, from your head to your feet you're all poison. Now just listen to me. Gregor's not a little beggar Jew, as you call him. He's my nephew, and if you touch a hair of his head, you'll regret it. The winter nights are long. You'll never close your eyes. You'll die a thousand deaths before I kill you."

Yonel grunted unintelligibly, spat on the floor, and went away, slamming the door behind him. Maria stood motionless.

Gregor waited a few minutes before opening his eyes. Then he raised himself onto his elbows and yawned, as if he were waking up.

"Did you have a good sleep?" Maria asked him weakly.

"Even better than at home."

He went out in the courtyard to wash up. When he came back he found hot coffee and two slices of bread and butter on the table. He ate with appetite, the coffee made him feel good. Sitting across the table Maria set forth her plan.

"I've spoken to Yonel," she said, her upper lip quivering. "You'll be seeing him often around the house, perhaps too often. Don't be frightened of him; he isn't as bad as he looks. Anyhow, he approves of my idea. Everything's going to be all right. He has promised to protect you."

Gregor wished at that moment he could have thrown his arms around her. He who had never told a lie suddenly saw that a lie can reveal a human being's true nature. Maria's eyes opened wide, and for no apparent reason, tears streamed down her hollow cheeks. Gregor had never seen her cry.

"You mustn't," he said gently, and without getting up he held out his hand and touched her arm, which was resting on the table. "No, Maria, you really mustn't. . . ."

"It's idiotic of me to cry," she said, wiping her face with the hem of her skirt. "You're too young to understand. But women are like that; all they can do is cry. When I'm unhappy, I cry; and when I'm happy, I cry too. If a woman doesn't cry, she must be dead. My sister Ileana didn't cry, but she was different. . . ." Noisily she blew her nose. "Don't stare at me; I'm not sick and I'm not dead. If I cry, it's just that I'm ashamed to have you stay in such a barn."

"I won't complain," said Gregor, smiling, "at least not before the end of the war. Remember, I'll be a deaf-mute."

Two days later she took him around the village. There were no more—and probably less—than three hundred people living there, most of them very young or very old, the others having been taken into the army. She pointed out the church, the school to which children from the next village went as well, the grocery, the notary's house, and the police station. The village people, already aware of his presence, stared at him and nodded their heads with a mixture of curiosity and pity. Ileana had enjoyed a certain notoriety, and the presence of her son brought all sorts of old gossip to the surface. "It's him, all right; he looks just like his mother." "That he does, may she be cursed." "Poor fellow, his mother sinned and he's the one God punished." "It's unfair, of course, but what can you do? The ways of heaven are inscrutable." Women at their windows, old men standing in the doorways, and the customers of the grocery all followed him with their eyes, as if he were a famous visitor, a prince. Maria introduced him to the notables.

"This is my nephew, Gregor. That's it, Gregor, make a bow there. You see, he can't talk, poor fellow; he can't even say hello. And he doesn't hear, either. Or if he does hear, he doesn't understand. There had to be a punishment, even if it was late in coming. . . ."

Gregor bowed, and moved his lips in a grimace, while the onlookers put on an expression of compassion.

"The poor boy, he seems so gentle."

"How did his mother happen to send him to you?"

"She lives in a large city; she's afraid of air raids."

"What about herself?"

"She isn't afraid of anything."

"Do you think he looks like Ileana? Those eyes . . ."

"Not the least bit. Look at him. He's a quiet sort, and she—ugh!—do you remember? The slut. She had a devil in her. . . ."

"That's right, he seems so good-natured, he looks as if he wouldn't hurt a fly, while she . . ."

"I can't understand. How could that slut of an Ileana have such a nice boy? I ask you?"

"Who's the father?"

Maria shrugged her shoulders.

"How should I know? I doubt if she knows herself." And she spat with disgust.

After they had made the rounds of the village Maria went home, leaving Gregor to stroll farther. Passers-by greeted him in friendly fashion and he nodded back. Spring filled the air with fragrance and promise, and the people went about their work with slow deliberateness, but not lazily. Far away, the war raged on, but they were oblivious to it. To them war meant a son at the front, a husband reported missing, a big brother in uniform. They said, "My son's in the war," just as they would have said, "My son's getting married."

During the following days Gregor came to know the village characters better. The priest, with his self-satisfied air of a false martyr, holding his hairy hands over his big stomach as if to protect it. . . . Constantine Stefan, the schoolteacher, a puny man, quite unnoticeable except when he opened his mouth to give out, excitedly, some pompous opinions; he talked a great deal and was incessantly in motion. . . . Mihai, the carpenter, nicknamed the Penitent, who sat on the ground in front of his hut, built of blackened wood, looking nervously first in one direction and then in the other, as if he were waiting for the arrival of God knows whom from God knows where. . . . Stan the blind man, near the entrance to the church: when he sang, it seemed as if his voice served him as eyes.

Gregor spent much time with them, listening to their joys and sorrows, the forbidden dreams that lay, hidden under seven layers of silence, among their memories. A deaf-mute was not dangerous, and they opened themselves up to him quite freely, laughing and crying, revealing secrets which their closest neighbors—above all their closest neighbors—did not know. They talked to him, also, about his "mother," how in times gone by she had turned the heads of all the men of the village, even the old ones. "Ah, well, fortunately she's gone away." "Ah well, too bad she's gone away."

The village bordered on a green and yellow valley where shepherds, lying on the grass, watched over their sheep, and played sad tunes on their long flutes. From far away they signaled to Gregor and he went to lie down beside them. With their eyes fixed on a point in the motionless sky they played heartbreaking airs, but he knew that at bottom they were happy, that they were in harmony with their lot and the lot of others. At sunset they gathered their flocks together by the call of the flute, without a single cry—and the air was filled with the chiming of bells and with nostalgia: farewell to the sun which leaves in peace, which never fails to return.

The only person whom Gregor never saw until that last day at the school was the mayor of the village, Count Petruskanu. The peasants spoke of him fearfully, with lowered voices, as if he were in league with some celestial or diabolical power. He lived in the villa beside the lake and was said to be so fabulously wealthy that only a man on horseback could cover the whole of his estate. In his luxurious manor, where the curtains were always drawn, he lived the life of a recluse, with an old nurse for a housekeeper. Every morning she went to purchase supplies at the grocery and stop in at the post office for the newspaper. Everyone hated her, without knowing exactly why, perhaps because she seemed to exude an odor of death. Swathed in a black scarf and shivering even in midsummer, she looked as if she were dying. Whenever she met one of the villagers on the street she spat contemptuously, not even bothering to see who it was. As for Petruskanu, he practically never showed himself, even at church. Every Sunday the priest went to the villa and said Mass in the private chapel which Petruskanu's father had built as a memorial to Countess Marcella, his young and beautiful wife who had died a year after their marriage. Petruskanu, his son, remained a bachelor. The priest had tried many times to give him advice or at least to talk to him. But Petruskanu had no desire for conversation. As soon as the Mass was over he had the housekeeper escort him to the door.

If Gregor could have spoken he would spend his time asking the villagers about their lives and that of his "mother," who still seemed to obsess those who had known her. From the scraps of information he was able to put together he gathered that she had possessed so strong a will and such boundless vitality that she had triumphed over every obstacle in her way. She was never content, however, with her victories, but turned them to derision, as if to further humble those whom she had already defeated. Actually she fought not to win, but to lose; the only trouble was that she kept on winning. After the war I'll find her, Gregor promised himself, yes, after the war everything will be possible.

But he could not speak, and this was fundamentally to his advantage. Because his curiosity was wordless, never rising to the surface, men and women spoke to him without inhibition, revealing their deepest and darkest anxieties, their guiltiest joys. He became not their mirror but their receptacle. Hardly a week had gone by before he was the best informed person in the community. He knew how to listen; he knew nothing else.

"My poor Gregor, you don't know how lucky you are. You're free. You've no family, no wife and children, above all, no daughter. Have you seen my daughter? The little bitch! She came home last week with a belly as big as a barrel. I beat her up, tore out her hair, knocked her against the wall. 'Who's the father?' I asked her. 'Who's the bastard that dishonored you? I'll bash his face in.' But she wouldn't say his name. She spat blood, but not a word came out of her mouth. So I'll be grandfather to a little bastard. . . . That bitch! What will people say? I'll be the laughing-stock of the whole village. What can I do, Gregor; tell me, what can I do?"

And another: "Come here, Gregor, and let's talk. Have you never wanted to get rid of all the words dancing in your head, to get them out of your system, somehow? No, I don't suppose you have, obviously. You're not like me; you're lucky. Well, do you know Mariutza? Don't look at me idiotically like that; you must know her; everybody does. There's only one Mariutza in the village, the daughter of the woodcutter who lives like a savage. You must have seen Mariutza coming back from the fields in the evening, with her hips swaying. She doesn't swing them any more; she's wearing a wide skirt now, trying to hide something that can't be hidden for long. She's expecting a child, Mariutza is, my child, and my wife doesn't know anything about it. If she finds out, she'll kill me; yes, she's capable of that; I know her. She's just waiting for a chance to do me in. She terrifies me; that's why I married her. She knows it, and that's why she hates me. What am I to do? You, you know nothing, you who are innocent of sin, give me advice."

And a third: "Do you see those people, in church and in the fields? All they care about is their own pleasure. And you think they're happy, don't you? You think they're good Christians. Well, they're liars, every last one of them. How do I know? Because I'm a liar myself. My whole life is a lie. I lie to the priest, to my wife, to my friends. You're the only one to

72

whom I don't lie. To the others I lie continually, to everyone. I don't tell them that my life disgusts me, that my wife disgusts me even more. What's there to do, Gregor, how can I live without lying?"

Impassive, Gregor listened and smiled inwardly. His mask protected him and made him conscious of a superiority. As the depositary of so many secrets he could have played the role of fate, setting off an earthquake in the village and a fire in the hearts of its inhabitants, overflowing as they were with bitterness and hate and revenge. Quite unsuspectingly they clapped him on the back and said gratefully, "It is good to have you among us. You, at least, are happy. You don't know what life's about, and that's fortunate."

Every one of them, in his own way, expressed satisfaction over the fact that the son of the prodigal Ileana should have come home. One offered him a glass of wine, another invited him to go walking and pick wild strawberries on the way. Perhaps it was because heretofore they had had no "village idiot" among them. He became "their" deaf-mute, just as the fat priest was "their" priest and the eccentric owner of the villa was "their" mayor. To them Gregor represented the fringe of consciousness, where words and images floated freely, unconnected to the shore; he was the incomprehensible element of existence, an island, near and yet far away, threatened with being washed away by the sea. When they confided in him they seemed to be delivering themselves to the powers of darkness with which part of him was somehow linked; they felt as if they were in the cemetery where they went to beg the dead to ward off evil. Half joking, half serious, they told him things that they would never have confessed to the priest, who would have spread them around without discrimination. With him they had less to fear than with the priest, for he would not reprimand them. With Gregor they were able to rid themselves of their guilt without incurring the penance that even the most lenient confessor would have imposed upon them.

Even someone as withdrawn and taciturn as Mihai, the carpenter, his initial mistrust overcome, encouraged him to pay him a visit. Gregor was quite pleased, and with reason, for

Mihai habitually avoided people. Whenever anyone came near him he scowled and lashed out, "What do you want now? Can't a man live in peace and quiet?"

Bare to the waist and sitting on the ground in front of his hut, Mihai invited Gregor to sit down beside him. Gregor did as he was asked. Out of the corner of his eye he observed the solitary carpenter, who stared out into nothing. Gregor was surprised to find that he was quite moving, as though himself an abandoned child.

"So," said Mihai with a touch of anger in his voice, "you're the son of the goddess Ileana. A woman like any other, after all, a mother like all the rest. So she had a son and it's you, is that it?"

He turned toward the boy and stared at him as hard as though he were trying to pierce the mystery, not of Gregor, but of himself. Although pretending indifference, Gregor was burning with curiosity. The carpenter intrigued him. Everything about him was out of proportion: his overly long fingers, his protruding cheekbones and eyes. His robust body was nervous; he squirmed continuously as though he were ill at ease. Mihai the Penitent. . . . No one knew what he had to repent for, what crimes he had committed and against whom. It had happened all of a sudden, when he was twenty-three years. One evening he had knocked at the door of his fiancée and said with a humiliated air that he couldn't marry her, that everything was over between them. No use weeping or fainting or throwing herself onto the floor, the wedding would not take place.

"But why, Mihai, why?"

"I don't deserve you. You are pure, you are innocent. You don't know what it is to be tempted or to sin. My sins are as heavy as the mountain and I can never turn away from them. I release you from your word. Go find a husband worthy of you, one whose past doesn't burn like a curse in his flesh. Forget me as quickly as you can, and forgive me for any harm I may have done you."

In spite of what he had said, his fiancée, after a moment of astonishment, sobbed and then fell, in a dead faint, to the floor. Mihai gave a long cry and ran away. The villagers could not recover from their consternation. The girl fell ill, and bad feeling toward Mihai grew. Various people tried to talk to his parents, but they refused to interfere. "He wouldn't obey us," they said. "He's a good-for-nothing who'll marry death, but we don't care any more."

The priest—an honest and warm-hearted fellow, since dead —went to tell Mihai what a sin it was to publicly humiliate the girl whom he had promised in the sight of God and man, to marry: to repudiate a betrothed was a grave and unpardonable act.

But Mihai would not listen and repeated his intention of remaining a bachelor. "I have my reasons."

"What about the girl?"

"She'll make out. She won't be alone for long."

The villagers mocked him, at the beginning with malice, later in fun. "You're telling big stories, Mihai. We've known you since you were born. We've seen you grow up. We remember the first time you took a razor to the few straggling hairs on your chin. Come on, Mihai, we know all about you! It's a lot of nonsense, all that talk about your sins. Come on, admit it, you're trying to make fun of us." Their refusal to believe him enraged Mihai. "What do you know?" he said, picking up a log, threateningly. "Leave me alone, or blood will flow!" "Careful, Mihai, anger is a sin too!" "Get out, I don't want to see you. When I look at you and see that we belong to the same species I want to spit on myself." "Easy there, Mihai; we know why you don't want to marry. You're afraid of women. We understand. Women scare you, admit it! They scare us, too." "Go away, your eyes dirty me! If you don't . . ." There was a murderous expression on his face as he raised the log, and his body trembled with fury.

With the passage of time they stopped teasing him and he came to be accepted by the community. His fiancée soon found a husband, but he had been taken into the army and for two years now there had been no news of him. His last letter was from the Eastern front, from Kiev. Because of his mental instability Mihai was declared unfit for military service. His fiancée, now the mother of three children, hung about his hut but he pretended not to see her.

"Ileana's boy, eh?" said Mihai, staring at Gregor obliquely. "It's funny, I just can't imagine her a mother."

He shifted his position until he could look Gregor in the face. He studied him attentively. Gregor realized that this tender-hearted giant was surely not a bad man and that he suffered. Below the surface, he had a good heart. The villagers actually loved him. He charged little for his work and made an effort to get along with everyone. If he kept clear of women, that was his business; and if he possessed vices, well, let him keep them to himself.

"I knew your mother, you see," said Mihai, in a trembling voice. "She was as proud and beautiful as a goddess. She could have corrupted even our Lord Jesus Christ. Did you know that? Sometimes I wonder if she didn't actually try. If a woman gives herself to more than one man, it's because a single conquest isn't enough for her; her pride demands more. And the pride of your mother . . . well, let's not speak of that. Words are only words, and your mother's pride humbled words—and not only words."

Gregor looked the carpenter straight in the eyes, making an effort not to betray his tenseness. This man, Gregor thought, seemed to cultivate his obsessions, to love and hate them at the same time, as if they kept him alive. If he could have allowed himself to speak, he would have said: "Mihai, go on, I beg of you, don't stop, go on."

"Yes, she was beautiful," the carpenter continued. "A real sorceress. She could have had all the men at her feet. And if she had said, Go strangle one another, they would have obeyed her. They crawled before her, but that wasn't enough; she was always asking for more. She enjoyed ridiculing the submissiveness of some and breaking the resistance of others, until she could ridicule them also. If you laughed, she would say, No, I want to see you cry, and if you cried she would say, No, I want to see you laugh. If you gave her your body, she said, It's your soul I want, and if you gave her your soul, she said, What do you want me to do with it? One winter day she said to me, I'll be yours if you'll bring me . . . Bring you what? A ray of sun. I wanted to choke her, but when she looked at me I melted like butter. You're dishonest and disgusting, I hate you, I wanted to say, but the words that came out of my mouth were, I love you. You haunt me even in my sleep. And you're no longer angry? No, Ileana. You love me in spite of my bad character? Yes, I love you the way you are. Then you're a real fool and don't deserve to have me love you. Out of spite I took up with another girl and we decided to marry. That, Ileana couldn't forgive. She kept trying to seduce me, but I made an effort to keep away. Sometimes she waited in the forest, where I went to gather wood. She called, but I didn't answer. She struck a pose in front of me, laughing in a way that made me quiver, but I didn't see her; I said to myself that she didn't exist, she didn't burn within my body. For a long time I held out against her. On the afternoon when she finally won, it was in an explosion of rage that we made love. Yes, she gave me her body, but so violently and with such a cold expression on her face that for a moment I said to myself: She's going to kill me. At the end she pushed me away. Lying under a tree I waited to see what was going to happen next, as tensely as if I had escaped from one danger, only to glimpse another. Ileana got up, pulled down her skirt, looked at me disdainfully, and said between clenched teeth, You're a disappointment. You're a pathetic specimen, like all the rest. I've no pride or joy in possessing you; in fact, I'm ashamed, disgusted. And she walked slowly away. I was too frightened to breathe, and yet I was thinking that I ought to have killed her. If I'd done that, I'm convinced that before she drew her last breath she would have loved me. She was a goddess measuring herself against death, that's the only explanation."

Mihai talked while watching Gregor, seeking some indication of whether or not he had followed the story. But Gregor remained impassive, breathing evenly and with a frozen expression. Suddenly the carpenter's face blazed with anger. He stared at Gregor as if he were an enemy, ready to punish him for the least gesture reminiscent of Ileana and her cruelty.

"You are a goddess's son," he said, leaning forward on his elbows in order to bring his face close to that of Gregor. "You're the proof that she was beautiful, that she existed, that she was a woman, that a woman like herself can have children, and that these children can live only on the sidelines of life, not understanding their fellow human beings or sharing their sins and their salvation. Was she capable of loving you? Do you love her? And your father, who is he? Is he happy?"

Gregor felt the carpenter's breath on his face and had to make an effort not to react.

"You're Ileana's deaf son," said Mihai exasperatedly, "so I can't hope that you'll enlighten me. I'll never find out whether your mother won her way, whether she finally succeeded in corrupting Our Lord. What do you think? Or are you capable of thinking? Personally, I'm willing to wager she did. And you're the fruit of this union, the result of her victory. Gregor, do you realize that you might be the Lord's son? And that your illustrious father made you dumb so that you couldn't tell? That's it, isn't it? You can tell me, I'm in on the secret. I knew your mother; she possessed me; she opened her doors to me; she told me everything."

Gregor felt scorched by Mihai's eyes. If he had opened his mouth or had reacted in any way, Mihai would have run away in terror. Mihai quite honestly took him for the son of Ileana, for the son of Jesus Christ, born out of a debauch. Once more Gregor resolved that after the war he would discover Ileana, the woman who had chased away boredom and kindled fires. He imagined himself, somewhere on the globe, in the rain or at the sunny edge of the woods, saying to her, "Woman, my mother is dead, and you are my mother. Your being my mother is what made me dumb and saved my life."

Thereafter he came often to sit with the carpenter in front of his hut. A secret greater than they bound them together. "Gregor, you're always with the Penitent," said Maria. "What do you want with him?" But Gregor played his role and did not answer. Even with Maria he took refuge behind the son of the whore, Ileana, whom God in his infinite mercy had deprived of the power to speak.

Another person sought out his company: Constantine Stefan, the old schoolteacher, whom the villagers avoided like the plague because they couldn't stand his endless chatter.

They knew by heart his witticisms and stories, his complaints about the lack of respect shown him by the younger generation, his recollections of the good old times when boys and girls were grateful to their teachers for what was taught them. "Yes, yes," peasants mocked, "you're right, but we've heard it all before." For the schoolteacher Gregor was the ideal prey. Shortly after Gregor had arrived, Stefan went to Maria and offered to give the boy private lessons.

"You're out of your mind," exclaimed Maria, her hands on her hips. "He's wooden-headed, can't you see? His brain, if he has one, contains nothing and can take nothing in. It's a piece of wood, I tell you. It's God's punishment and a just one!"

"Let me try," said the old man plaintively; "you can never tell. He's no idiot, that's certain, no more than lots of my former students who talk stupidly all day and a good part of the night. Yesterday I saw Petru in front of the police station, and he . . ."

Maria saw no reason for subjecting her nephew to this flow of words and cut him short.

"Don't waste your breath; the answer's no."

"Why? Give me some reason. Are you against education? Against progress? Against culture?"

"I'm not against anything. I simply haven't got money to throw away; it doesn't flow in the streets, you know."

"Who's talking about money?" the schoolteacher exclaimed. "Am I asking you for money? I don't need that. Who do you think I am? A profiteer, a materialist? As I was saying last week to . . . Well, never mind. Let's get back to the subject. I'd like to give your nephew free lessons. My contribution to the war effort! I'll do it with pleasure and . . ."

"No," said Maria, relentlessly. "It's no use your trying. The answer is no."

"But why, Maria? Why?" Constantine Stefan protested. He was not thinking of Gregor at the moment. It made him happy to have a listener and he had no intention of stopping. Under the spell of his own eloquence he mingled childhood episodes, poetry learned by heart, and recalled the predictions of his teachers. . . .

Maria, brave Maria, became increasingly impatient.

"That's enough. You bore me, and soon you'll have me tired as well. Besides, I have work to do. Let my nephew alone; he's been ill and needs rest. Look at how pale his cheeks are, and how hollow. The least bit of exertion could be harmful. Don't you have eyes, heart? Do you want to kill him?"

Finally she stemmed the flood. But the schoolteacher waylaid Gregor in the late afternoons when he could have him all to himself. Gregor listened without emotion. For the old chatterbox had also had his own love story with Ileana. Clearly, in the whole of this lost village, she hadn't left a single heart intact.

"Yes, my boy, I knew your mother," said the old man, spitting on the ground. "She offered herself to me—I may as well tell you—I was attractive to her, I guess, that's all. Life and women are beyond explanation. Only nothing happened. I was shy; in fact, I still am. Yes, I had the ripe, forbidden fruit in my hand, and I didn't dare bite into it. I think back all the time of what a fool I was. Every time I said something to your mother I was paralyzed. She was my pupil, of course. Everyone here has been my pupil at one time or another, that is, except the mayor. And perhaps Nikolai, but that's another story— when he was eight years old he was arrested for murder. Your mother, when she was twelve years old, perhaps even a little less, already behaved like a woman, blindingly beautiful, capricious. The boys, why she drove them crazy; they'd have killed their fathers and mothers if she'd given them the word. Slaves, that's what they were. Myself also; she managed to throw me, too, into a state of confusion. In her presence I felt insignificant, completely stupid. And yet always and in every subject she was the class dunce. She refused to make the slightest effort. 'I'll get along in life without your books,' she claimed. No homework for her; mathematics she didn't like and grammar was sheer horror, yes horror, along with geography and history. 'What use are they to me?' she would say, tossing her head; 'I'll get along.' Often I swore I'd punish her, but when she opened those innocent, dark eyes I felt as if the earth were opening beneath me and I would fall in and disappear. I was ready to throw myself at her feet, right in front of the whole class, and implore her pardon. She knew what power she had over me. One day she stayed in the classroom under the pretext of speaking with me about the geography lesson. There was a sad look on her face. 'I know I give you trouble,' she said, lowering her head. 'I don't want to hurt you, really I don't. I'm too fond of you for that.' 'Then you should work harder,' I said, concealing my emotion. 'Education counts these days, Ileana. Later on, when you're grown up, you'll be sorry you didn't take full advantage of it.' 'I'll do what you say, I promise.' 'Very good.' To reward her good resolution, I said I'd tutor her until she caught up with the rest of the class. So she stayed every day after school, after the others were gone. But it wasn't the tutoring that interested her, of course; it was me. She stared at me with quivering lips while I was explaining the lesson, but she didn't take in a word I was saying. The words stuck in my throat, I stammered and perspired. One day, quite accidentally, I swear it, my hand touched her hair. She didn't move, but I didn't dare make the same gesture again. Your mother had more nerve than I; she took my hand and taught me how to stroke her hair. That night I couldn't shut my eyes, and the next day in class I seemed to be sleepwalking. When we were alone together your mother was a model of composure. 'Today I'm going to teach you how to kiss a woman,' she announced calmly, and she did. I was consumed with passion and rage and shame and told myself it was a dangerous business. 'What are you doing, Constantine Stefan?' I said to myself. 'Have you no modesty? No principles? Have you forgotten she's a minor, that you can get into all sorts of trouble?'' I appealed to my reason, but it did me no good. Your mother was stronger than me, stronger than me and all my principles. One afternoon she pretended to be warm, and I offered her a glass of milk or water. She shot me a mocking look: 'What a lot you have to learn!' she told me. Then, looking at me scornfully, she proceeded to undress. Just like that, right in front of me, as if we were husband and wife. Seeing my embarrassment, she said, 'You're lucky to have me to teach you.' And I tell you she was barely twelve years old. A tigress, a divine tigress, capable of defeating an army of supermen. I watched her deliberately take off her clothes, and a beast shouted in me, a beast that was to lay me low. Your mother went over to the window and drew the curtains. With my last remaining energy I rushed to the door and ran away, as fast as if the devil were at my heels. When the villagers saw me stumbling blindly over the cobblestones they thought I'd gone mad. I was the only one to know that, on the contrary, I had saved my reason. Now, of course, I'm sorry. Devil take reason and timidity! Life wouldn't be worth living if it didn't include a bit of madness. What a sight she was, little Ileana, naked and trembling, with her arms crossed over her little belly. A beauty she was, and she loved me, but I was a fool and a coward."

There was one thing the schoolteacher didn't know. Ileana had alerted her classmates, and they had watched the whole scene until very near the end. By sheer luck he had failed to see them or hear their laughter.

"The tutoring came to an end," he went on breathlessly, "and your mother returned—through my fault—to being the class dunce. But I still loved her. I don't know what I really loved, the child or the woman. Both, I suppose. But she had destroyed something inside me. Before, I was happy and at ease among the children; I taught them to read and write and sing; I pointed out the beauties of nature, the enchantment of living things, the unsuspected depths of certain ideas that are passed down from one generaion to another. Sometimes I took them to the woods and talked to them about trees and plants and animals. It seemed to me that God was listening to us, that God himself was a schoolchild. But when your mother was there I lost my ease, I was no longer myself, and my teaching suffered. I failed the other children, who were not to blame."

And he went on to describe the pupils toward whom he had felt guilty. Grown-ups now, all of them, they had doubtless forgotten. Not he. He would never forget.

Gregor thought of children going to school and of those who would never go to school again. The old man was crying, but Gregor's face remained immobile. Children are the first to be devoured by war. Suffer little children to come unto me, particularly Jewish children. Tell them nothing. Don't cry or make them cry. Don't tell them what fate awaits them. Don't tell them that invisible clouds are darkening the sky, or that I am calling them unto me, these Jewish children, in order that my beloved sons, soldiers of love and the cross, may strangle them and throw their bodies into the river that will carry them down to the sea.

Without realizing it Gregor had been transfigured. The voice of Gavriel vibrated within him, regulating his breathing and giving depth to his silence. He hid himself behind Gavriel's face, beneath Gavriel's star, and this was why he was able, almost without an effort, to keep silent.

Little by little Gregor learned everything about the village. With piercing eyes he looked through walls and grimacing faces. He knew why one man seemed glum and another gay; nothing surprised him. He could have guessed at what anyone was doing at any given hour of the day. "Hello there, Gregor, can you spare a minute?" The villagers could no longer get along without him. By surrendering to him the keys to their existence they had made him the custodian of their liberties.

And the priest, instead of taking umbrage, went along with it. One Saturday afternoon Gregor was standing with bowed head, in front of the church, listening to the blind man sing. Suddenly the priest came up from behind him and pushed him inside. Instinctively Gregor fell to his knees, as if to pray.

"No," said the priest, "get up. You can pray another time."

As a deaf-mute that knew the tricks of the trade, Gregor didn't move. The priest raised him to a standing position.

"Come with me, my boy; don't be afraid."

The priest had gleaming eyes and a strange smile set in the middle of his pudgy face. Murmuring "Blessed are the simple-minded, for theirs is the kingdom of Heaven; you don't know temptation, you don't know how lucky you are," he pushed Gregor toward the confessional. At first Gregor did not understand that he had been forced into the priest's section of the box.

The priest, meanwhile, entered the penitent's section, folded his hands, bent his head, and began to whisper, *Ave*

Maria, purissima . . . "I have sinned, my child. In the name of the Lord I beg you to give me absolution."

Gregor was tempted to reveal his disguise; he had to bite his lips in order not to laugh. The scene was almost ridiculous. He thought of Gavriel and controlled himself.

"My sin is heavy and weighs heavily on my conscience," the priest was saying. "And yet, Lord, it was for you that I committed it, for you alone. . . ."

The curiosity of the young Jew was aroused: "He too has a story," he thought to himself. "Perhaps it's about Ileana. Well, why not? Why should Ileana have spared him?"

But the priest's story had nothing to do with Ileana, who had left the village before his arrival. The priest had committed no carnal sins. He was against sin, but not against crime.

Several weeks before, a Jew, who must have jumped from a death train, had come to him for protection. Heedless of danger, the priest had taken him in.

" 'Here's a chance to save his soul, to bring him to the light,' I said to myself. Kindness is a weapon, and I decided to use it. One evening, when I thought he was ready, I called to his attention the fact that his people's trials were nearing an end. 'God will have mercy upon them as soon as they repent,' I said. He listened politely: 'Yes, Father; thank you, Father.' 'Don't thank me, thank God. He commanded me to do good; He is the source of my will and the goal of everything I do.' 'No!' he said firmly standing upright before me. 'No?' I echoed, dumb with astonishment and sorrow. 'No, Father,' he said implacably and pitilessly. 'I won't go along with it. You want an alibi, but I won't supply one for you.' "

The priest tried to discuss, to cajole, to protest to the Jew that his intentions were all of love and Christian charity.

"But in the heat of the discussion I lost patience; I lost my temper and fell into the trap. I accused him of ingratitude and vulgar materialism, of thinking only of his earthly life. But he shook his head. 'No, Father, I owe you nothing; you owe us everything. For two thousand years you've crucified us in the hope of rediscovering in yourself the man whom you've travestied as God. Stop thinking about our salvation and perhaps the cemeteries won't be so full of Jews.' 'But you're alive, my son,' I exclaimed, 'thanks to me you're still alive, thanks to the Christ who dies every day in order that you may go on living!' 'No, Father, we die every day, not him!' 'Very well, never mind about Christ. Let's speak of God; you owe Him thanks for having saved you.' 'No, Father, no. Thank God in time of war? Of course I know how He likes to be thanked; that's all He really cares for. He demands gratitude of His beggars; it's positively human of Him, isn't it, because it allows Him to believe in His own benevolence. What do you expect, Father? Like women, He's jealous, adores compliments, gifts, sacrifices? Like a woman He thinks that everything is His due; like a woman He needs men. He *is* a woman, I tell you.' "

The priest nearly choked over these last words and had to pause in order to regain his composure.

"I knew he wanted to hurt me, and I lacked humility. In the face of his blasphemy I began to weep, not with pity but with rage. I wanted to strike him on the face and humiliate him, I even wished for his death. Satan was talking through his lips, and shouldn't every good Christian chase him away? This is just what I did. I showed him the door and told him never again to set foot in my house—which is God's house. With impressive calm he put on his coat and walked toward the door, where he stopped and looked at me, with pity rather than hate. 'You see, Father, I was right. And you don't even know who I am.' I started to overtake him, to bring him back and ask his pardon, but he was already swallowed up by the night. A few hours later he was captured and turned over to the Germans. Even under torture he did not denounce me. I never saw him again. I don't know what happened to him. But his words of farewell are still with me, devouring my reason. In the middle of Mass I can hear his voice say, 'I won't go along with it. Do you know who I am?' Sometimes I catch myself answering, Yes, I know. You're the Son of Man, and you were right. I'm afraid; I'm afraid of having lost my soul and my salvation. I'm going mad. . . ."

He hid his head in his hands and for a long time Gregor heard only his heavy breathing. For the second time he was tempted to reveal himself, to turn to the priest and shout in his face, "You don't know who it was that you chased away; well, I'll tell you. It was I, it was Gavriel. I curse you, and may my curse precede and follow you all the way to the grave!"

Fortunately the priest got up, somewhat abruptly, and led Gregor out of the church, looking more troubled than relieved. His hand pressed down on Gregor's shoulder and again he murmured, "You're lucky my boy; Satan's interested only in intelligence."

In front of the church Stan was singing, sadly. He seemed to mistrust Gregor, and Gregor, for his part, had held himself aloof and had never sought his company. Sometimes he would sit near him, but Stan went on singing as if he weren't even there. Gregor was always to remember Stan's favorite song:

Forget, kind passer-by, that you have fed my hunger;
Forget and go your way, for I'll remember longer . . .

With an enormous straw hat on his head and his cane between his legs, Stan sang for hours on end until he was totally exhausted and fell into a stupor so frightening that people turned their eyes away. Kindly people brought him hot soup and corn bread, which he ate with awkward gestures. The priest's housekeeper looked after him and spoke to him almost tenderly. He seldom replied, and then only in unfinished sentences, but he let her do what she would. Gregor liked the way he sang; his hoarse voice stimulated the mind instead of lulling it to sleep. Only blind people can catch the essence of a song and convey it without mutilation.

The days unfolded slowly and peacefully. Summer brought back life and gaiety; people's faces wore an appearance of lasting happiness. Old men and women lolled in front of their huts and talked of the past; children talked of the future. Almost shamefully Gregor came to the conclusion that there are possibilities of enrichment in war. Some people acquire money, others decorations and claims to glory, still others snatches of vision and anxiety which lend significance to their life by raising it to the level of consciousness. There is a chance of changing one's self, of ripening, of learning in a flash what might otherwise have taken years. Such a man thinks: "I'm a war profiteer, I ought to be ashamed." However, this very shame contributes to his enrichment.

War taught Gregor that men—all men except saints and those by whom they are murdered—lead a double life, one giving sap to the other, but separated by the same abyss that separates birth from death, actual being from the image it casts over both past and future. Constantine Stefan was more than a schoolteacher, the priest more than a prayer-machine, and Mihai was better fitted to disputing with his creator than to making tables and stools.

Even today, in a street of Calcutta or Tel-Aviv, if Gregor's eyes fall upon a passer-by with a haggard or resolute air it is because he sees in him a reflection of his own secret anxiety; he would give anything to decipher and disarm it and to affirm thereby the solidarity of destinies bound together for and against man. Every death leaves a scar, and every time a child laughs it starts healing. Good morning, good evening, are you happy? Ghostly bluish silhouettes, ridiculous in their exaggerated ambitions. The rhythm of their march toward death—perhaps his own as well—remains alien to him. Marching, if we are strong, in the dust, and if we are not, in the mud, we take a step, a few steps together and then our paths draw apart, and only dust and mud are left. What, then, is man? Hope turned to dust. But whenever Gregor thinks of the remote village in Transylvania he knows that the opposite is equally true. What is man? Dust turned to hope.

He admits that, had it not been his apparent meeting with Gavriel, and he insisted on *apparent,* he would not have been able to endure and his being would not have been revealed to him. The sequence of events has a mystery all its own. He admits, too, that were it not for the meeting with Gavriel (and he insists on attaching the adjective *earlier* to it) he could never have endured. Because he was not Gregor, but Gavriel, he managed to live through these few weeks—weeks set apart from the rest of his life—without worrying too much about the fate of his family, without breaking forever the bonds between himself and his fellow men, Gregor would have burst, more than once, with sorrow or anger; he would have drowned in his own tears. The strength of Gavriel saved him. It very nearly lost him as well.

Gentle and docile, the nights shortened, in deference to a summer, which continued to burn furiously in the valleys and on the mountain tops. During the day the village seemed deserted. Here and there an old man dozed, with a straw hat pulled down over his eyes, leaning against the wall of his yellow hut, in the yellow sunlight, or under an apple tree whose branches offered the wind temporary refuge. The women, with their red or black hair rolled on top of their heads, worked in the fields and implored heaven to send rain. The children, devoured by impatience, prayed for time to pass more quickly and vacation to begin. As every year at this time, Constantine Stefan lost his voice in a vain effort to impose discipline.

According to custom, he was engaged in rehearsing with his recalcitrant pupils a play to be given at the end of the school year. The children, who had no mind for anything but games, took part only in order to avoid punishment. Why learn by heart a text that had nothing to do with their studies? They saw no point to it. History, geography, and arithmetic were all very well, but what good was theater? They hung back and protested, but the teacher insisted. Every year, come hell or high water, before an audience composed of the notables and people of the five adjacent villages, his play was given.

The actors could only be involuntarily comic. Constantine Stefan should have chosen to give comedies. Unfortunately he had a pronounced taste for drama and, even more for tragedy. Mistrustful of laughter, because he feared himself to be its butt, he was intent upon overwhelming. Little Rumanian peasants who murdered the Hungarian language were no great help. The only one to be overwhelmed was the director, and that for reasons which had little to do with the content or the meaning of the play.

This year the cast had an unexpected recruit: Gregor. According to instructions from the Ministry of Education, the schoolteacher had chosen a timely subject: the Jews, or more precisely, hatred of the Jews and its justification. Constantine Stefan's overflowing enthusiasm and imagination inspired him with a bright idea. He would present the figure who, ever since the birth of the religion of love, had stood for baseness and betrayal: Judas Iscariot. The priest, who was duly consulted, declared himself delighted, but set one condition. It was all right for the play to speak of Christ, but he should not be shown. Knowing his public, the priest wanted to save the Son of God from being made into an object of mockery.

The director did not find very much enthusiasm among the players; they were sullen and seemed to delight in thwarting him. For one thing, none of them wanted to take the part of the traitor. Pontius Pilate? All right, Saint Peter? With pleasure. A Roman soldier? Why not? But not Judas; he was fundamentally antipathetic to them. In vain did Constantine Stefan explain that it was all make-believe: You'll be Judas for two hours and then you'll return to being yourself. He called upon the priest to bear him out, but the priest's eloquence was to no avail. The disciple Judas inspired deepseated mistrust. This was only natural. Almost every Sunday at Christmas and, above all, at Easter the priest stuffed their heads with Judas's irreparable crimes. A coward, a liar, an informer, the symbol of everything detestable! Had he not, for thirty pieces of silver, sold the Savior of mankind to the Romans? He was impure to the touch and even his name could not be pronounced without spitting on the ground or brandishing the fist in the direction of an actual or an imaginary Jew. Take the part of this traitor? No thanks. Too dangerous. Constantine Stefan was at his wit's end. He cursed the Jews; this, too, was their fault.

Then he had a second bright idea. Gregor's presence in the village suddenly seemed providential. The despised part was perfectly fitted to the son of Ileana, the woman who had sown discord in so many marriages and in so many souls. Wasn't it so? Breathless, he hurried to Maria's house to share with her his solution.

"The perfect solution," he said, rubbing his hands as if in self-congratulation. "He won't have to speak or even to move, really. He'll appear on the stage at the appropriate moments of the last act, that's all, without a word, or a gesture, just as a presence; he'll look on and accept what happens. A silent Judas, there's something original for you, a Judas struck dumb by God! Moral: He who sins by his power of speech shall lose it. My dear Maria, the more I think about it the more I realize that your nephew is ideal for the part. God sent him here, and I'm taking him in. You can consider it an honor, mind you. Of course you're willing, aren't you? You simply can't say no; the fate of the play is in your hands."

"I'm not willing at all," said Maria somberly.

"What, not willing? You refuse? Impossible! I need your nephew, the village needs him, Christ needs him. It's a matter of duty, like military service. You don't want your nephew to be a deserter, do you, Maria? Remember that we're at war."

"I still say no," said Maria, as if she had some presentiment of evil to come. She made a gesture as if to wipe her hands on her skirt, although her hands were perfectly dry. "Leave us alone, Constantine Stefan. Gregor isn't one of your pupils. And I don't want him to be a laughing-stock. He's not strong, and this might kill him. As for duty, you know perfectly well that boys of his kind aren't called up for the army; they don't even know that there's a war. Leave him alone, I tell you. Find someone else to be laughed at."

"You don't understand," said the schoolteacher, growing red in the face. "Judas isn't a comic character. He's tragedy itself, just like your nephew. How can I get it into your head that they fundamentally resemble each other?"

"So now you're insulting him," Maria interrupted, passing from protest to anger. "How dare you?"

"No, no, Maria. You've misunderstood me . . ."

"That's enough," she put in again, not allowing him to finish his sentence; "you've really gone too far. My poor nephew is the soul of innocence. He's pure and good and has never hurt anyone. It's no, I tell you. I refuse. Gregor's not a clown, called in to amuse the people. Go away, and don't speak to me about it again, ever, do you understand?"

Just then Yonel, still sober, appeared at the door.

"What's going on?" he asked. "Why are you quarreling?"

Constantine Stefan, hoping to find an ally, explained the matter with many gestures.

"He's quite right," said Yonel sententiously. "I agree. For once here's a chance for Gregor to do something for the rest of us. He owes us at least that, doesn't he?"

90

"Gregor is my nephew," said Maria brusquely. "It's up to me to say what he may and may not do."

"Quite true," said Yonel mellifluously; "you're right there. But why won't you let him be in the play? That's what I can't understand."

"Mind your own business!"

"Don't lose your temper, my good Maria. It's bad for your health. I don't know why you make it into something so big. According to the teacher, there's nothing to it. No one's asking our dear Gregor to work in the fields or make any other sacrifice for this village, which you must admit has treated him like one of its own children. He's asked only for a couple of hours of his time. If I understood correctly he'll get up on the stage, win the audience's applause, and go away. How can that hurt him? If you ask me, it may even do him good. Poor fellow, he doesn't have much fun. He wanders about all day long, feeling quite useless, and probably depressed. Thanks to the schoolteacher's bright idea he can at last enjoy himself. I can't help feeling sorry for the boy. Always alone. I wonder, sometimes, what he thinks of us. If he imagines we're all dumb, like himself."

"Too bad *you* aren't dumb," muttered Maria, glowering.

The schoolteacher saw that things were starting to go his way.

"So, will you give him to us, Maria? Yes? Yonel's on our side, and you trust him, don't you?"

"No, nothing doing," said Maria between clenched teeth.

"Anyone would think you were afraid, that you were trying to protect him."

"I'm not afraid."

"Then why are you so stubborn? Do you know what people will say? That you didn't dare. And they'll wonder why. They'll think your attitude suspicious."

"Too bad. You'll not have Gregor."

But in the end she had to give in. To ignore the trap that Yonel had set for her might be dangerous. Constantine Stefan might well go around saying that her stubbornness must be inspired by fear.

"Very well, take him! And go to the devil!"

With exuberant joy, the little schoolteacher began to dance about. "Thank you, Maria! Yonel, thank you! You've saved my life. I'm so happy. Thank you, thank you!"

Maria turned to Yonel, after Stefan had left.

"If a single hair falls from his head, you'll pay dear for it. My threat still holds."

"What can possibly happen to your little Jew? Nothing. He'll cause people to laugh, that's all. You're making it all such a big thing."

"We'll see," said Maria, shrugging her shoulders.

"Nothing will happen," repeated Yonel, with a sudden intimation of fear. He was no longer so sure, and regretted that he had stepped in. What if something did go wrong? Maria would keep her word, he knew that. "Everything will be all right, you'll see."

He made a move in her direction, but she paid no attention and went to do her wash. Uncertainly Yonel followed her for a moment with his eyes. Then he went out, swearing, "It's the fault of the Jews!"

The great day was set for Thursday of the following week. Stefan took Gregor to his class and introduced him.

"Here's our Judas. So you see, God doesn't abandon those who believe in him. I ask you to be nice to this poor fellow, who suffers for the sins committed by his mother."

Impassively Gregor let him do as he would.

The next day the schoolteacher burst into the classroom in a state of almost uncontrollable agitation. He had just heard the most important news of his whole life: Count Petruskanu was coming in person, to see the play.

"My dear boys and girls and . . . colleagues," he said solemnly, after he had recovered from his emotion. "I trust you realize the importance of what I have just told you. I'm going to ask each one of you to do his very best toward making the play worthy of the Count's attention. The experience you are going to have will leave its mark on your lives and you will be proud—I hope—to tell your children about it."

The young people were impressed and pledged their support in chorus. Never in his whole teaching career did Constantine Stefan have more obedient pupils; in their zeal they anticipated all his desires.

Maria alone seemed worried; she had a presentiment of danger, to which she could give no concrete shape.

"That bastard Yonel!" she murmured to herself throughout these days. "I'll get even with him. He won't get away with it no matter how long I have to wait."

Too late to withdraw.

As for Gregor, he kept calm. The hustle and bustle of the rehearsals amused him. They wanted him to play a part? He'd play it. And he was as excited as the rest of them over the prospect of a glimpse of the mysterious Petruskanu, who like a god, would not allow himself to be seen by his subjects. From the moment of his arrival in the village, this man had intrigued him.

"Don't worry, Maria. Everything will be all right. I'm a better actor than any of them; you know that, don't you?"

"I wish the whole stupid business were over. That idiot Petruskanu! Always turning up at the wrong time!"

"You and your forebodings!" said Gregor teasingly. "I've grown up, Maria, you don't seem to realize that. I'm no longer a child."

"That's just what I'm afraid of."

Worry made Maria less talkative than usual. She counted the days, the hours, as if to exorcise an evil that was about to be born. She was constantly in motion, went to church three times a day, used every means to make the time go faster and to put it to good use.

Before this Gregor had not opened his mouth, even when he was alone with Maria. But now his discipline broke down and she did not even reprimand him.

"Can you tell me why Petruskanu, so contrary to his habits has decided to be at the play?" he asked her.

"How should I know? I'm not inside his head, thank God."

"But you must have some idea. What is it?"

"What a nuisance you are! He doesn't confide in me."

The least remark made her nervous. She set herself against the whole world: on one side herself, on the other the rest of the human race, arrayed in all its hostility. Even her nephew seemed to be among her enemies. Suddenly Gregor had an idea.

"Look here, Maria, did Petruskanu know Ileana?"

Maria did not answer. Gregor repeated his question. She raised her head, let it drop again, and replied. "I haven't the slightest idea."

Gregor tried various stratagems to draw her out, until finally she exclaimed in exasperation, "You annoy me with your questions. You're some deaf-mute aren't you?"

Maria's reaction strengthened Gregor's conviction that he himself had something to do with the Count's surprising decision. There was nothing more to be done to draw out Maria. He decided to wait until after the play: at ease, Maria would be more assured, more talkative.

Meanwhile, as a good actor, Gregor struggled to accommodate himself to the character of Judas. Who was he? Christ's best disciple and closest friend. From one day to the next, and for no apparent reason, his loyalty was shattered and Judas became a traitor. Why? Why this sudden change? According to the Gospels there was an obscure story of money. Thirty pieces of silver. Absurd and inconceivable: The money adds to the mystery rather than explaining it. Christ's companions had no interest in terrestrial things—these had nothing to do with their aspirations. There had to be other reasons, more hidden than these. If the disciple abandoned his Master for thirty miserable pieces of silver, it meant that both men were more vulnerable than they knew.

Gavriel used to say that the difference between Christians and Jews was that for Christians everything that comes from God is good and everything evil bears the mark of man; the Jews, however, press their search further and more blasphemously, crediting God with evil as well as absolution. The first act of Abraham, the first Jew—his readiness to sacrifice his son—was an accusation against God and his injustice. After that Moses shattered the tables of the Law, in anger not only with his own people but with the God of his people. The Midrash contains a troubling legend along these same lines. Cain says to God: "Why did you make me commit this crime?

Why did it have to be me? You could have prevented it, but you didn't. Why not?" The answer? evasive of course. All that is left to us of Cain is his curse. For a long time Gregor had wondered why Cain didn't kill himself. The reason was this: Cain wanted to make life hard for the Creator of men and for their creations. If Christians insisted that Judas had killed himself, it was to absolve Christ of his own death.

Without knowing why, Gregor felt an ineffable joy when he thought of his playing the part of Judas. In front of the church Stan, the blind man, was singing:

"Forget, passer-by, that thanks to you I smile,
That thanks to you I dream and see sights lost to you a while."

Somewhere, in the distance, there was a war.

3

The villagers went about preparing the school celebration with much more enthusiasm than in previous years. Constantine Stefan was recognizably at the peak of his glory; great and small submitted to his orders. No longer was it difficult for him to assert his authority. No one made fun any longer of his diminutive size or constant chatter. He walked in a ponderous and dignified manner; he seemed to have grown six inches; people gave way before him.

The play was to be given in a long wooden shed resembling a military barracks. Mihai was to construct the stage and the police to provide three kerosene lamps for lighting. The townspeople would be seated on school benches and the notables on chairs in the front row. Constantine Stefan worked uninterruptedly, taking care of every detail. He seemed to be everywhere at once: he rehearsed the players, supervised the carpenter, and scolded the young girls for their slowness in decorating the room. Nothing was left to chance. "He's like a bridegroom on the eve of his marriage," said Mihai. "Like a general on the eve of battle," said someone else. For Constantine Stefan this was surely the greatest day of the war.

"I'd give a year of my life to have it behind me," muttered Maria, who became more nervous every hour.

Yonel was afraid to face her anger and kept away. The priest was unusually friendly when he met Gregor on the street, and the boys and girls of the school outdid themselves to be nice to him, to protect him. He was carrying the weight of the play on his shoulders and they accorded him the honor due one who had voluntarily undertaken a dangerous mission which they had all refused. He was the hero, feared, respected, and pitied.

The next day. Thursday.

Gregor was anxious. It would not be a day like others. A new crossroad.

The village was frantic with activity. The schoolteacher had become unrecognizable, talking to himself and not answering when addressed. At one moment he would shout without cause, at another smile beatifically. He struck Saint Peter across the face, then tearfully embraced him. A few minutes later he did the same thing with Pontius Pilate. The tension was driving him mad.

The play was to begin at three o'clock. The director and the principal actors did not sleep a wink the night before and neither did Maria. Gregor awoke with a start. He had dreamed that someone was holding out a stick and saying, "Take this, you'll need it." To which he replied, "I don't want it."

In the morning the schoolteacher realized that there was still much to be done: pieces of furniture to be moved, blankets to be sewn together before they could be strung up as curtains, last-minute instructions to be penciled on the walls.

"I need several more days," he complained, "it's going to be a catastrophe. Just wait and see, just wait and see."

The villagers looked up at the skies: it would be a beautiful day. At two o'clock they all started moving, leaving their fields and their houses empty behind them. The men wore their Sunday suits and the young girls, with their hair freshly washed and combed, smelled of lotion. "Hello there, are you coming? Hurry up!" "Yes, neighbor, I'm on my way. Wait for me." A procession, as during Easter week, but without bearers of icons.

The only villager who had to be forced into going was Codreanu, the thief. Flanked by two stout peasants he was brought to the flower-decked shed, gritting his teeth and cursing everyone he met along the way. "Another minute and you wouldn't have found me," he complained. But the villagers had thought of everything, even of preventing their homes from being robbed while they were away. For safety's sake it was better to have him at the play. "It'll do you good, Codreanu," they told him. "You might learn something."

By half past two the shed resembled a fair, a market day in the city. Shouting, laughing, spitting, clapping friends on the back, pulling mustaches. The older ones smoked yard-long pipes, while the women sucked and cracked candies. "So, neighbor, what part is your boy playing?" "A saint, neighbor. My boy's a saint. What about yours?" "A Roman soldier. With his muscles he'd be miscast as a saint."

Maria hid in a corner, biting her lips and wringing her hands. Whether she was swearing or praying, she couldn't say. People spoke of her sister and herself and Gregor, but she answered distractedly, without seeking to conceal her ill humor. "How lucky that your nephew is here, Maria! Without him they couldn't have put on the play. The Lord must have sent him to us." "Or the Devil," Maria answered.

There were a few visitors from neighboring villages. "We heard there was something going on over here, so we thought . . ." "Welcome! Our holiday is a big house, room for everybody." With visitors there was an exchange of news and snuff, talk of business and marriages and, among the women, gossip. "Are you Carolina's mother?" It was Carolina's mother. "Then are you coming to see the mare? Will he come to see the mare?" He will come to see the mare. "Look at Vassili there. He's sleeping before the play's even begun. Listen to him snore!" Vassili was snoring.

"He's arrived," cried the peasant who had been keeping watch. Domnul Petruskanu has arrived. I see him."

Three o'clock. Clothed in rags and with charcoal on his face, Gregor watched his companions who, behind the scenes, were reassuring one another. Among the audience there was silence and an undercurrent of whispers. Then, suddenly, the sound of chairs scraping on the floor and legs pulled aside to make way for the illustrious guest. Gregor was overcome by anxiety. Under his charcoal mask, he turned pale.

Petruskanu scorned the public's respectful interest. He sat down and the rest followed his example. The schoolteacher wiped the perspiration from his forehead and whispered his last instructions. "Be quiet while I make my little speech. Don't budge. You there (pointing to Gregor), you be particularly careful." One of the boys took it upon himself to watch over Judas in case he hadn't understood.

Shhh! Constantine Stefan adjusted his tortoise-shell glasses, which he wore only on special occasions, and advanced to the front of the stage. He bowed so deeply that it seemed as if he could never straighten himself up. But the cough of one of the onlookers helped him to regain his balance and his composure. He unfolded a sheet of paper and began to read a patriotic speech. Love, honor, duty, sacrifice, war aims, they were all there. The peasants didn't understand a word, but he was talking only to the front row and particularly to the only person who could understand and enjoy this choice language. The fact that Vassili was fast asleep and Codreanu was sneezing didn't in the least disturb him. Vassili was snoring so loudly that his neighbor had to clap a hand over his mouth. There was shushing on the left side, and the right side replied with even longer shushing. The audience was growing impatient. Even in church, even at the cemetery the priest wouldn't have made so boring a speech.

Gregor took a step toward the curtain, feeling a violent urge to see Petruskanu, but his self-appointed guardian grabbed his arm. "Don't move, you!" It was lucky that Gregor's face was blackened, because his cheeks were aflame.

"Here's to victory, here's to our country and its regent!"

Reluctantly Constantine Stefan brought his speech to an end. The relieved peasants applauded. The old shepherd, Vassili, imagining that he was in the midst of a storm, woke up and leaped to his feet. His neighbor pulled him down, laughing. The speaker withdrew, leaving a deafening roar behind him. Then the two boys in charge of the curtain pulled back the blankets on either side. The play had begun; no exit was possible. What would happen, would happen, inevitably, inexorably. And now—silence.

A play in three acts, showing how, on the day of the crucifixion, the disciples of Jesus had decided to avenge him by punishing the traitor. First act: they weep for the death of their Master. Second act: they decide to judge the man who is guilty. Third act: they confront Judas. Gregor did not have to appear until very near the end of the last act.

Meanwhile he tried repeatedly to look out from behind the curtain in order to see, not the players, but the terrible Count Petruskanu, who had come to see the play—he was certain—solely on account of him, Gregor. But his guardian still prevented him. Gregor's heart was pounding.

With wild hair and bloodshot eyes Constantine Stefan dashed about hysterically as if caught up in a demonic dance. He prompted the actors, making more mistakes than they did, wept with rage, struck his fists against his forehead: "It's a fiasco! A fiasco! I'm done for!" He ran from one place to another, murmuring, "It was better at the very first rehearsal! They're killing me! I'm done for, I'm done for, I'm done for!" All of which was grossly exaggerated. The spectators found the play highly impressive. Every speech won applause, and their faces were filled with a mixture of pride and emotion. Only Petruskanu remained stiff and impassive, hardly batting an eyelash.

As soon as the curtain was raised on the third act, the schoolteacher signaled to Gregor: "Watch out, my boy; you'll soon be going on."

Gregor didn't know where he was, but he was far away; his mind was free of the tyranny of thought and exploring the boundaries of time, where past and future meet. This once, he didn't have to pretend that he hadn't understood because he really didn't understand. Not the language, not the situation, not the anxiety which caught at his throat. Who was this clown? What did he want of him? What was he saying?

"Watch out," the schoolteacher repeated. His glasses were fogged over. "Are you ready?"

When Gregor failed to react he threw up his arms in despair and whispered an order. Four strong arms picked up Gregor, and a second later he found himself on the stage. Maria exclaimed out loud and he heard her. She put her hand in front of her mouth, but her eyes bulged out of their sockets.

"Judas! Traitor!"

"Judas! You did it for money!"

"You betrayed the Son of God!"

"You killed the Savior!"

Some twenty of them clustered around him threateningly and berated him.

"You thought you could get away? There's no escape from the wrath of God!"

"Hiding, were you? God's eye is everywhere!"

Some of them went through the motions of beating him up; others, with improvised conviction, heaped insults and injuries upon him.

"To think that you were the best of us all!"

"To think that you were his favorite disciple!"

The whole cast, including the Romans, was to take part in the last act, which Constantine Stefan had intended to be an apotheosis of passion: justice triumphant! And at this point the audience began to join the actors. Anything for action! So far the play had dragged; it was all talk and lamentations. The peasants were definitely bored; they let Vassili sleep and snore in peace since, after all, he wasn't missing anything. In fact they would have liked to join him were it not that they were still intent upon admiring the talent of their own children. Here and there some old man, with his head sunk upon his chest, had drifted into a blissful slumber. Then, all of a sudden, the whole thing came alive, became clear. On one side the villain, on the other, the virtuous, the righteous. Here was a language they could understand. Everything had become perfectly simple.

One of the peasants cried out, "What are you waiting for, son? Spit on him!" And another, "Are you afraid to touch him? You have fists, don't you? Use them?" And a third, "If you don't make him spit blood and regret the day he was born, you're no son of mine!"

Gregor saw Maria get up from her seat and go over to Yonel. She spoke with him beseeching and threatening him, but he shrugged his shoulders helplessly. Then she disappeared, toward the back of the stage, probably to warn Constantine Stefan. Meanwhile the play went on. Gregor came back from very far away. Someone was holding out a stick and saying, Take this, and he said, No, I don't want it. He was dreaming, and a voice within him said, "I don't want this dream."

"Why did you betray him? Speak up, you dog; we're listening. Why did you sell him?"

"If you're a man, defend yourself!"

"You committed a horrible crime. Have you nothing to say for yourself?"

The peasants had surged to their feet. Their nostrils were quivering and they shouted at the top of their lungs, with their wives echoing them. They were a mob, and the mob wanted blood. If they had found stones, they would have stoned him, like a mangy dog; in their collective madness they lost all self-control. Gregor heard a strange buzz in his ears and drowned himself in it. Help, help? No, he would not cry for help. He stiffened himself, and his body stiffened also.

The first blow blinded him. It lasted only a second, and he opened his eyes, thinking, I won't close them again. And he kept them open even when he was struck again. Pain spread through his body but he did nothing to lessen it or drive it away. I've always been afraid of physical pain, he said to himself, but here I am enduring it. He was surprised: my body is able to surprise me.

The blows rained upon him from every side, accompanied and urged on by the shouts of the audience. Cold-bloodedly he looked his persecutors in the eye, one after another, passing straight from one to the next. He was not playing, and neither were they. They were locked in battle. His cold-bloodedness only increased the general fury and the blows fell even more brutally than before.

"Make him talk!" shouted the crowd wildly.

"Make him cry!"

"He's got to confess!"

"He's got to repent!"

The peasant Vassili woke up and gave vent to his fury: they didn't let him sleep. He asked his inattentive neighbor:

"Does he refuse to ask forgiveness? The bastard! Come on, let's show him he can't betray Christ and get away with it!"

"On his knees! Get him down on his knees!"

"Beat him up! No mercy!"

"That's right, no mercy! Kill him!"

Codreanu, the thief, took advantage of the distractions of his guards and slipped out of the shed. Only he was grateful to Judas.

"Still standing, is he?" Whom does he think he's making a fool of? Of the Lord, is it?"

"Go ahead, boys, hit him. In the name of heaven, hit him, hit him! Do you want us to come up and give you a hand?"

Gregor let his eyes wander slowly over the roomful of people who, for some obscure reason, wanted his death. He did not feel the blows; he heard them only as they fell with dull thuds upon his body. He was wounded, but he was unaware of it; his skin was bursting, but he was able to ignore it. Pain had not yet penetrated his consciousness.

Convulsed, the crowd was delirious with an ancient hate, suddenly reawakened. At a single word these people would have marched backwards through time to add another cross to those of Golgotha.

In the first row the priest, his arms folded across his stomach, was lost in blissful meditation. Mihai, the penitent, observed the scene skeptically but took no part in the uproar. Stan the blind man smiled, enigmatic.

"On your knees, traitor!" shouted the mob with a single voice.

"Spit out your crime! Spit it out in blood! He must be made to speak. He must."

Only yesterday these had been friendly faces. Only yesterday these people had talked to him, gripped his arm, offered him an apple, a cluster of raisins, a kindly word. All of them had seemed to say, "God gave you a raw deal, but we are better than God; we love you and we want to make it up to you." They had made a charitable gift of their compassion; yes, they were rich in compassion and, thanks to him, they could boast of it. And now here they were asking for his death. They haven't changed, Gregor said to himself without bitterness, and I haven't changed either. We have remained what we were, neither more nor less, and yet in the farthest corner of their being, and of mine too, something has been transfigured. Conditions are no longer the same. Do they know that I'm not Judas, that I'm not the son of Ileana? What is this blind force that has destroyed their kindliness and pity? Exactly what has happened? Standing in stubborn pride, draped with blood, he stared at them from his pedestal.

Suddenly he saw him, and for an interminable moment the crowd ceased to exist. With his legs crossed and a cigarette in his hand, Petruskanu was studying him. His head was inclined slightly to the right, and there was an expression of intense anxiety on his finely cut, angular face. Their eyes crossed and at this instant a deep and imperishable bond was created between them. They were no longer alone. Gregor wanted to smile to reassure him. No, I'm not in pain; I'm not ashamed, really; no, I'm not guilty, not toward them. He frowned, and Petruskanu did likewise. Gregor was flooded by an undefinable feeling of happiness. Silently Petruskanu asked, *"Do you want my help? I have only to stand up and this horde of people will bow their heads in fear. Do you want it?"*

"No, friend, not now, not yet. I can hold out."

"So be it. We'll wait. But know that I'm here, that I'm watching."

"I know, friend, I know."

The attack continued and the attackers invested it with all their heart, their passion: they were enacting a rite. Gregor did not feel the blood running down his face. Neither the blood nor the face were his. They belonged to someone else, two thousand years dead, but kept cruelly alive to expiate the crimes committed by others.

Mihai the carpenter, Mihai the penitent, was the first to decide to come to Gregor's aid. Without stirring from his place near the door he raised his voice and for a second it dominated the outbursts of his rage.

"Stop! Stop! You'll kill him, you imbeciles! Can't you see that it's only a game, that he's not Judas, that he's Gregor, our Gregor, the son of our Ileana?"

"What of it?" an angry voice answered. "His mother was no saint, was she? She deserved to be punished, didn't she? She gave us enough trouble, didn't she? She made fools of us, didn't she? Don't you come to her defense, Mihai! No pity for Ileana, Mihai! No pity for Ileana's son!"

Mihai tried to argue, but they refused to listen and cried, jeering at him, "You're a meddler, that's all you are, Mihai. Quiet! Let justice be done! Vengeance! He who sent Christ to death deserves to die. He didn't care about us; why care about him? Like mother, like son. Remember your duty, boys. Avenge your parents. Ileana was our Judas; she sold us for less than thirty pieces of silver. Go to it, boys, and God bless you!"

The carpenter shrugged his shoulders and was silent. And the killing went on. They all knew that Gregor wasn't Judas, and yet their blood thirstiness did not abate. On the contrary, it increased. This was the most glorious hour of their lives, the one that linked them to history. Judas reawakened the memory of old wounds and fed their hate. Ileana, that was the enemy. Suddenly they realized that the danger was still there, that beneath their feet the earth was still unstable. The presence of Ileana's son overturned their world. Foam on their lips, they cursed Gregor.

Once more Gregor turned toward the inscrutable Petruskanu, who was looking at him through half-closed eyes, studying him while drawing on a cigarette. He, too, knew that Gregor was not Judas but the son of Ileana, and he wanted to see how Ileana would react in the face of this mob, drunk with repressed and unrequited jealousy.

"Do you want my help?"

"No, not yet. You can see, friend, that I am still standing; I am their past, and I am stronger than they."

"Prouder than they."

Gregor wanted to smile. He owed to Ileana his power to stand firm as a rock, not to cry aloud, not to give in to pain, not to take part in the game. After the war, he was thinking, I'll seek out this woman and say: I didn't let you down; Petruskanu is my witness. Petruskanu was staring at him, seeming to smile, as if he had guessed his resolution.

Mihai tried again to reason with the mob and again he was shouted down. The peasants and their good wives had no intention of letting him dam their enthusiasm or spoil their celebration. When he insisted, with increasing vehemence, they threw him out of the room. And Gregor's world could count one less pillar. The priest did not move; he reflected upon the transmission of sin from one generation to the next and the strange, but just, ways of providence. Maria had still not returned.

As the attack grew more violent Gregor discovered that he was stronger than they; they were suffering and he was not. The scene had the unreal, oppressive quality of a nightmare. The pain, there, on him, in him, an alien presence, was that of a nightmare. He felt the pain, but at the same time he knew that when he chose he could stop it.

His face, streaming with blood, was like a mask carried by an African sorcerer as he conjures the dead to reveal themselves to the living and manifest their desire to become human once more. The red was streaked with black, blood with soot. Petruskanu's stare was more insistent.

"It's time for me to intervene. They're going to kill you."

"No, friend, wait a little longer. They won't kill me because they're afraid of my death."

Petruskanu's bloodless lips quivered imperceptibly.

Then Gregor was seized by a burning desire to take part in the show and direct it. "I haven't much more time," he said to himself. "I must act while I can still stand; not on my knees. If I wait too long my body will betray me." And he continued to himself, "You have no right to lie to Petruskanu or to conceal part of the truth from him. Not from him. From the others, yes, that's all they ask; they feed this lie and are fed by it. But he is different. He deserves your speaking to him, face to face, openly, without need for disguise. The others are afraid of the truth—yours, their own—and they strangle it. He deserves better. You have survived only in order to meet this man, silent and hard, who was waiting for you, like a guide, at the crossroad. To lie to him would mean taking a detour, and betraying the significance of the meeting: to die lying is no less serious than to live in a lie.

Gregor spread his legs in order to stand firm upon the stage and slowly, very slowly, he raised his right arm. The other actors, believing that he had decided to defend himself, were ready to throw him down and trample him. One man in the audience picked up a chair and was going to use it. He had to act quickly to forestall him. Every second, every breath, every gesture counted. Time was pressing. A thousand veils were rent: the Prophets emerged from the past and the Messiah from the future. Quickly! Something had to happen. Gregor breathed deeply, and his voice rang out firmly as he spoke to the audience: "Men and women of this village, listen to me!"

In their amazement they froze, incredulous, as if death had surprised them in the midst of battle. Projected out of time they were like wax figures, grotesque and idiotic, without destiny or soul, clay creatures, damned in the service of the devil. Their upraised arms hung in the air, their mouths were half open with tongues protruding and features swollen; the slightest breath would have knocked them over and returned them to dust. All breathing ceased. They were afraid of discovering themselves alive and responsible. The priest was bent over as if he were about to fall on his stomach; he seemed to have lost his eyelids. Then, their faces drained of hate gave way to animal fear. The silence was heavy with blood. Suddenly an old man recovered sufficiently to throw himself upon the floor and to cry out in terror, "Merciful God, have pity on us!"

And he burst into sobs.

And another, imitating him, exclaimed, "Merciful God, forgive us our sins!"

And a third, "A miracle! A miracle, brothers! Pray to Our Lord to have pity on us, for we are miserable creatures."

"Yes, yes, yes! A miracle, a miracle before our eyes! Our dear Gregor is no longer dumb; he is speaking! Our own beloved Gregor! God had made him speak! Look and see for yourselves: God has accomplished a miracle before our eyes."

As one man they fell to the ground, moaning and groaning; some thought they were dying, others imagined themselves already dead. The stage was strewn with the actors' bodies, and only Gregor was left standing. Once more the whole shed was filled with noise. Some beat their heads against the floor, others smote their breasts, while the women lamented in shrill voices, as if at a funeral. The police, flat on the floor, did not dare look at one another. Petruskanu alone did not move but continued to sit stiffly upright, with an implacable air. His cigarette had gone out between his fingers, but he did not notice. His upper lip was trembling slightly and his expression hardened as he looked at Gregor.

"Men and women of this village," Gregor repeated, "listen to me! I have something to tell you."

The women crossed themselves, the children sobbed, the actors' faces were white as chalk. The clamor died, lips continued to move silently.

"I have something to say," continued Gregor. "First of all, I am not who you think."

"We know that," said the old man who had first announced the miracle. You're not . . ."

"I'm not Judas," said Gregor, feeling like the prophet on the mountain top, with God's word and the lightning of God's word running through him.

"No, you're not Judas," echoed the first old man. "We know that, my boy, you don't need to tell us. You're Gregor, our Gregor, one of our own children whom God has chosen to favor. What we didn't know is that you're a saint. Forgive us. In the name of our womenfolk and our dead, we beg you not to hold it against us. It isn't you that we wanted to kill; you know we love you, you know that. It was Judas who deserved to die. Him! the traitor! Have pity on us, poor ignorant sinners that we are. Don't let God punish us. You are a saint, and we know it now. A saint—Our Lord had chosen to do a miracle through you. In the name of this miracle we offer you our humility, our remorse. Don't reject us."

Petruskanu pinched his lips tightly together.

"I'm not who you think I am," said Gregor, surprised by the power of his own voice.

"We know!" cried out the old men, writhing with anguish. "We know!"

"No, you don't know," said Gregor.

Again they started to protest, but Gregor quieted them with a gesture and his voice became as cutting as a sword.

"You've shifted your ignorance, that's all. First you took me for Judas, and I wasn't Judas; now you take me for a saint, and I'm not a saint either. Judas is the saint, not me. You struck Judas, you wounded a saint. Only he can forgive you, not I."

The priest panted for breath and held his head between his hands as if to prevent it from bursting; Gregor's voice cut through and strangled him. Then the door opened upon Mihai. Taking in the situation at a glance, he gave a shout of triumph.

"Repent! For years I've begged you to give up your evil ways, to cast away your sins, and you have refused to listen."

Gregor swallowed his saliva; his swollen eyes were aching.

"Only Judas can forgive you. Beg him! Only he can pardon you. I can't act in his name. I'm not Judas."

"We know that," sobbed the old men. "You're not Judas, you're Gregor, the son of our dear Ileana, the most beautiful among us, the one with the most generous, the most open heart. If God chose you to bear witness to His glory, it's because your mother, too, accomplished miracles, but we were too blind to see them; it's because without our knowing it, Ileana became a saint. You are the son of a saint, and you must forgive us. We're damned if you reject us."

"Ignorance is still speaking through your mouths."

"Then tell us what to do, what to say."

"First, tell me this: are you guilty—yes or no—of injustice to Judas?"

"Yes," said the first old man, after a moment of hesitation.

"I want an answer from all of you."

"Yes," they cried out, men and women together. "We are guilty."

"He is the victim; not Jesus; he is the crucified; not the Christ. Have you understood that?"

"Yes, yes."

"I don't hear the priest. Doesn't he agree?"

The priest lifted his face towards Gregor. His lips moved, but no sound came from his mouth. His neighbors elbowed him, pressing him to obey. "Speak, Father, speak, or else we're lost. Can't you see that it is God who forces you to submit."

"Yes, yes," the priest muttered with an immense effort.

"Yes, what?"

"I'm guilty; we're all guilty."

He trembled from head to foot, knowing that he could not be saved. He had lived in ignorance and among lies, content with easy explanations. Now, at the hour of punishment, everything had crashed down and it was too late to start over.

"Say after me, 'Judas is innocent and we humbly implore his forgiveness.' "

All of them complied. Only Petruskanu did not take part in the confession but continued to stare at Gregor. Gregor threw back his head; the moment had come. He let the silence become more heavy before he said, in a lower voice, "I'm now going to tell you something else you don't know."

He paused for a moment in order to lend more weight to what was to follow. The peasants leaned forward, expecting the worst.

"I'm not Ileana's son," said Gregor, articulating every syllable.

For the second time that afternoon the village was struck by lightning. As pale, as if bathed in the deathly light of the end of the world, the peasants stared incredulously a one another. Had they heard correctly, or was it all a dream? Each one looked into his neighbor's eyes for confirmation. Petruskanu could no longer control the trembling of his upper lip. Gregor perceived his dismayed expression and smiled as he said, "Ileana is a saint, but I am not her son."

With his body rigid, upraised arm and blackened blazing face, he looked a wild, ragged prophet, far from the multitude and even farther from his own self, standing on the mountain top uncertain as to what God wanted him to do: to curse or to forgive, to chastise men or to give them the consoling balm of grace and hope with which to rebuild their life, their faith, their way.

For a brief instant he weighed the two possibilities. Words surged to his lips, words charged with vengeance and unhappiness, placed under the sign of ultimate justice. He could explain the situation and throw at them the secrets which they had confided in him, leaving hate in his wake. They would hate one another openly instead of hating the Jews; they would no longer wish to appear on the streets; wives would not be able to endure the presence of their husbands. You there, or you, with the scar on your right cheek, if speech has been restored to me it is in order that I may use it. And I say this: stop coveting your wife's younger and more beautiful sister; leave her alone and do not sow fire and poison in her body. And you, yes, you with the drooping mustache, you're the informer who turned in your best friend to the police and got him sent to prison. And you beside him, with the big donkey ears, you're only a dirty thief who stole the widow's sack of flour; it's on your account that she's starving. Yes, Gregor thought, I could and should go all the way, open all the sluices. After each case I'd pause long enough to choose the next victim, so that they would be crushed by fear and anxiety, and justice would be done.

But he saw Petruskanu and quenched his thirst for vengeance. What did the others matter, he was there for Petruskanu, it was to him alone that he was speaking.

"Men and women of this village," he said, raising his voice, "stand up and be reassured. You have nothing more to fear. I have one last confession to make. But first, stand up."

Further commotion followed. Some obeyed while others rose only as far as their knees. All of them concentrated their gaze upon him, hanging on his lips. Suddenly they perceived the danger. This stranger who was not the son of Ileana, who was no longer mute, knew too much. He could destroy them.

"Yes," said Gregor, speaking to Petruskanu and, through him, to his subjects. "This confession will be my last. That I am not Judas you already know. And I have told you that I am not Ileana's son, either. All I have left to tell you is this: my name is not Gregor. I am a Jew and my name is a Jewish name, Gavriel."

He was silent and there was a smile, not of triumph, but of pity on his face. The peasants opened their mouths wide in astonishment. This was the last thing that they had expected and it was too much for them. The priest collapsed onto his chair, and the villagers stared at the stage without comprehending. In all their minds there was a single thought: we are the victims of a Jew who holds us in his hands. If he goes on making these confessions, the earth will swallow us up.

The old man who a few minutes before had called him a saint was the first to regain his composure. Brandishing his fists threateningly, he cried out, "Liar! Dirty liar! You've deceived us, you've betrayed our trust, you've made fun of innocent people, and you shall pay for it!"

His words provoked a general explosion. Becoming themselves once more the villagers quickly caught up with the new turn of events. Their hate returned quickly to the surface, hastened by bitterness and by fear.

"Liar! Traitor!"

On the stage the boys and girls standing in a semicircle around Gregor did not yet dare draw any closer. The danger was from the audience where the grown men pressed forward with black resolute eyes, and knives in their hands. From the rear the women urged them on.

"Go on! Give it to him! Make him dumb again! Cut out his tongue!"

With painful clear-sightedness Gregor held his breath and waited. He was still living in his own time, separated by centuries from these men who advanced upon him. He was waiting for death; he knew that it would come, that it was on its way. Death was somewhere in the room, preceding the men and drawing them forward; death was the black light that gleamed in their eyes. Motionless, he saw it coming. A small voice whispered: You are going to die, but your death has a meaning; Gavriel and Petruskanu are not two persons; they are one. He questioned himself: Am I afraid? No, he was not afraid. He thought: I am going to die and I am not afraid. I shall make my death a gate."

Meanwhile the peasants moved forward like soldiers preparing to assault invisible barricades. Their bare feet, gliding over the floor, made a strange rustle, sweet to the ear, like the murmur of a human voice. Imperturbable Gregor watched death as it moved to seize its prey. Death has not one face but a thousand faces, he thought to himself, not one hand but a thousand hands. So this was death, this force which sealed men and women indissolubly together, making them opaque and stubborn and hostile. I have learned nothing. Where is the good Constantine Stefan? Half dead behind the scenes, crazy with despair. The third act is not yours, schoolteacher! And not mine either. Death has written it, death will ring down the curtain and harvest the applause. "Bravo, bravo!" the living will cry, "Well played!"

The executioners were moving close to the stage, about to invade it and avenge their honor in blood. Gregor did not flinch. At this same moment, in the crimson fields of Galicia, smartly turned-out officers were shouting the order: "Fire! Fire!" A hundred Jews, ten thousand Jews were tumbling into the ditches. He would not die alone.

Imperceptibly he turned to bid Petruskanu farewell. Once more their eyes met. Then things happened so precipitantly that they were outside the village before the peasants in their wagons and the police on their horses had time to pursue them. Petruskanu had leaped onto the stage and silently led Gregor behind the scenery and out the rear door. They ran to the carriage. Petruskanu had pushed Gregor inside, dismissed the driver and taken the reins. The two horses whinnied and set out in a westerly direction. Sunset bathed the horizon in blood.

"I know a place where you'll be safe," said Petruskanu. He had the deep, clear voice of a man accustomed to silence and solitude. "We'll spend the night there, and then I'll take you to the partisans."

Gregor did not reply. Petruskanu's tone of voice did not call for an answer. The earth grew peaceful, the sky came to life. The wind rustled in the trees and gently caressed the blades of grass on either side of the road. An hour later the carriage came to a halt in front of an isolated house in the woods. Petruskanu jumped out and Gregor followed him inside. Petruskanu had no need of a light to orient himself. He threw open the windows and night came in. Then he took off his coat and brought out of a closet a short-sleeved white shirt and a light gray suit.

"Outside, to the left, there's a well, go wash up. You'll be frightened if you see your face."

While Petruskanu took care of the horses, Gregor washed himself. The cold water restored his strength; he returned to his true self; his memory functioned and spread throughout his body. At the same time he was overcome by a weariness which had nothing physical about it. He went back to the house, where Petruskanu offered him a cup of coffee, which he gulped down, his throat burning. Then he put on the shirt and the suit, both of which were too big for him.

"One of the partisans will fix them for you," said Petruskanu.

They went out again and sat down on the grass. There were bright stars in the deep blue sky.

"Tired?" Petruskanu asked him.

"Terribly tired." He reflected for a moment and then added, "It's a strange feeling, a weariness which is neither physical nor mental, which affects neither the body nor the brain but only the memory."

"Not weary of living, are you?"

"Perhaps."

Gregor wanted to talk about Gavriel. Some other time. He was sure of meeting Petruskanu again. Either him or someone else with the same voice and face and generosity.

"I knew Ileana," Petruskanu was saying.

"I know."

They were both silent.

"How do you know?"

"I knew the minute I saw you."

Petruskanu sighed, and his eyes wandered from one star to another as if to measure their distance.

"It's on her account that you did what you did, isn't it?"

"Yes and no," Petruskanu reflected. "For her and for you also. I liked seeing you face the crowd, face pain and injustice impassively, contemptuous of everything that could have destroyed you. Ileana could have done the same thing. Perhaps you are her son, after all."

"Perhaps," said Gregor.

They did not exchange another word in the two hours that elapsed before midnight, when they left. Everything had been said.

114

"Look after Maria," said Gregor as he sat in the carriage.

"I'll look after her."

Toward three o'clock in the morning they came to a small town. Petruskanu said that the partisans were hiding in the nearby forest. He let Gregor down at its edge and, without descending, held out his hand.

"Goodbye, Gavriel. And good luck."

"Goodbye," said Gregor, with a catch in his throat, "and good luck. Know that I shall not forget you."

"I know."

In the darkness Petruskanu seemed to be smiling.

"After the war I'll look for Ileana," Gregor added, "and thank her."

"After the war . . ." said Petruskanu dreamily. "After the war . . ."

Then brusquely he tugged at the reins and disappeared.

autumn

1

What silence! The forest is listening, Gregor reflected, his head hanging, as they walked along side by side in the darkness. We speak of the forest as having a soul; it has a memory as well. It listens and remembers.

How far away is the sky, stranger! A madman's gaze walks across it. The moon is full, but its cold, spectral light makes it seem unreal. We are prisoners of this forest which, like a living being, holds its breath and curious, advances, leaning forward, on the alert, so as not to lose the least rustle, the least whisper. Nothing must escape it, nothing must occur outside its embrace. We are prisoners of this madness.

A tormented man or a dreaming child, perhaps they are one and the same, will come here one day, seeking rest or the asking of questions, or piercing visions, and from very near and from very far away—everything depends on the depth of his sincerity—he will perceive the sound of our steps and of our heavy breathing. And we shall live on in him.

The miracle of the forest: nothing that is said in its midst is lost. The saint and the solitary, they too are perhaps identical, come here not only to purify their bodies and their passions, but also to listen and tremble, to tremble as they listen to this roaring voice which, before creation, before the liberation of the word, already contained form and matter, joy and defeat, and that which separates and reconciles them, from all of which the universe, time, and their own secret life were fashioned.

Outside the voice of the forest is drowned out by the chattering and lamentations of those who traffic in their future and in anxiety, their own and that of others. Here it keeps its miraculous quality, its beauty, which ends by becoming force. Sometimes, beyond uprooted time, a cry of astonishment and terror reaches us, the cry of the ancestor who, opening his eyes for the first time on a world already in motion, realized that he had been deceived.

"It's madness," said Leib the Lion, "pure madness."

He refused to admit what was self-evident, that the earth and sky of Europe had become great, haunted cemeteries. Angrily he cried, "If what you say is true, then you are mad, then I am mad myself."

They were walking with no other purpose than to be alone. The others had stayed in the bunker which served as a command post. At intervals, far from the sentries, they stopped, sniffing the air in every direction, fearful of being overtaken by a patrol. The thousand voices of the night, which punctuated the silence, were stifled and broken among the branches, where the moon forced a passage. Where is Gavriel? Gregor wondered. In the wind, among the leaves, in the silence? Everywhere. He was the wind, the tree, the night. He was the gaze that searched the sky, waiting for a sign, for the apparition of an angel. Where is Gavriel? Who is Gavriel?

"We're living in a time of madness," said Gregor. "It has descended upon us, not like lightning but like the plague. We've returned to the Middle Ages, Leib. Only now neither the priests of the Inquisition nor their victims understand what drives them to act or in what god's name the fires are lit. It's a universal eclipse. Everything is falling apart; past, future, present, hope, humanity, progress, all these are nothing but words. Are you sure that there is a tomorrow? No, tomorrow has already been, is already extinguished. Time only exists in the measure to which man is there to endure or bless or deny.

But there are no more men. It's the end of the world, Leib. Everything is finished, I tell you. Gavriel was right: the Messiah is not coming; he got lost along the way, and from now on the clouds will obscure his sight. There are no more men, Leib, I tell you. Here and there, a few, but they are hiding in caves, like frightened animals, while the others mistake themselves for gods because they are thirsty for blood. If this goes on, we shall witness a new deluge: a sea of blood will envelop the earth, and the ark will be engulfed."

Incredulous, Leib nodded and ran his hand over his forehead as if to dispel a pain. "We must find Gavriel," he said.

"Find him? Where and how?"

"I don't know.'

"What makes you think he's still alive, that he's still in the same prison? It's been weeks since they captured him. How do you know he hasn't been deported?"

"I don't know. But we must ask."

Gregor was about to say: it's useless to risk it, Gavriel is dead. But he was unable to speak such simple words: Gavriel is dead.

"We could bribe someone in the prison, a guard perhaps."

"Yes, perhaps we could."

Leib halted suddenly. So did Gregor. Once upon a time Leib had seemed to him invulnerable. Near to him Gregor still felt secure, and unafraid of Pishta and his gang.

"Just the same you must admit it's strange," said Leib. "It took a war to make our paths cross again." His eyes blazed in the dark, and Gregor was once more a schoolboy.

"That's the purpose of war," said Gregor, concealing his emotion. "It intensifies and underlines everything strange. War broke out in order that our paths might cross. War has fun; it overturns law and order, shakes the trees, and says to men: Get yourselves out of the mess. Suddenly children are older than their parents, and war says to them both: Go on, look each other in the face, and we'll see what happens. But nothing happens. Fathers and children are content to look each other in the face, and they die without having understood the game they have been playing. Then war laughs. Why not? It has every right to. It plants you in front of a stranger and says, Love him, kill him, humiliate him, and you obey without asking yourself whether it is right. An hour later you will be loved or killed or humiliated in your turn. At bottom we know all this, but we play the game as if it were for fun. That's what's strange."

"You've grown up," said Leib, touching his arm.

"Grown old."

Leib threw back his head. "Our own war, against the gang, do you remember it? That was when? Ten years ago? More? Less?"

"I don't know. Maybe ten days. Sometimes I wonder if it was really I who waited for you every morning so that we could walk together through the snow, the doorway that opened onto our battleground. Sometimes I wonder if it's really I that question myself about my past, whether I'm not shut up in a dream that is not my own."

Leib scrutinized the sky, and then said in a contained voice, "You've grown up. It's terrible how we've grown up, all of us."

And they continued to walk through the listening forest.

2

A few hours earlier Gregor could never have imagined that he was going to meet his childhood friend. After Petruskanu had gone he plunged into the forest and felt it close behind him. Suddenly two armed shadows rose up at either side.

"Who are you?" said a voice in Hungarian.

"I'm a Jew."

"Do you speak Yiddish?"

"Yes."

He almost added "naturally." But he restrained himself. Certain Jews from the interior of Hungary didn't speak Yiddish. Patriotism demanded that they speak nothing but Hungarian.

"Say something in Yiddish."

"I'm looking for the partisans," he said in Yiddish. "Are you the partisans?"

But his question got no answer, and the interrogation continued.

"What is the prayer recited upon waking in the morning?"

"*Mode ani lefanecha.* I thank you, Lord, for having restored my soul."

"And before going to sleep?"

"*Hamapil hevlei sheina.* Blessed art thou, O Lord, our God who makes the bands of sleep to fall upon mine eyes."

From then on the whole conversation was in Yiddish.

"Where have you come from?"

"From over there."

"From very far?"

"Far enough."

"Are you alone?"

"Yes, alone."

"Who brought you here?"

"A friend."

"A Jew?"

"No."

"Why did he do it?"

"Because he's a friend."

"Did he know that we lived in this forest?"

"Probably."

"Did he say so?"

"Yes."

"What's his name?"

"I can't tell you."

"Why not?"

"I don't talk much about my friends."

"Are you sure that he isn't with the police? That he isn't trying to trap us? That he didn't report us to the enemy?"

"Quite sure."

The two shadows drew back, their guns still cocked, and held a brief consultation.

"All right, then. We'll take you with us."

They proceeded to blindfold him, a useless precaution since the night was pitch black. One of them stayed behind, as a lookout; the other took Gregor by the arm and told him to follow. After half an hour they halted, and Gregor heard his guide whisper a password and receive an answer. They went down an underground stairway; at the bottom a door opened and Gregor was pushed into a room which he could guess was full of silent people. There the blindfold was removed. The bunker reminded him of Maria's hut. A kerosene lamp, hanging from the ceiling, cast a yellowish light over the tense faces of a dozen men, all of them young except for the one with the beard who must have been over forty. Nearly the doorway, which was hidden behind a heavy wool blanket, was a young girl with black hair, a rapt melancholy expression. The others clustered around a boy sitting at a table, who seemed to be their leader; he had a gentle, dreamy look, crossed occasionally with glimmers of irony. Gregor searched his memory; he had seen him before. He tried to remember, but they began to interrogate him, all of them, that is, except the leader and the young girl. Gregor's replies were terse and reluctant. Obviously the partisans didn't trust him and that displeased him. "What is it! Do I look a stool pigeon?" But the partisans didn't care how he looked; they wanted information. All right. This was understandable, but Gregor could not contain his impatience. Yes, he lived in the town below, near the Orthodox church. Yes, the two-story building on the square was the school. And where was the old synagogue? On Rose Street, and the head of the Jewish community was called . . . Yes, Josovits, that was it. Where were his parents? Gone. Where? Far away, along with the rest of the ghetto population. When? Gregor wasn't quite sure; it must have been about two months ago. With which transport? He didn't know, because he himself had left the ghetto before the transports began. Yes, he had gone into hiding, in a cave up in the mountains, and then in a village. After that a friend, who was not a Jew, had brought him to the forest. His friend's name? That he wouldn't say. They insisted, but Gregor held out against them.

The bearded fellow was angry. "Hell, you can trust us. We trust you, don't we?"

Gregor shook his head. "No, I'm sorry, but that's not the question."

The young girl, standing motionless near the door, kept her eyes fixed upon him. So did the leader. They were the real interrogators. Once more Gregor strained his memory in an effort to place the boy's gentle but stubborn expression, his strong chin and reassuring calm. He must hear his voice. And so, with an almost insolent manner, he turned toward him and asked, "What about you? Have you no questions?"

"No none."

"Are you satisfied with my answers?"

"I don't give a damn about them." There was an iron light in his eyes as he added, after a brief pause, "I knew them already." Before Gregor could react he got up and held out his hand. "There's only one thing I'd like to ask you. Did you ever know a boy called . . ."

"Leib!' shouted Gregor. "Leib the Lion!"

They shook hands. The partisans looked on in surprise, and the young girl leaned over darkly, as if some danger were at hand.

"Do you know each other?" asked one of the others.

"Oh, we made the war together," said Leib.

"Only mountains never meet," said the bearded man, who was known as Zeide, which means the grandfather.

They all surrounded Gregor, talking and listening to him as to an old friend. After all, if Leib had stood up for him he must be all right. Most came from nearby villages; they had met Leib in the ghetto and followed him into hiding. They knew that the ghetto had been evacuated, but they had no idea of what had happened to its inhabitants and imagined that they had been taken to a *puszta* or work camp. Soon the war would be over and they would be reunited with their families. The allied armies were advancing on every front and the Germans seemed headed toward irrevocable disaster. Victory was near. Dumfounded, Gregor listened to them. He realized that they were unaware of the fact that the Germans were carrying out the "final solution." In London and Stockholm and Washington this was common knowledge, but no one had told the Jews of Transylvania: Beware! You're being led to the slaughterhouse.

The young girl continued to stare at the new arrival mistrustfully. It was plain she didn't like him, and he wondered why. Leaving the group he went over to her.

"My name is Gregor," he said; "what is yours?"

She didn't react. Gregor couldn't understand the reason for her hostility.

"Clara, that's her name," said Leib, looking at her affectionately.

"Clara," Gregor repeated, as if to himself.

Behind him the others went on talking. They were discussing the situation at the front and the difficulties that lay ahead. The Fascist government at Budapest was even more anti-Semitic than that of Berlin. "Man is alone, the Jew is not," the bearded fellow was saying. "We must never fail to help one another." This seemed to be his favorite saying. Clara slowly lowered her head, and her expression hardened as if she had penetrated a faraway mystery. Gregor blushed with shame at the thought that she would never consider him an ally. Suddenly she burst into laughter.

"You're funny looking, do you know? Who rigged you up this way, a circus director?"

Gregor looked down at his clothes. He had forgotten how large they were on him.

"I apologize," he said with embarassment. "This outfit was given me by a friend."

"He has good taste!"

"Don't go making fun of him!"

"Get out of those clothes. Give them to me. I'll fix them for you. Otherwise, I'll laugh every time I see you."

"I don't like your laugh."

"Come outside," said Leib. "You can take the suit off out there. Clara will fix it and call you when it's ready."

In front of the entrance to the bunker Leib explained, "We live here like hermits. We have a cache of weapons, bought or stolen. About a hundred of our fighters are scattered through the forest, and our underground bunkers are well hidden and strongly defended. If the police come, we'll fight to the last rather than be taken. We don't want to work in German war plants. Our relatives are doing it, and that's more than enough."

Gregor wanted to shout out, "Little do you know! The Jews of our town are running about heaven, looking for a cemetery." But he stifled the words. Later, he thought, later. A door opened behind him and a hand held out his suit.

"Let's go back," said Leib when he had put it on.

"Now you're smartly turned out!" said Clara.

"We'd better get some sleep," put in the bearded fellow, and the others agreed.

"Leib," said Gregor, "I have to talk to you."

At the same time he shuddered. Later, a voice said to him. Give him one more day of peace.

"What about?" asked Leib.

"I'll tell you outside."

"Speak."

"Not here."

"Why not? I have nothing to hide from my friends."

"But I'd rather speak to you alone."

Leib hesitated for a moment and his expression became severe. "All right then," he said, "let's go out."

"Can I go with you?" asked Clara.

Leib made a sign to indicate that it was up to Gregor.

"No," said Gregor. "I want to be alone with him."

"Leib tells me everything."

"I don't though."

"Go to hell," she said furiously.

"Enough," said Leib. "Don't fight."

The other partisans stood around embarrassed, waiting to see what would happen.

"Are we going to sleep or aren't we?" asked the fellow with the beard.

"Go on and sleep," said Leib.

"I'll wait for you," answered Clara.

Gregor went toward the door and Leib followed, frowning in disapproval. Once they were outside Gregor said brusquely, "I have a story to tell you, a Jewish story, something very funny. A messenger called Gavriel told it to me."

"I don't like Jewish jokes. They're too sad, and I don't like Jews to appeal to my pity."

"My story calls for anger, not pity."

"All right, then, I'm listening."

Gregor ran his hand over his lips. How was he to begin?

"I'm listening," Leib repeated, with irritation.

Gregor began to tell him the facts as he had heard them from Gavriel. The facts. The facts alone. The facts of the massacre of the Jewish community. He passed over the messianic aspect of the story. That could wait for another time. For the present the facts would suffice.

"It's the same thing everywhere," said Gregor. "The just man has a thousand truths, and that's his tragedy; the murderer has one alone, and that's his strength. And he's applied his strength in Poland and Hungary and the Ukraine. I wonder if up there, beside the heavenly throne, there isn't a master assassin, giving out these orders. There's no other explanation. Who has it in for us? What have we done that's so terrible? What's the curse that seems to precede us to point the way?"

Walking beside him, shaken to the depths of his being, Leib was silent. Every now and then he sighed. He wanted to scream, but down below the police were doubtless listening for the least sound from the forest.

"It's madness," he murmured, "sheer madness."

"Of course," said Gregor. "A madman's story."

"I can't believe it. You can't kill a whole people. Its unthinkable."

"Exactly. Unthinkable," said Gregor.

"Unless the human race has reached the end of the road."

"This is the end. People will go on living without knowing that they're already dead."

"If it's true, then the human race has lost its reason."

"It has lost its reason, Leib."

"Then it deserves total destruction. That's Sodom and Gomorrah."

"The inhabitants of Sodom didn't kill children before their mothers' eyes. The citizens of Gomorrah went in for vice, not for death. Our generation is worse than theirs. It's the generation of the guilty. We all have a share in the crime, even if we combat it; there's no escape from the trap. There's the madness of our generation, complicity between executioners and victims, imposed upon the latter without their being aware of it. Gavriel's story teaches us that the Messiah has come too late, that he's killed anew every day by men and by God. God, too, is killed every day. Who'll dare speak tomorrow of divine grace and mercy or of man as a savior? The inhabitants of Sodom left God in peace. They didn't lay hands on children."

Gregor talked and talked. During the two months with

Maria he had accumulated words which now burst from his lips.

"Are you sure that Gavriel didn't simply imagine these horrors?" Leib asked him.

"Quite sure."

Here and there the icy light of dawn came through the branches, Gregor shivered, and quickened his step in order to flee from it, preferring the darkness. Leib leaned against a pine tree and stared at him without speaking. Then, in a low voice, he asked, "Are you sure that Gavriel exists? That he ever existed?"

Gregor clenched his fists and the blood rushed to his temples. If I don't shout I'll choke. He mastered his voice, which sounded out calm.

"Sometimes I doubt the existence of Gregor, but never that of Gavriel."

Leib waited for him to go on, but Gregor was silent. I really ought to laugh, he was thinking, but I can't do it, not yet.

"Look here," Leib said at last. "Gavriel knows things that we don't know. We ought to try to free him."

"Of course, Leib, of course . . ."

"That is, if . . ."

"If what?"

"If he's still alive."

"Even if he's dead we should bring him back, and resurrect him."

They made their way back to the bunker, where the others were awake and waiting. They felt that their chief would have important news for them and there would be time to sleep later. Clara poured hot tea into the earthenware bowls. Haimi, the youngest of the partisans, had a ravaged face, with eyes reddened by fatigue and insomnia. In the wavering light of the kerosene lamp the others seemed dirty and sullen.

"Do you want some tea?" Clara asked Leib.

He did not answer. He stood by the table, before his increasingly nervous companions, with the veins of his neck swelling. In his turn he asked himself whether he should spare them the truth. He weighed the pros and the cons and could not reach a decision.

"What about you, Gregor? Will you have some tea? Aren't you as thirsty as the rest of us?"

He did not notice the nasty tone in her voice and nodded "no." His hands could not have held the bowl. Clara put the teapot on the table and stared at Leib, her nostrils quivering. He had changed; something was preying on his mind. Haimi rubbed his eyes as if to fight sleep and Zeide stroked his beard. As the tension grew all of them breathed harder.

"I have something to tell you," Leib began. "I must ask you: no tears and no resignation."

In a clear, dry voice and clipped, concise sentences he told them of the death of the local Jews, evacuated from the ghetto to a destination no longer unknown. He spoke without emotion as he reported the facts of the situation. It was a problem and as such called for a solution and for definite action to follow.

Gregor saw their faces register horror; some hardened, others opened wide to sorrow. Haimi put his hand up to his throat and left it there for a moment while he questioned himself as to the meaning of his gesture; then he gave up and contented himself with buttoning his shirt collar as if to protect himself from the cold. The bearded fellow swung his head from right to left and took on a haggard, hunted air. Clara lowered her eyelids and pinched her lips but held herself erect, resolved not to give way. At a certain point she cast Gregor a look filled with pity and defiance, and he knew that one day he would love her.

When Leib had finished his report there was an unbearable silence, one that bound them together until death. All of them bowed their heads. Let fate lead to the bitter end; they were ready to follow. Clara closed her eyes and reopened them immediately, settling them heavily, in judgment, upon Gregor. It was on his account that they were suffering; he was their bond and their fate, the heir to Gavriel's role, a messenger incapable of deciphering his message. Who is our Master? Who is our questioner? Who answers for us, and before whom must we justify ourselves?

"Give me some tea," Gregor said to Clara.

He wanted to show that he was capable of breaking the

silence, but his voice, weak, died away in his throat. Clara continued to stare at him, without hearing. The partisans had eyes only for their chief and seemed to be listening to him even if for some minutes he had not spoken.

"Give me some tea," Gregor repeated. "I'm thirsty, and my throat is dry."

Clara poured some tea into the bowl and handed it to him. The warm liquid made him feel nauseous. Inattentively he dropped the bowl, which smashed on the floor. The partisans shuddered. Haimi wept secretly, as if he were the one to break it.

"Man is a solitary animal," Zeide murmured.

This time he did not finish his sentence. He had got the idea that men were there to kill rather than to help one another, that they were there to massacre the Jews, letting them go hand in hand to death, defying solitude.

Leib's expression became dreamy and pained; like that of a man left standing on the pier while the ship carries away part of himself.

"You're less cruel than I thought," Clara said to Gregor.

Again he knew that one day he would love her and one day he would stop loving her.

Haimi was the first to get up.

"I'm on duty," he said, finding an excuse to leave.

"After the war," said Zeide as if talking to himself, "after the war, I will go to every town in the world, I will stop in front of every man in the street, and I will spit in his face."

Whereupon he followed Haimi outside: "I am also on duty." Never had there been such enthusiasm for standing watch, so few complaints of sleepiness or fatigue.

His hands crossed behind his back, Leib paced nervously up and down the bunker. Clara put out the lamp and opened the door. With the gray light of dawn, a breeze swept into the room. Gregor shivered. The challenge of a new day lay ahead. Clara sat down, exhausted, at the table, and waited. Gregor would have liked to sit down beside her, but he did not dare. He looked from one to the other, wondering if he was in the way. Leib stopped suddenly and announced his decision.

" 'Operation Gavriel,' " he said firmly. "To save the only Jew who has information about the fate of our brothers is an obligation. But before we lay plans I must alert the other partisans in the forest and speak to their leaders. I'll be back late this afternoon."

He went over to Clara, brushed her face, her lips lightly with his hand, and then, withdrew brusquely, without having kissed her, almost as if in anger. Leaning upon her elbows, frozen, Clara followed him with her eyes. After a long pause she turned toward Gregor: "I'd like to be alone," she told him.

Gregor went out to visit with the sentries. In clusters of two or three the partisans were whispering to one another. Gavriel, they said, must be mad; anyone who could invent such a story, anyone who would remember such a story must be mad. Farther on, alone behind a bush, Gregor caught sight of Haimi. The poor boy was struggling desperately to contain his tears. He was rubbing his eyes and sniffling.

"What's the matter friend?" Gregor asked gently.

Making an effort to maintain his self-control the boy shrugged his shoulders, as if saying "you won't understand."

"You're suffering," said Gregor.

"I'm sorry," said Haimi.

"Sorry? What for?"

"Sorry that I showed it."

He couldn't have been more than twelve years old, and Gregor was at a loss as to how to comfort him. Would he ever grow up to be a man? Would he ever know the happiness of embracing a woman, of saying to her, "You are beautiful. Come, tell me your secret?"

"You mustn't be ashamed," he said. "Only grown-ups play at hiding their feelings. Let them have their day; they have nothing more to hide, really. Laugh, cry, when you feel like it."

"I don't want to cry," said the boy, sobbing.

"I do," confessed Gregor.

Gregor waited for him to calm down and then, smiling, made him talk. His mother? Long since dead. His father? Killed. During a mission. He belonged to Leib's group. A

133

fearless, intrepid fighter. A giant. He always volunteered. Nothing frightened him. "The Germans are afraid of us," he liked to say; "so much the better." But one day he fell into an ambush. A chance bullet.

"A wonderful man, my father," said Haimi. "I don't know how he let himself be killed. I really don't know." And he shrugged his shoulders as if to say: My father, the most wonderful father in the world, wanted his death to teach me a lesson. But you don't understand. What does it matter to you that he's dead? Haimi hid his face in his hands. Gregor was overcome with melancholy; he felt awkward and useless and guilty. I, I never cried, he said to himself. *My* father wanted me to be strong. "Keep your sorrows to yourself instead of selling them cheap," he used to say. He wanted me to be like him. My father was a wonderful man.

"I wonder if he knew he was going to die," said Haimi.

He was sure that his father had died without warning, that death had not left him time to face and fight it. Otherwise he would surely have overcome death. Indeed, he never spoke of death. When he was told that a comrade had fallen, he listened intently but said nothing and tried to change the subject.

"There, there, don't cry!" said Gregor soothingly.

"Why did he never speak of death? Because he knew it was coming?" Haimi took out his handkerchief and blew his nose noisily.

Poor boy! thought Gregor. Our solitude will never equal yours. You know already that the heart of man is only a cemetery; the more open it becomes, the greater is the cold. At your age a loss opens a deeper wound, takes on a more total meaning than treachery. If your father is dead, it means that God is unjust, that life is a farce. It means that God doesn't love man or deserve his love. That fact is the stumbling-block on which he will build his idea of the world. In the beginning God created man in order to kill him; he created him because he has no pity.

"I'm ashamed to have cried," said Haimi.

"I'm ashamed not to have cried," answered Gregor.

Haimi grinned. Gregor wanted to put his hand on his shoulder, talk to him about himself, the war, friendship, to tell him that no one dies too early or too late because death does not come by chance: for if they were to miss each other—man and death—the earth would stop turning. But he chose to be silent. Words or tears, words and tears.

Leib returned worried. The afternoon was at its end. A tarnished sun was sinking and twilight was gathering in the forest. Overhead the sky was of a pale blue and there was a flaming arc on the horizon.

The partisans sat on the grass in front of the bunker to listen to Leib's report. The other groups had reacted violently to the news he had brought them. Two women had attempted suicide and saved, could not stop crying. Several of the younger partisans had demanded retaliation against the town and to set it on fire. But eventually Leib had persuaded them to follow his plan. First, to make sure that Gavriel was still in the central prison. If so, they were to concentrate their efforts upon freeing him. Two comrades were to be sent to find out if he was really there, and in order to save time Leib would make contact with them, three days later, at the Hotel Corona on the main square. After that he would decide on the next move.

"That's all," he said in conclusion.

All of them wanted to go. "I know the town." "I look like a peasant." "I have a friend who could put me up." And Haimi: "I am so small, no one would notice me." Leib let them talk for a few minutes and then raised his arm.

"I didn't ask for volunteers," he said softly. "I'll pick out the persons best qualified." He paused long enough to smile and added, "As a matter of fact, my choice is already made."

They held their breath. The trees gradually filled with darkness. Peace everywhere, a harmony between heaven and earth. The future existed; every moment contained it. With past and present it was one of three layers of bark that protect eternity; break any one and you enter into solitude. That which will be has already been: "There's the tragedy," Gavriel had said. "I shall die, therefore I am dead; and there the laceration of conscience begins. Do I want victory with every breath? What victory and over whom? I do not even know who the enemy is."

"Gregor," said Leib, "follow me!"

Less than twenty-four hours, that was all the time he would have spent in the bunker.

"You too, Clara."

They followed him inside and Clara lit the lamp. Then the three of them sat down at the table, Gregor across from Clara. From without they could hear the whispering of the other members of the group, who did not approve of the choice.

"I know you're exhausted," said Leib; "you need sleep, and so does Clara. But the time is short, and every hour precious. There are still ghettos that have not been evacuated. After we've talked with Gavriel we can spread the alarm and alert the people to flee."

"Flee?" exclaimed Gregor. "Where? Do you trust the Hungarians? I don't."

"Neither do I, but that isn't the question. First we must find Gavriel."

Clara did not take part in the conversation. She listened, her thoughts elsewhere.

"You must be off soon," Leib was saying. "You know the town, Gregor, and you will know how to avoid suspicion. Your mission: to approach one of the prison guards, to question him, and, possible, to bribe him. As for you, Clara . . ."

He looked over at the girl, his gaze resting first on her lips and then upon her eyes. "Your job is simply to go with him and protect him. You'll pretend to be lovers, so as not to attract attention."

Leib's voice was quiet and assured. "Have you any idea where you can sleep?"

"We have a choice," said Gregor. "In my cave in the mountain, or in an abandoned house in the ghetto."

"I leave it up to you. We'll meet Tuesday afternoon at the café of the Hotel Corona. Pretend you don't know me. Is that agreed?"

"Agreed."

Leib turned questioningly toward Clara.

"Agreed," she said.

Leib gave them some money. Gregor still had his false

papers. Clara didn't have any, but it was too late to get them.

"When shall we go?" asked Gregor.

"In an hour."

Gregor got up abruptly and left the room. Let them be alone.

Three days that Gregor was never to forget. Long walks around the dark silent prison. Hand in hand. Unprotected they walked for hours. They paused to kiss each other and secretly study the face of a guard talking to a sentry or of another hurrying off to a lovers' tryst.

As a child, Gregor had always averted his eyes as he went by, hoping not to be seen by the faceless prisoners who, from within, envied his liberty. Now they all had faces; they all had the same face; the face of Gavriel. Gregor no longer lowered his voice. Love. It's only a game, he said to himself. Clara and Leib are in love, and he's my friend. She thinks of him when she kisses me. Soon they'll be together again and leave me alone. And yet he liked to kiss her. He thought of her, of no one else.

In the evening they left the town by passing the slaughter-house, hurriedly although no nauseating odor followed them. An hour later the silence of the cave welcomed them. Here Clara was no longer the same. She behaved like a stranger.

"Do you want to sleep?"

She made no reply.

"Do you want to talk?"

"No."

"I could tell you a story."

"If you like."

And so he told her Gavriel's story as thought it were his own. The true story of the true Gavriel. From time to time she interrupted to say. "I don't care."

Monday morning they managed to start a conversation with a guard whom they had seen several times in front of the prison gate. He recognized them and called them over.

"There you are again!" he exclaimed good-naturedly. "You can't think of anything but love. I don't blame you, though. Nowadays there's no time to waste."

Clara made a flirtatious answer, and they arranged to meet him at six o'clock in front of the Hotel Corona. They had three hours to waste and sat down on a park bench to warm themselves in the sun.

"Do you think Gavriel's still here? Nearby? That maybe he hears us? That he sees us?" asked Gregor.

"I don't care," said Clara, blushing, and then, more loudly: "I don't believe he's here." And then, "I hope that he's not here. Besides, he doesn't really exist, this Gavriel of yours." She looked Gregor in the eye. "I'm afraid." And she repeated, in a whisper: "I'm afraid."

Gregor was troubled and did not ask for an explanation.

At six o'clock they met the guard. They invited him to dinner and toasted his health. "To friendship! To love! To war!" Clara questioned him, obliquely, about the Jews that had disappeared from the town.

"Where did they all go?"

"Away."

"Good riddance!" said Clara.

"Good riddance," echoed the guard.

Gregor admired her coolness. She played well.

"Didn't any Jews manage to hide?" she asked.

"Not a one. They were trapped. Like rats. All packed off together. The ghetto's empty. Finished."

"Good!" Clara exclaimed.

They ordered another bottle of wine. "Let's drink to the vanished, to the looted houses, and burned synagogues." Clara went on with her interrogation.

"When the police lay hands on a Jew, what do they do with him?"

"Into prison."

"And then?"

"They turn him over to the Germans. Germans love Jews, you know. They want them for presents."

"And what do they do with them?"

"They load them into trains which go off at night."

"But there aren't any more transports here, are there?"

"Not here, but in other places: Debrecen, Szeged, Budapest.

What do you think. It's easy to clear our country of Jews? Well, I tell you, it isn't. The more you get, the more there are."

As he drank he became more and more talkative. He laughed, and his two companions joined his laughter. At intervals he kept saying how fond he was of them. Eventually he asked what he could do for them.

"Thank you, Janos; we're quite happy. There's nothing we need."

"Lovers always need an 'empty' cell," Janos said with a sneer.

"Thank you, Janos. We love each other in the open. We have nothing to hide."

Later in the evening she told him an elaborate story. She had an uncle who had worked in a remote town for a wealthy Jew. The dirty Jew had escaped from the ghetto and wasn't recaptured until after the last transport had gone. She wanted to know whether he was still around, perhaps in the prison. Why did she want to know? Before leaving the ghetto he had buried his money in the garden. If he was still alive he could be forced to say where it was. This way Clara would have a dowry. Otherwise she'd have to get married empty-handed, without even a trousseau, and later on her husband would reproach her. Janos couldn't resist such an appeal.

"I have an idea how to help you," he said.

"Help us?" asked Clara, pretending to be surprised. "How can you help us?"

"I'll ask around. If he's in my prison, I promise you I'll make him sing."

"How can we ever thank you."

"I was young myself once."

And he added, teasingly, to Gregor, "My boy, you're marrying a woman with a quick tongue. Mark my word, she'll hurt you!" Then, in a more serious vein, he took out a notebook and wet the tip of a pencil.

"All right. To business. What's his name?"

"Whose name?"

"The name of your Jew. How am I to find him if I don't know his name?"

Gregor was about to say Gavriel, but Clara spoke first.

"He doesn't go under his real name, Janos. You can be sure of that. He's clever enough to have false papers. Those Jews, they think that with money they can buy anything."

"Then how am I to find him?"

"I'll describe him to you," said Gregor. "A Jew can change his name but not his face. He'll always look like a Jew, won't he?"

"Yes. I can tell one a mile away."

"Well, he's tall and thin. Black beard. Feverish eyes. Twenty or thirty years old, it all depends."

"Depends on what?"

"The mood he's in."

"Is that all?"

"Yes, that's all," said Clara.

"Are you sure?"

"No," put in Gregor. "There's one important detail: He always laughs a lot."

Janos put the pencil down beside his glass.

"Laughs a lot, did you say?"

"Yes."

"Why? At whom?"

"At everything. At himself, perhaps."

Janos shook his head incredulously.

"I thought Jews couldn't do anything but moan and groan."

"You don't know them, Janos. They laugh at you. They laugh, but you don't hear them. You're too busy making them cry," Gregor said, laughing.

Janos lost himself in thought for a minute, and then became gay again.

"Don't worry. If I find him, he won't want to laugh again."

He drank a last glass, put the notebook and pencil back in his uniform pocket and stood up.

"I must go. I have a wife, and she doesn't laugh often."

He promised to meet them again the next day. The same time. The same place. With information, if he was lucky.

"And you'll ask me to your wedding?"

"We'll give our first child your name."

Janos took a deep breath to throw off the effects of the

140

alcohol, kissed Clara on the forehead, and stumbled away. Soon after Clara and Gregor followed. It was already dark, and a policeman advised them to get home before the curfew. The old men of the civil defense corps were going around the streets knocking at windows and shouting, "Lights out! Lights out! You're breaking the law." Clara and Gregor slipped out of the town. When they arrived at the cave, Gregor fell onto his cot, while Clara stood at the door, looking out into the darkness.

"You act well," Gregor told her.

She went to lie down on the other cot and said, "At three o'clock tomorrow we're meeting Leib."

"Is he acting, too? If so, what's his role?"

"Leib isn't acting. He is what he is."

"How long have you known him?"

"That's none of your business."

A strange fire devoured Gregor who, with all his strength invited sleep which did not come.

"Talk to me," said Clara. "When a boy's in love he talks; don't you know that?"

"Does Leib talk much?"

"No, but he's different."

They held hands; they looked into each other's eyes; nothing else mattered.

"Talk to me," said Clara. "Otherwise we'll be noticed. In wartimes silence is suspicious. Say anything at all. Why you love me, for instance. Aren't you supposed to be madly in love?"

Gregor was put off by the coldness of her voice, but he played along, and started talking.

"You are dark and I love the night that rises up in you like a song. Your neck is slender and when I press my lips to it then I know that I have lips. Your gentle hands weave the knot of our love; they express the unspeakable, and that is why I love them. Hands that don't go together betray the hearts that accept the lie; they have not yet learned to lie as eyes lie and mouths lie and even hearts. But ours do go together and they weave a truth worthy of us."

For the first time in his life he said things which surprised him; he began a sentence without knowing where it would take him. At intervals Clara interjected, "Me too! I feel the same way!" but the dryness of her voice proved the contrary. Gregor fell back into his emptiness. Did she see him or was she listening to him?

Clara continued to play her part well. The café of the Hotel Corona exuded boredom. Both the local people and the occupying troops were drawn to the streets by the afternoon sun. Smartly turned-out German officers, ragged Hungarian soldiers, and a host of women, all apparently relaxed and happy. Who says that war breeds hate? It seems, rather, to breed love, especially when it has the savor of forbidden fruit. Love one another, for shortly you will die, you will be victims and executioners. Love one another, and seize a moment of happiness from the future. In time of war the real victories are behind the lines, where young girls, lonely wives, and widows ask nothing better than to be conquered and are not particular about the conqueror. A soldier, German or Hungarian, has only to hold out his hand. No woman can resist him. One or another, what's the difference. If Hungarian women are unfaithful to their husbands, it's the husbands' fault. They could have kept out of the war. After all, war is men's creation; women never would have invented it. And adultery is just a way of showing their indignation. One protests the best one can.

"Don't look so funereal," Clara was saying. "You don't want us to be caught, do you? Sadness is a Jewish identification card. Come on, cheer up, smile!"

Gregor made an effort, but in vain. The town seemed to him as unreal as a stage setting. Clara and he were playing lovers, but what roles were the people around them playing? He had a feeling that at any moment the curtain might drop.

"Talk!" said Clara. "Lovers always have a lot to say. Or don't you really love me?"

"What do lovers talk about?"

"Everything. About nature and destiny."

"Do you think there's such a thing as Jewish destiny?"

"Yes. But it's an anti-Semitic destiny."

Twenty minutes before three. The hour of their appointment with Leib. He arrived on time, limping and leaning on a cane. So very young, and wounded in that way! The waiter led him solicitously to a good table, near the terrace of the café, but he chose to be seated closer to his friends. He ordered ice cream and a newspaper. The waiter brought them with alacrity. He took in Gregor and Clara with a glance. What a splendid couple, he thought. Gregor felt ill at ease. Acting for the benefit of strangers was one thing, but before a friend was another. Leib sat—only his profile visible—behind his newspaper. He, too, was acting. Better than I, Gregor reflected.

Eventually Gregor managed to make his report, looking into Clara's eyes while he spoke to his friend. Clara's smile was meant for Leib, and Gregor blushed to see how she drank in Leib's words even when they were not directed to her. Whenever the waiter passed, Gregor at once changed the subject.

"Six o'clock, Janos is coming. That's when we'll know. You come back around eight. If we're not here, wait for us. All right? Approve? If you do, turn the page of your paper."

Clara kept her eyes fastened upon Gregor. The newspaper rustled. The next step settled, Gregor could find nothing more to say. He wanted to leave quickly, the idea of going on with the game was more than he could bear. But he had not yet paid the bill, and the waiter was serving on the terrace.

"Say something, Clara," he begged her.

"Take care of yourself," she said gently addressing Gregor but speaking to Leib; "you're all I have in the world." There was a light in her restless eyes, which were no longer dissembling.

"Go on, Clara," Gregor said encouragingly.

She did not hear him, but she continued. "You're my only link with life. Please do be careful. For my sake. For ours."

Leib started to get up from his chair, and the waiter hurried over with the bill. He left him a generous tip, and the waiter thanked him effusively. Leib gave him back the newspaper and stood leaning on the edge of the table, as if he were dizzy. Neither Clara nor Gregor could speak. I ought to pray, Gregor

143

was thinking, but I've forgotten how. Clara lowered her eyelids. Finally, with a sigh, Leib started to leave.

"Say something," said Clara, "quickly; I'm frightened."

Gregor nodded mutely; he had the sensation of falling into an abyss.

"Say something! Do something!" Clara muttered between her teeth.

To whom was she talking, to Leib or to Gregor? With an impulse of desperation he pulled her towards him and kissed her lips. From the doorway, where he had paused to catch his breath, Leib saw them. For a fraction of a second his eyes met Gregor's, and smiling, he limped through the door in the direction of the park.

"You've become a good actor," Clara remarked.

Arm in arm they left the café. From the sidewalk tables friendly looks were cast in their direction. What a handsome couple! What it is to be young!

"I'm no longer acting," said Gregor.

"Go ahead and eat," said Janos, nudging Gregor with his elbow.

Gregor was not hungry. Gavriel is alive, he kept saying to himself, trembling with impatience. If Janos is in such good spirits, it must be because he has found Gavriel. Nothing else matters.

"Eat, I tell you; it's delicious! You aren't sick, are you?"

Near the window a respectable looking old man was dozing under the cold scrutiny of his wife. She obviously wished he were dead; there was the gleam of a knife-blade in her eyes. Janos caressed his glass with his right hand, while with the left he wiped his drooping mustache.

"Too bad your girl friend didn't come," he said, winking.

"She isn't well. You know how women are, always complaining of some ailment. One has to be indulgent."

"It's too bad, just the same. I have a surprise for the two of you."

Once more Gregor's heart pounded. Gavriel, he thought; his surprise is called Gavriel. Gavriel's alive, and he's spoken to him. Soon I'll speak to him myself. I'll give him back what belongs to him and resume my own name."

"A surprise?" he said aloud. "What can it be?"

"Not so fast, boy, not so fast! First we'll eat and drink well, and then . . ."

He winked again.

"Too bad, though, that your girl friend chose to stay home. I like women in my audience."

Gavriel is alive, Gregor kept thinking. He was glad to have persuaded Clara to let him come alone. Not that he had told her the real reason; he had made up one that was likely enough. "I can't go on with this masquerade. In front of Janos I don't care, but in front of Leib. This evening I'd like to see him alone." Clara turned scarlet, from either anger or shame, or both. "I didn't think you were such a coward," she said. "You don't dare to go to the very end." "Yes, I do, Clara. I shall go to the end, but alone. Without you or Leib. It's easier. One can aim higher and move farther." "Where to? What for?" "That I can't say. I don't know where the road leads. It has chosen me, and I follow."

The discussion had necessarily been short. Before Gregor's obstinacy Clara could not contain her anger, and passers-by whispered, "A lovers' quarrel." "Leib will be disappointed not to see me this evening," she objected. "He'll understand." "But *I* don't understand." "That doesn't matter to me." She threw back her head and retorted hatefully, "I'll never forgive you!" Then she walked away without even shaking his hand. "Go after her, my boy, and ask her forgiveness," an elderly gentleman advised Gregor. "You'll love each other all the more after a quarrel." Gregor turned his back, feeling relieved, and went in the opposite direction. A few more hours of patience, of impatience. A grave event was at hand; an event which concerned Gavriel and bore Gavriel's name. He's alive, still alive. Eventually Janos will take me to the prison. I'll manage to smile when I finally see him and say: "I didn't forget you," and he'll answer with a laugh. And after that? After that, nothing. Gregor could not see beyond their meeting.

"Too bad," Janos said again, continuing to drink. "I'd have liked to see your girl friend's face when she heard my secret."

Janos had arrived punctually at six o'clock. Jailers are meticulously punctual, never early, never late. Representing, as they do, both liberty and the absence of liberty, they are the incarnation of time. Janos ordered an enormous dinner. All the while Gregor was burning to make him talk: Is he alive? Is he here? Have you seen him? Has he suffered? But he controlled himself. Gavriel's survival depends upon me; a premature question might be his death warrant. Time went by, and soon Leib would be there. Janos ate and drank in a leisurely fashion, at ease in his own notion of time. The trouble with jailers is that waiting doesn't bother them; they're in no hurry. To them an hour is an hour and a year a year.

"Go on and eat," said Janos, nudging him with his elbow.

Gregor tried to do justice to the meal. Fish, sauce, vegetables. "Soon," he kept thinking. Soon a weight will be lifted from me. Was it the effect of the wine or the prospect of seeing Gavriel, he became gay and imitated Janos' way of drinking and laughing. He felt infinitely indulgent toward the whole world, including the cold woman sitting beside her old husband and sharpening a knife in her eyes.

"So you're going to marry the girl," said Janos, with a malicious gleam in his eyes.

"Yes, I am. We love each other."

"Aren't you a bit young to get married?"

"I'll be older soon enough."

"And what are you going to do?"

"When?"

"After you're married, of course."

"I'm not sure. First the army. And after the war? I haven't thought about it."

Janos promised his help in case Gregor wanted to be a jailer. One of the softest jobs you can hope to find. Gregor listened politely, but distractedly. Janos was drinking too much, and his conversation was rambling. Gregor glanced at his watch. Soon, soon a limping boy, with a cane, Leib, would appear at the restaurant door and he must convey the message that Gavriel was alive and that he expected to be taken by Janos to see him. Soon. It was already half past seven, and Leib would be there at eight o'clock. On time. Leib was punctual, like a prison guard. There's something of the prison guard in us all.

"After you're married," Janos went on repetitively, "you'll have a family on your hands. Better come to me for a soft job."

Gregor paid no attention. For the moment, he tasted only the joys of expectation. The waiter brought them some black coffee, bitter, undrinkable. Even the watch hands seemed to be moving forward impatiently. Only a quarter of an hour more. Should he interrupt Janos and ask him abruptly: What about the surprise? No, to risk it was too great. Words kill. At the beginning there is always the word. *Fire!* a lieutenant was calling out somewhere, and a line of men and women tumbled into a ditch. Somewhere a sergeant was calling out in Russian or German or English: *Forward* and the world would count a few less people. Patience, Gregor! Open your mouth and you may tumble Gavriel into his ditch.

"I don't care about love," the guard was saying. "I'm interested only in hate. Love makes a man weak, but hate makes him strong."

With a broad sweep of his arm he seemed to envelop all the inhabitants of the globe in fire and blood. Then with his right hand he picked up his glass and emptied it, while with the left he pushed up his mustache.

"Wine makes a man strong too," he said. "When you drink you forget your own weakness and see that of others. Soon you forget that you're drinking. The presence of a full bottle on the table is an insult. If you want to be a jailer, you must learn to drink, my boy."

"Yes," said Gregor.

Their table was the noisiest in the room. Near the window the old man was peacefully dozing before his wife. Farther away a Hungarian officer was flirting with a handsome woman whose husband was off fighting. He talked and she laughed; it was plain that beauty and heroism were about to conclude a short-term alliance. To the right still farther, a German lieutenant was reciting something—a poem, perhaps, in the ear of his female companion, who didn't understand a word he was saying. So much the worse, or perhaps the better, for both herself and the poet. Women listen, in ecstasy, above all when a smartly uniformed officer is reciting an endless poem about death—a German officer always speaks about death, for he is its confident and devoted servant. *Fire!* and a line of men, women and children, silent and barely astonished, tumble into the ditch. Just as in a poem, *nicht wahr? Ach,* the power of words in certain mouths!

But in the expectant mood of this evening Gregor felt nothing but pity toward the entire world. Toward the unaware old man and his embittered wife, toward the Hungarian officer and his loud-mouthed companion, even toward the German lieutenant, who sang of the glory of love, war, and blood. Ten minutes before eight. Gavriel is alive. Do you hear, officers and gentlemen? The man of God is alive; soon he will pick up his stick and march on, imposing his rhythm and his silence upon you.

Eight minutes to eight. Leib would appear at any moment. Gregor tried to figure out a way of signaling to him that his mission, or at least its initial phase, was accomplished. A nod would be sufficient.

"Well, then?" said Janos, with a fatherly air. "What do you say to working with me?"

"Nothing could please me more. But first I must go into the army and do my share of killing. Today no one is a man until he's shed blood. The more he kills the more of a man he is. No wonder our German allies call themselves supermen."

"Good, good. I'm not speaking of the present. But after the war, will you come to see me? I'll teach you the trade, or rather how to enjoy it. War or no war, there are sure to be prisons, and jailers will always be in demand. Don't worry, you'll be happy."

"I'll come to see you on the very day of victory," promised Gregor.

It was nearly eight o'clock. Gregor's eyes were fastened on the door. I have good news, Leib, he would say with a smile. This idiot Janos imagines that he's giving me a surprise! The hands are moving on; there are only a few minutes left. Leib will understand at a glance, and Janos won't even notice; he's too busy drinking and talking. Go to it, Janos, drink and talk. And, above all, don't look at me. Pay no attention either to me or to the lame fellow who will be here at any moment.

Eight o'clock. The waiter was busying himself with the table nearest the entrance. Gregor leaned forward in order to see the door. The waiter was serving a family of five, which was visiting the town. The mother was scolding the daughter: "No dessert unless you finish your potatoes!" The little girl obeyed. Leib was late! Patience, Gregor; he'll come. But what if he's been caught, Gregor asked himself. Impossible! For three days I've been walking through the town and I haven't seen any of my old friends or the friends of my father. The police no longer stop people to ask for their papers. The town must already be *Judenrein*. Leib can go about fearlessly, like myself. The Jews are all gone, never to return. So why should he be late? His watch must have stopped; such things happen, especially in time of war. Watches have more sense than men, and they refuse to move. That's why Leib is late; the watch hands have led him astray. But he'll be coming; you can count on him, Gregor. Do you understand? Count on him. Leib has never let his friends down. As long as his friends need him he'll escape danger. I need you, Leib. Gavriel needs you. And Clara. Be careful, Leib; don't take any foolish risks. Don't delay. Show yourself. Open the door and come in. And look at me. Gavriel is alive, and he, too, is waiting for you.

The little girl had finished her potatoes. Proudly she pointed to her empty plate. "I've finished, mother."

"So they weren't so bad, were they?"

"Can I have my dessert?"

Her father was silent. Near the window the old man was still sleeping under the murderous gaze of his wife.

Five minutes past eight. Patience, Gregor. Nervousness attracts danger. Don't be nervous. Imitate Janos; he has no nerves. Drink, talk, and laugh like him, that's the best weapon against fear, the beast gnawing at your stomach. Why do you suppose Janos drinks? Is he, too, fighting fear? The same fear as yours?

"As I told you, I have a surprise for you and your girl friend," said Janos, scratching the tip of his broad, flat nose.

"Yes, you did tell me."

"Aren't you curious to know what it is?"

"Yes, but I can wait."

"What will you gain by waiting?"

"Nothing."

Outside it was growing dark. The waiters pulled the curtains because of the blackout. Quarter past eight. Already. Patience, Gregor! Make an effort, don't give your feelings away. Leib can't be far now. Leib is Yiddish for lion. The name is fitting, for the lion is king of that jungle.

"So do you want to hear about the surprise or don't you?"

"I do, naturally," said Gregor.

"If you'd rather wait until tomorrow, just say so. I'm not in a hurry."

Janos was in a jovial, teasing mood.

"I'm not in a hurry either," said Gregor.

Twenty minutes past eight. Where are you, Leib? I can wait until midnight, if necessary. I obey my will and it obeys me; we are one and the same, proceeding in the same direction. Don't worry about us; I'm not losing my mind. But where are you? Hurry up, friend. I know that a wounded war veteran, a lame man, walks slowly. But you must try to hurry. It's late, Leib; Gavriel is alive, and it's late.

"The bottle's empty," declared Janos, wiping his mustache. "Now for the surprise!"

Don't shake, Gregor said to himself, don't shake. I know what he's going to say, so I must keep calm. Watch out for your nerves. Make yourself smile. Control your smile.

"Pull your chair closer," said Janos; "I don't want to shout. What I have to tell you is nobody else's business."

Gregor obeyed. Half past eight. His heart was pounding faster and faster; he wanted to get up and run, to exhaust himself. Patience? That's easy to say. Leib was thirty minutes late, and that was too long. In thirty minutes a lot can happen.

"It concerns the fellow Clara was talking about," Janos said teasingly, as if Gregor didn't know, "the rich Jew."

"Yes," said Gregor, indifferent.

"The surprise has to do with him."

"Yes?"

"Sit up straight. You'll fall off your chair."

Gregor breathed hard and perspiration collected on his

forehead. He swallowed his saliva. Where should he look, at Janos's lips or his eyes? His eyes.

"I've found him," said Janos, lowering his voice.

It was what Gregor expected, but the surprise overwhelmed him. Tears welled in his eyes. Say something, Gregor; don't sit there staring. Betray nothing.

"Have you nothing to say?"

"Thank you."

The guard leaned forward, his face close to that of Gregor.

"He's in the prison. Not far from here. Cell ninety-one. Top secret. The Germans have been advised. Tomorrow he'll be taken to Budapest. From there, on the first transport. Soon there'll be nothing left of your Jew but a memory, a bad memory."

Twenty minutes to nine. Gregor felt torn between Leib and Gavriel. He wanted to think of both together, because to choose one of them meant to betray the other. He chose Leib. The delay in his arrival meant that something had gone wrong.

"Where do the transports go?" he asked.

"Sh!" said Janos. "Not so loud!"

"All these Jews, where do they take them?"

"Sh! They go to eternity," said Janos, winking. "Do you get the idea?"

"Yes, they go to eternity."

Janos nudged him.

"Pleased?"

"Pleased?" said Gregor without understanding.

"Pleased with my surprise."

"Of course I'm pleased. And Clara will be even more so."

"Too bad she didn't come. I'd have liked to see her face when I told her."

"She isn't well. You know how women are."

Gregor started to talk, saying anything at all to fill the time. Leib's ruining our plans. What next? If he doesn't come in five minutes, it's all over. I'll wait until nine o'clock. He ordered another round of wine, but the waiter shook his head; too late, closing time. The restaurant began to empty. The old man woke with a start; his wife hid the knife in her eyes and smiled. The little girl whispered into her mother's ear that she had to go to the toilet. Janos called the waiter and paid the bill. It was nine o'clock.

"How fast the time goes," Janos sighed.

"Very fast," echoed Gregor.

Leib wasn't coming; Leib won't come. Gregor tried to keep calm. Nothing serious, Gregor. Nothing can happen to Leib the Lion. The delay? There must be a good reason. Probably at the last minute some more urgent mission caused him to change his plans, and he had no way of letting me know. It's that simple. Everything's simple in time of war. He'll have gone directly home; perhaps he's waiting for me.

"Shall we go?" said Janos.

"Yes."

They were the last to leave. The waiters were stacking the chairs, and the room took on a lugubrious air. When they were on the street Janos said that he was going back to the prison to question the Jew.

"It's my wedding present," he said. "You'll have the information you want tomorrow."

"Thank you, Janos. Clara and I shall be eternally grateful."

"Come, come; no sentimentality. Let's wait and see. He looks like a tough nut. Pig-headed. But trust me. He'll talk."

The wine made Gregor's head feel heavy. His chest and shoulders ached; his eyes burned, but his brain still functioned, fashioning plans, looking for ways out, weighing one risk against another. He perspired. How could he save Gavriel from torture? Tell Janos to postpone questioning him until the next day? Impossible. The prisoner was to be turned over to the Germans in the morning. Janos would be suspicious. Something else. Quick. Otherwise Janos might kill him.

"Janos," he said abruptly, "one more favor. Take me with you. The time is short, and it's important that I be in on the questioning. If I'm there, he won't dare hide the truth."

Janos shot him a hard look ranging him from head to toe.

"Aren't you a bit young for such things? You'd throw up a good meal."

"No, I really want to, Janos. I'll behave."

"You'll be sorry."

"No, I won't."

Janos thought for a moment and then shrugged his shoulders.

"All right, if you insist; come with me."

Gregor stopped to breathe. Janos loomed up like a giant beside him.

"We'll go in to see him after midnight, when there's a change of guards," Janos said.

He proposed a short walk to stretch their legs and clear their heads of the wine. Was that all right? In his company Gregor needn't worry about its being so late. No policeman would stop them. Janos walked pondorously, as if dragging his feet through the mud, and stopping to spit on the ground. His face darkened and he lost his good humor. Angrily he scratched his nose. Gregor, absorbed in his own thoughts, paid no attention.

"All the same . . ." Janos muttered.

"All the same, what?" said Gregor for the sake of showing interest.

"There's something I don't understand. You never told me your Jew's name."

"Gavriel."

"A queer duck."

"Queer?"

"He doesn't fit your description. That bothers me. I don't like to see a Jew change so fast."

They were walking through the deserted main square. The windows were dark and the houses were huddled together as if to protect themselves against the plague. The town: a cemetery. The inhabitants were dead, only their shadows survived them. Shadows of houses, of children, of pregnant women. The trees, too, seemed unreal; death lurked in them in order to attract its prey. Their footsteps in the night were nowhere recorded, not even in memory; they only enlarged the cemetery. Did Leib hear them, or Gavriel? By now Gregor was convinced that the broken appointment with Leib signified the end of an epoch, of a friendship. Here I am, walking calmly beside a torturer, indifferent to the danger of which he is the incarnation and deaf to the cries of those who tumble into the ditch. Careful, Gregor; you're losing your way! Don't think of Leib, it's too late for that. There'll be time to think of him tomorrow. Tonight your thoughts belong to Gavriel. Soon you'll find yourself before him, in his cell, and you'll say . . . What shall I say? I'll say: once again you're cheating the Angel of Death. When my friend sees that I'm on good terms with his jailer he'll be astonished. But I'll find a way to signal to him with my hand or head or eyes, to tell him that this is an abominable but necessary game. I am a Jew, Gavriel, like yourself, and my deliverance depends upon yours. "Soon," Gregor thought, and he trembled with fear or joy, perhaps with both together.

Janos stumbled heavily along, finding it more and more difficult to raise his legs and seeming to mark time.

"It still bothers me. For two months our town has been *Judenrein,* or so we thought. But it wasn't true; there was still a Jew among us. I can't get over the fact that he managed to hide out so long."

"What do you expect?" Gregor said, rambling. "It's the Jews' trade, and they've learned it. They show themselves, they get beaten up. No sooner in their skin than God remembers them and gives them some dangerous and useless mission. Jews resemble their God. They're always hiding. The world's not only *Judenrein;* it's *Gottrein* as well. Soon there'll be no more Jews and no more God. Nobody will hide any longer. That will be hell. We shall be alone."

Gregor talked on, in order to overcome his trembling, to transform joy into fear and fear into joy. Fortunately Janos was so preoccupied that he was not even listening. They had come to the narrow street where once the indestructible old Jewish synagogue had welcomed the faithful gathered together there to praise God and his chosen people.

"Let's go back," said Gregor.

Janos did not hear, and he had to repeat the sentence, tugging at his companion's sleeve.

"All the same . . ." Janos muttered; "I don't understand."

Their footsteps echoed afar as they marched through the dead city, like two friends who have so much to tell that they cannot say goodnight and must go on walking. And yet soon Janos would stand before Gavriel as his torturer. Under certain circumstances, can a torturer be a friend? Why not? He is no less of a man than the next; he is all men, and their friend.

"I don't understand," said Janos for the tenth time.

Gregor looked at his animal-like face: the obtuse angles of the profile, the receding chin, thick lips, flat nose, bull's neck. If he were out of uniform, would I recognize him as the torturer of Gavriel?

"What don't you understand?"

How late was it? Ten o'clock, perhaps. A little more or less, what did it matter. Not yet midnight. Gregor remembered Clara's accusation: "You're a coward!" Am I really? No one who hasn't drunk his cup to the dregs has really lived. Who doesn't go to the end, can know only a truth that is partial and mutilated. A man must commit every act, undergo every humiliation, lay claim to every reason to blaspheme, or else he cannot be whole. There was the trap. To save a friend, that's called living. But to betray a friend—the same or another—is called living as well.

"All the same, it's funny. Do you know when your Jew was captured?"

"When?" asked Gregor in a whisper.

"Just today."

Gregor felt as if he had been struck in the face. "I don't understand," he said, and yet he began to understand.

"Neither do I," said the guard, spitting.

Then he gave some details. During the afternoon two policemen had seen someone suspicious in the vicinity of the abandoned ghetto. They asked to see his papers and found them in good order, but nevertheless they took him to the police station. Why such zeal? Because of Janos. Having found no Jew in prison Janos had spread the alarm: the police should keep their eyes open. These two officers were lucky. At the police station it was discovered that the papers were forged. The prisoner denied that he was a Jew until he was ordered to take off his clothes; then he had confessed immediately.

There was nothing left now of Gregor but fear. He choked

and bit his lips. To feel pain, to put your finger on the wound and deepen it until you become the wound. And nothing else.

"What language did he speak?"

"What's that? What language? Hungarian, of course! He speaks Hungarian, like you and me."

Gregor swallowed.

"When they whipped him," Janos went on, "He asked for more."

"Have you seen him?"

"Yes, I have. They beat him up and then brought him to us. When I heard of his arrival you can imagine how happy I was; I ran to greet him."

"You really did see him?"

"I told you so? With my own eyes. That's why I'm trying to make you see. The description you gave me yesterday doesn't fit."

Everything was clear, painfully clear. No more hope.

"First," Janos went on, "he has no beard; second, he's fair, not dark. You wouldn't make much of a policeman. Poor observer."

Gregor walked silently behind him, as if through a cemetery, swaying from right to left in imitation of his gait.

"And the bastard had the nerve to claim that he'd been wounded in the war! He was limping and carried a cane. Well, they broke that over his back quickly enough. After that he walked as straight as you or me. Standing up against the wall of his cell he dared look me right in the eye. 'Aren't you ashamed of pretending to be a soldier?' I asked him. 'No. And you?' 'I don't deceive anybody.' 'That's why you ought to be ashamed.' "

Before he knew it Gregor saw that they were on the street overhung by the ruins of the synagogue. The building next door, where the Rabbi had lived, was still intact. A German sentry was on duty at the door. Later Gregor learned that it had been requisitioned by the German military command. For a long time it troubled him that a foreigner, whose face he would never see, should have lived in the room where once a holy man had communed with his soul. Is there any link between one man and the one who succeeds him in time and space? There must be, since the successor is who he is and not another. Poor rabbi!

"For two whole months he made fools of us by wandering around the streets, rubbing elbows with German officers and Hungarian women, as if he were on top of the world instead of being a trapped beast."

Janos was choking with indignation.

"Now I see why you told me that he was always laughing. You were right. Perhaps you aren't so stupid as you look. Of course he was laughing. Inside. I can just see him in a restaurant or theater, with his cane leaning against his leg and the airs of a bemedaled hero. No doubt men got up to offer him a chair and women stared at him with admiration."

Janos was shouting at the top of his lungs, but the windows on the square remained shut. The dead slept, and in their dreams they saw the ditches filling without end. Janos halted, and brandished his fist at an invisible enemy, dead or alive, what did it matter.

"He can wait now, the dirty Jew! He's nothing to lose by waiting. Tonight I'll take him in hand and I can promise you he won't laugh any longer!"

His shouts echoed, strangely out of place, in the darkness. Shouting is not permissible in a cemetery. Only the dead have a right to speak.

Gregor wanted to tell him: "My dear sir, do you know that I hate you with all my heart, with a hate that I promise to keep alive as long as I am living?" But he said nothing. He wasn't sure that either his hate or the night was real. Janos started to walk on and Gregor followed. What could he do? He must do something, but no action made sense. Gavriel was dead, Leib was in prison, and he, Gregor, was walking with a jailer. He must make up his mind. But how? Should he go with Janos to the cell and see Leib the Lion tortured? That would prove to Clara that he was capable of going to the very end. But I no longer want to prove anything, either to myself or anybody else. Yet Janos must be prevented from taking revenge on Leib. What if I were to tell him that I, too, am a Jew in hiding, that I, too, laugh inwardly at his people of murderers? No. Why not? Because Janos wouldn't believe it.

Or was it because he, Gregor, feared pain? Because he wanted to see Clara again and justify or humiliate himself in her presence. It was all too easy to share Leib's fate and his martyrdom. What good would it do to the partisans in the forest? Come, Leib. The story is starting all over. Where are our lanterns? Broken. And the gypsy who egged on Pishta and his Gang? Go to it, boys! The Jews are unarmed and at your mercy. Jump on them and give us their blood in which to wash away our sins. . . . No, Leib; we shall go on, even without lanterns. We'll fight our battles separately. Not alone, but separated.

"Wait a minute," said Gregor. "I'll be right back."

"Where are you going? Are you looking for a place to . . ."

Without giving him time to catch on, Gregor disappeared into the night. The real problem isn't hate, no, not hate. But shame, yes, shame.

3

The faces before him were sealed, more inscrutable and intense than usual. Gregor saw them through a fog a single face many eyes. They're sad, he thought, not at all surprised. The heavy presence of the war, the daily sacrifices; another light gone out, another tree felled. To them Leib was not so much a chief as a comrade. Every one of his words and gestures enriched their hope by giving to it simplicity and humility: we shall prevail, for inasmuch as it has any meaning, victory is within the domain of man and of that which elevates rather than denies him. We shall prevail, because by taking up arms, by defying those who claim to speak in the name of destiny, theirs and ours, we have already won a right to victory, and whatever may happen it will be neither vain nor transitory. Victory, according to Leib, was more a necessity than a certitude. And now? He is a prisoner and they are sad; that is why they stand there, pale and fearful, and stare at me.

"Tell us," Zeide said, taciturn.

"I've told you everything."

But still they waited. They were not satisfied with his reply.

Gregor felt forced to add: "There's nothing more to say. You know it all."

Outside the sun was mutely battling the forest. Here and there the overhanging vault was pierced, and a ray of light slid down from the length of a tree to lose itself in the foliage, here green, there touched with gold. In spite of the heavy, damp heat, Gregor was shivering. He had not slept all night. He had walked, without a halt, through the fields, hiding in the wheat at the least suspicious sound and avoiding the villages along the way. At noon he had arrived, breathless and perspiring, at the bunker and thrown himself down on the grass, while Haimi, the first to see him, ran to alert the others. In a second they were all about him, worried, concerned: "Are you hurt?" "Are you thirsty?" "Do you want a glass of water?" It was only after they were sure that he was safe and unharmed that they asked those questions that really mattered: "Where is Leib?" "Why is it that you came back alone?" "When will he come?" No one asked: "What about Gavriel? Did you find him?" Gregor wanted to tell them that Gavriel was dead, but that they didn't really care. Their Gavriel was Leib, and his name trembled on their lips. Even the sentries deserted their posts and came to ask for news. "We didn't see Leib. Why not? Where is he?"

Zeide was the first to understand. He closed his eyes, concentrated. When he reopened them he was no longer the same man; the strength and the responsibility of leadership had come upon him. At once he took the situation in hand, reprimanded the sentries, and sent them back, then he turned to Gregor:

"We'd better talk inside."

Zeide led the way. The others followed. Clara stood near the table, resting her arms on it. Gregor blushed deeply when he saw her. He started to move in her direction, but her mask of hostility caused him to recoil and turn away his head. At a sign from Zeide, whose authority no one had disputed, Gregor sat down at the table, opposite the rest.

"Speak," said Zeide. "Omit nothing."

He wanted to know everything. All the details. The picture had to be clear. Gregor spoke quickly, words tumbling from his mouth. As he spoke, he furtively glanced at Clara, who stood, motionless and tense, her lips half open, weighing his every word. In order to spare her, Gregor spoke in the first person singular: I said, I thought, I saw, I got such and such an impression, I reacted in this or that way. They listened with concentration, and as he spoke his voice grew strong and clear, freed of fatigue: it was the voice of the perfect witness. His account was chronological and coherent. The meetings with Janos, the meals, the laughter, the lies. Nothing was left out. Beyond sorrow a certain pride emerged. To these men he became one who had returned from a wild country, filled with dragons and other monsters, a man who had seen destiny at work. Every one of his sentences translated a portion of an infinite evil, of a murderous truth. They thrust their heads forward in order not to lose a single expression, a single pause. Someone unknown to them spoke through his voice. Suddenly he stopped talking, and the ensuing silence had the power of a curse; imperceptibly, they bowed their heads.

"Go on," said Zeide, as if emerging from a dream.

"That's all. There's nothing more to be said or done."

Gregor wiped the perspiration from his forehead. The very fact of having spoken gave him a sensation of well-being. We are brothers and we shall win. I will no longer have to carry the chains of a captive leader.

"Finished?" said Zeide. "Start all over!"

Gregor let a few seconds go by while he caught his breath. He was thirsty, but he did not dare ask for a drink. What has happened is beyond their understanding, he thought. They refuse to admit that Leib is lost, that their group is orphaned and decapitated. They can't believe it. It's not too surprising. Leib arrested? Unthinkable. Leib the Lion, the indomitable, will surely break his chains and tear apart his cage. Alone he can stand up against the whole Hungarian army, Panzers included. To his comrades Leib was a Samson, triumphant over all ruses devised against him. He was not simply a Jew armed with anger, he was the wrath of all Jews, from the days of the temple's burning to their own day. Leib humiliated, locked up, accepting defeat without bringing down the walls and rending the earth? No, not Leib the Lion. In their minds Leib was still the indomitable guide who would lead them across the desert to the faraway Promised Land. With both hands they

161

pushed the facts away. By taking refuge behind incredulity they hoped to exorcise fate.

"Start all over," Zeide repeated, when Gregor had finished for the second time.

"From the beginning?"

"From the beginning."

"Very well. It was this way. We had an appointment to meet. It was yesterday . . ."

"It was yesterday," echoed Zeide. "Go on."

Gregor began again. Some thirty eyes stared at him. Clara ran her eyes over his forehead, his lips, his eyebrows. The others studied his perspiring face, his dilated eyes, his quivering nostrils and the hands laid discreetly on the table. No one interrupted to ask for further explanation. The more Gregor spoke the farther removed he felt from this place, without approaching any other. He was back in the town, wandering from one street and one defeat to another, circling seven times the walls of the prison, which stood out like a church above the low buildings around it, retracing the route he had followed the preceding days and trying, unsuccessfully, to correct some of his errors. His thoughts did not follow his voice but took an opposite direction. I never met Janos; I never asked him to look for a Jew who had changed his name and was always laughing. Too late. The Jew in question is no longer laughing; someone else will laugh in his place. As Gregor spoke his voice carried him farther and farther away. He was there and he was elsewhere. These men who tracked him to the most secret places of time, real and imagined, it is I who bring them to life: I am their fear and their pride. At this point he became calm; as long as he talked he was safe. He would have liked to talk for days and nights, but the events themselves carried him forward inexorably and he, their prisoner, had to submit. The end was rising up to meet him; there was no way of delaying or circumventing it.

"That's all. Leib didn't come. He won't."

Nobody moved. Gregor looked at his hands, spread out upon the table, hoping they would not tremble.

At Zeide's command he began for the third time to tell his story. From the beginning? From the beginning. Gregor wanted to protest, but he restrained himself. He was becoming feverish, but continued. Do you want my voice? Take it. We'll start again. The human voice brings people together and separates them. Brick by brick, stone by stone the voice builds walls, a man knocks his head against them, it hurts; it no longer hurts. Eventually the voice becomes a prison. From the beginning? Yes, from the beginning. The voice is a desert. Whoever is thirsty drinks his own blood. I am thirsty. I am burning. They don't even notice. So what. We'll start all over. It's my voice you need? Take it. In the beginning God created the heaven and the earth, and that evening Leib was supposed to meet me at the restaurant. Do you understand? I don't. Never mind. Let's go on.

As Gregor spoke he became someone else. Listening to his own voice, he found it false. This isn't the true story; you're holding that back. The repetition of the truth betrays it. The more I talk the more I empty myself of truth. They listen to me in awe, as if I were speaking from a mountain top, my head touching the sky, and yet they don't know me, I don't know them. Except for Haimi, Zeide, and Clara I don't even know their names. Not that that means anything. A name? It locks doors; it doesn't open them. I'm the last to have seen Leib alive; that's what matters. And so they listen to me. They'll spend the rest of their lives listening. One day someone—a hurt woman, a frightened child—will look at them questioningly: "Where are you? Your thoughts are far away." And with a disturbed expression on their face, a finger to their lips, they will say, "Be quiet, woman, be quiet, child!"

The bunker was poorly ventilated and stuffy. But the partisans didn't notice, and neither did Gregor. Deep inside he was frozen with cold. These journeys into time, these repeated trips exhausted him and left him without moorings.

He had said nothing for some time, but Zeide and his friends were observing him like scholars, waiting for nothing less than a miracle. You who tell so good a story, give it a different ending; tell us that what you said isn't true, tell us that Leib is free, that he'll return tomorrow or next week. Suddenly he met Haimi's enflamed eyes. He was struck to the heart. Haimi is angry; he holds me responsible for the logic of events. If I hadn't come, Leib would still be alive. Gregor had to grant that Haimi was right; he saw the day coming when this youngest of the partisans would vent upon him his hatred of the jailers. By the mere fact of my having toasted with Janos, of having shaken his hand and existed in his eyes, I have brought back a portion of him with me and I shall never throw it off. Gregor went away. Janos returned.

Gregor decided that at the first occasion he would take Haimi aside to talk to him about Leib whom he had known before any of them, when they were both boys, younger than anyone present. We waged a war that will last as long as I live, and as long as it lasts, Leib will be a part of it.

On the other side of the table, around and behind Zeide, all the faces were merged into one, incredulity and sorrow written upon it. They mistrust me because I have spoken. I should have been silent. Not that my silence would have made them any less suspicious. To them I am the instrument of death. If Gavriel were present, they would be capable of strangling him. Leib sacrificed himself for Gavriel, and I am the link between them.

Haimi's eyes were wet. Zeide leaned his chin on his right fist, which was propped upon the table. Gregor felt Clara's eyes on his dry lips. Who is the hunchback behind the new leader? He told me his name, but I've forgotten it. He's not really a hunchback; he just looks like one because his head is down between his shoulders. Only about twenty years old with big, floppy ears, a thin, embittered face, capable of hate. What's his name? Leib introduced him to me. I can still feel his damp, limp hand's shake, but his name escapes me. It's important to remember. Memory ought to hold even the most insignificant things, and a name isn't insignificant. I'm too thirsty, that's why my memory is hazy. My lungs are bursting. A glass of water. A few drops on my tongue and lips, and the barriers will fall. I'm ashamed to ask; ashamed to speak of water. I don't know why, but I'm ashamed, and that prevents me from speaking and gives a false meaning to my silence. Why do they stare at me, unblinking and hostile? They see that I'm ashamed, but they don't know why; they're trying to find the meaning of my shame. They can't know that my shame comes from the fact that I'm thirsty and that I've forgotten the name of the damp-handed hunchback. I should explain it to them, before they go off on a false track. I should tell them that I'm not—at least not exclusively—a stranger separating Leib from his life and death. I'm one of them. Each one of us is, to someone, a key with many uses, without it doors neither open nor shut. Leib would have understood, and you, too, must understand. Leib asked me to go to the town. You are all witnesses to that. He was the one who decided to use my key. Amid the dangers of the town I was not alone, for I felt myself bound to you; I was your extension. We were members of one group, one body; it is with each one of you that Janos clinked glasses and shook hands. I was Leib's fate. But now you are mine. We can choose neither our lives nor our destinies, nor the code with which to decipher them.

Gregor was bathed in sweat and trembling, not with fear but simply with cold. He felt dirty and impure; already he was behaving as though he were accused and guilty. With a surge of energy he decided to regain control of the situation. I have spoken, he said to himself, and my words have dug a ditch between us. I must now build a bridge between us, that they may share my shame as I share their silence.

"Give me a glass of water," he said hoarsely.

No one moved.

"Since yesterday evening," he said, almost shouting, "since I left the restaurant not a drop of water has touched my tongue; my throat is burning and there's sand in my lungs. I'm suffocating."

Nothing. His voice didn't carry. It was as if he had not spoken. Zeide was still scrutinizing him with his chin leaning on his right fist. The hunchback seemed to be maliciously amused. Haimi was still trying not to cry, his mouth twisted as if in pain. Lugubriously, the others waited for a miracle or for the killing of the miracle-maker. Outside the light took on a metallic glare.

"Suppose that I'm guilty," Gregor cried angrily. "What right have you to condemn me?"

Their expressions became cold and cutting; they cut into his flesh and Gregor turned suddenly toward the door. Clara observed him, without pity, with hate, with curiosity. He was sure that she would not refuse him a glass of water. She knew the truth, she must know it; she knew that Leib was his childhood friend, that, in a way, he had been his childhood. But she, too, stood stiff and unreachable. Gregor found the expectation unbearable. Were deaf-mutes to judge him? There is a wall between us, he reflected. I speak words and hear them and their content is familiar, but when they reach their ears they are no longer the same. I asked for water and they think they have heard a confession.

"Very well then," he said, raising his head. "Since you choose not to understand, I'll tell you a story."

And for the fourth time he told them of the events leading to the arrest of Leib. He added nothing, omitted nothing, word by word he repeated what they had heard three times before. Only his voice had changed; it was heavy with resonance and shook with anger contained and intense. Even if the story was identical with those that had gone before, it sounded new. They listened as if they were hearing it for the first time. Their bodies were tense; some panted and others held their breath. Clara, still rigid, seemed to be listening with her eyes. The power of repetition, Gregor thought. Perhaps the mystics are right in choosing to repeat a single sentence or prayer all their life. A thousand times one still makes one. Yet one multiplied by a thousand differs from one multiplied by ten or by one. In taking a single word by assault it is possible to discover the secret of creation, the center where all threads come together. The dozing old man, the woman with a knife in her eyes, the obedient little girl: the sum of all these was Leib's arrest. The ten thousand Jews who were burned every day in Silesia, Gavriel's laugh, the fellowship of the partisans, all these added up to the misunderstanding of which one man was the victim. Now Gregor understood everything, both his own guilt and that of his audience. The injustice perpetrated in an unknown land concerns me; I am responsible. He who is not among the victims is with the executioners. This was the meaning of the holocaust: it implicated not only Abraham or his son, but their God as well.

At the end of the story Gregor was moved to see a tear shine in Haimi's eye. Some day, he thought, I shall take him aside and talk to him.

"Now," he said in a low voice, "I'd like a glass of water. I'm thirsty."

A long moment passed. Then Clara rose and brought him a drink. His hand did not tremble. He swallowed; and then the weight of his shame fell upon him once more. He put the glass down on the table and shouted, "What in the name of God do you want from me? I've told you everything. I've explained everything. Why do you stare at me that way?"

Clara had gone back to her place near the door. The sun was setting and the forest was filled with shadows. The tops of the fir trees were outlined against a somber sky.

"Any questions? Go ahead and ask them, but stop treating me like a stranger!"

He saw the hunchback whisper something into Zeide's ear. They all thrust their heads forward in order to hear better.

"We'd like to clear up a few details," Zeide said at last. "You know the part that Leib played in all our lives. That's why we must go to the end. For later on."

"I'm an empty man," Gregor said with despair.

He stopped short. A man? It was the first time he had referred to himself in that way. His father used to say: "You must prepare for the day when you will be a man." And now he was one. Where, exactly, was the boundary line? When had he stopped being a child?

"An emptied man," he repeated, in order not to allow time in which to recapture an abandoned position. "What I knew, you now know. What I saw, heard, did, you have now seen, heard, and done. Together we have gone the limit; beyond there is nothing."

"True," Zeide admitted. "You have spoken. Nobody denies it. And we have listened without interrupting. But you forget the value of questions. Hear us now." Zeide had spoken. quietly.

"Go on, Zeide, I'm ready. Ask your questions, all of you, and I'll give them back to you white and washed. You want proof of good conduct, assurance of innocence. That's what you want, isn't it? You'll get it!"

Gregor's fury had fascinated the hunchback. He shook his heavy head and broke into sullen laughter, incredulous of everything that Gregor was saying.

"Let's begin with you," said Zeide addressing Gregor. "Give us your questions." Gregor was amazed. "Of myself? I have none."

A childhood memory: he was about eight, shortly after the death of his grandfather. It was a spring day. His father had taken him up into the mountains. Gregor liked the fields, the horse-drawn carriage, and to be alone with his father. His father, contrary to his habit, talked to him that day. "One day you'll be a man and there will be no one for you to question. What will you do?" "I won't have any questions." "I hope that you will!" "Tell me, father, why are the clouds afraid of the sun? Why do beggars always hold out their hands? How does a blind man know that it's dark and time to go to bed?" His father smiled. "Very good, son. You're starting well. You'll see: answers change, but questions are always the same."

"You have no questions?" Zeide repeated.

"Yes, Why do beggars always hold out their hands? How does a blind man know that it's dark and time to go to bed?"

The hunchback sneered. Gregor found him repulsively ugly. He was astonished: I'm capable of hate. Perhaps that's what makes him sneer.

"We have some questions," said Zeide, looking at him out of sorrowful eyes.

"I'm listening."

In a calm voice Zeide put him through the interrogation, while behind him the hunchback ridiculed both questions and answers. At first Gregor answered in a determinedly relaxed manner, but little by little he became aware of the humiliation of the spectacle. What were they driving at? Why was Zeide trying to confuse him? What did he want to prove?

"Why did you make your appointment with Janos for six o'clock?"

"He set the hour. It was the time when he got off duty."

"Why did you tell Leib to come at eight?"

"I needed time to talk to Janos."

"Did Leib's lateness worry you?"

"Very much."

"Talk to us about your worry."

"It was in my eyes."

"Then talk to us about your eyes."

"They ran through the streets, searching the doorways and questioning the passers-by."

"Did your eyes visit the prison?"

"No. I knew they couldn't pierce the walls."

"What do you reproach yourself for?"

"For not being in Leib's place. Or Gavriel's."

"What do you regret?"

"That I'm not Leib or Gavriel."

The hunchback seemed to be dancing. It seemed to Gregor as if he might break into applause. What was his name? If I could remember, I'd be saved. But my memory is somehow closed. The worst enemy? Memory. The hunchback is making fun of me because my memory has failed.

"What are you after, Zeide?"

"The truth."

"There are many truths. Each one denies the others."

"I want the one that contains them all."

"Even if it's inhuman?"

"Even if it's inhuman."

The hunchback was enjoying himself. What was the hunchback's truth? His body, which life seemed to penetrate reluctantly, out of spite or vengeance? And Zeide who goes on with his ridiculous game? Are you looking for a scapegoat? He's dead. Leib was arrested and sacrificed for nothing. At this hour Leib must be going through the prison gate, helmeted guards on either side. They'll be taking the 7:32 train which today will be on time. Tomorrow he'll arrive at a transit camp. When will the next transport leave for Germany? Who knows? With a little luck Leib will have time to attempt an escape; with a little luck the war will be over before the camp is emptied; with a little luck death will lose its power. The front was advancing, the enemy is retreating and victory is near. Welcome, Leib! How did you manage to get back? It's all imagination. And so? Who says miracles have gone forever?

Zeide did not relent, but Gregor's thoughts were elsewhere,

trying to invent miracles with which to save his friend. He'll get away. Leib will never surrender. He's strong, stronger than war. One day he'll appear, and we'll ask him: Where have you been all this time? And he'll shrug his shoulders and say, I fought against war and crushed it. Leib can't die. Leib will resurrect himself. Does death surround and imprison us? Yes, but it's within man's power to make a breach in any wall. That's what will happen with Leib. We shall prevail.

But the hunchback was trying to destroy it all. There's a limit to everything. No one has a right not to believe in miracles just because it's a time of war or to make fun of those who believe in them, because their faith is in itself a miracle. Gregor wanted to throw himself on the hunchback and punish him. If he didn't do so, it was because he was overcome by a weird sensation: his body was becoming a stranger to him: his face was covered with wrinkles, his eyes were extinguished, his strength had ebbed away. He was struck by an absurd idea: the hunchback and I have become one. If one of us raises his arm, it is enough to commit the other, to judge and condemn him. Gregor shook himself. It was time to stop the game. If I don't intercede now, he thought, I'll lose all interest in winning.

"Enough!" he shouted, bringing his fist down on the table. "I've had enough. Enough of your suspicions."

Zeide started and, amid the general astonishment, the hunchback gave a cry of victory.

"I'm going to talk," said Gregor.

The twilight lay heavily on the trees and sank into the depths of the forest. The air thickened, and in the distance the sky changed color as the angels of darkness captured the light. Clara bit her lips; Haimi stared at Gregor with anguish. Zeide looked at him uncertainly, as if he did not know whether to encourage him to speak or to be silent. They were apprehensive of what he was going to tell them.

"You're suspicious of me," said Gregor, "And you're right. I'm suspicious of myself. You're wondering if it isn't my fault that Leib was arrested; so do I. I take all responsibility. But it wasn't an accident. It was a betrayal. It's too easy to blame chance. You want someone guilty: here I am."

He talked rapidly and dryly. The hunchback spat on the ground, Clara stiffened and Zeide scrutinized him curiously, his face showing scorn and pity.

Without pause Gregor began again, for the last time, to describe the dinner with Janos, but gave it now a grotesque interpretation. He and Janos were accomplices. Janos was an old friend of his father; he had come often to his family's house. He, Gregor, had betrayed Leib, and Janos, in return, had promised to obtain the release of his parents. What could be more simple and logical? A simple transaction. And as he proceeded with this lie Gregor discovered that there was some truth to it. Now that he had proclaimed himself guilty everything that had been enigmatic became clear.

Why had he chosen to denigrate himself before his comrades? Out of spite? In order to make fun of Zeide? To push Clara to the edge and test her strength? To turn the weapons of the hunchback against him? Whatever the reason, it gave Gregor a satisfaction he had never known before. As if he had said to Zeide and the hunchback and the other judges: You think you can dirty me; I can do it better than you. Look: I have ordered the *Yetzer Hara,* the spirit of evil, to come out of myself and be seen. All of its unspeakable desires, I make mine; I acknowledge in myself the most disgusting acts and ambitions, those which since creation have sought a sick conscience in which to live and flourish. By words at least, Gregor had pushed himself to the uttermost limits of evil from which, by expressing it, he hoped to be freed. Suddenly he understood why, on *Yom Kippur,* Jews beat their breasts and accused themselves of crimes they had never committed: exorcise evil. The scapegoat, driven into the wilderness, comes back with the face and nimbus of a superman.

"Yes, I betrayed Leib the Lion," said Gregor with mock remorse.

But his hearers did not realize that he was making fun of them, and of good and evil as well. Haimi struck his forehead and sobbed, "But why, why? Wasn't he your friend?"

Gregor was sorry. To lie to a child is like giving him poison. Tomorrow, he said to himself, I'll ask him to go for a walk and I'll talk to him.

"Exactly," said Zeide, disbelieving him. "Why should you have betrayed your friend? And the rest of us with him."

"I told you. Those were the terms of the bargain. I betrayed Leib to Janos, and Janos promised to give me back my parents."

"How did you know they were still alive?"

"I didn't. But I said to myself that if there was one chance in a thousand I ought to make use of it."

It was a weak argument. Gregor hastily invented another.

"To tell the truth, I never was fond of Leib. I envied him, his strength, his calm, his superiority. He was always the leader."

"So you really betrayed him?" Haimi shouted despairingly. "Really?"

Gregor turned away. To provoke anger was exactly what he had wanted, but he had not forseen Haimi's suffering. He turned to the hunchback, who stood behind Zeide, still sneering as if to say: I've imposed my will. There you are on your knees and soon you'll put away your pride and beg our forgiveness.

"I really betrayed him," said Gregor, laughing at last.

He was speaking for the future. Later on he would never deny the essential truth of what he was now saying. To live is to betray the dead. We hasten to bury and forget them because we are ashamed; we feel guilty towards them.

"Why are you laughing?" asked Zeide.

"Involuntarily," said the accused, but he was lying. He was laughing at his judges, at himself, at fate, for fate was laughing louder than he.

"Forgive me," he said. "My laughter was pointless. I'm tired. Too much for one day, don't you agree?" And he went on, "You want to know why I betrayed Leib? Simple. It was by mistake, unconsciously. Only afterwards did I take responsibility."

This explanation held. The wine, the drunken talk, the slip of the tongue. After all, his judges couldn't believe that the betrayal was premeditated. What mattered was to convince them that he had had their chief arrested. Meanwhile Zeide was unrelenting.

"Exactly when did it happen?" he insisted.

Gregor made a quick calculation. Leib had been arrested the previous afternoon, so the betrayal must have occurred before.

"When? The day before yesterday, during our first meal together."

There had been two meals with Janos. Clara had been at the first, but that was nobody's business. It was something between the two of them, and she would not deny it. But in order to avoid dangerous questions in this, Gregor took over control of the conversation.

"I was drinking, you understand. Too much, I admit it. Janos, too. We were testing each other. First I thought I was playing the game alone, but by the end of the meal I had proof to the contrary. Janos was playing too. All drunks are frustrated actors. And Janos was better than I at both drinking and acting. My head was reeling, his wasn't. He was taking in every word and storing it in his memory. Whereas I listened and talked and forgot. Once I used the wrong name immediately he pricked up his ears. 'You know two Jews? Who's the other? His name is Leib? Who is he, exactly? Where's he hiding? What's his connection with Gavriel?' And that's how he caught me. I shouldn't have been drinking. I didn't know that I couldn't hold my liquor."

Haimi, unable to control himself any longer, burst into sobs, and no one thought to comfort him. Zeide had a vague look in his eyes and stroked his beard reflectively. The hunchback scratched his ear. Only two black candles were lacking to make the scene of excommunication complete.

Gregor felt himself in full possession of his faculties; he had not imagined that he could be so strong. They believed me, he was thinking. In a minute it will be all over. Who will be the executioner? The hunchback. Ugly, cruel, and full of hate as he is, he's cut out for the part. He'll carry out the sentence without ever knowing that the victim was making fun of him and all the others. But then no one will know, except perhaps Clara, and she will remain silent until the end. No one would know that Gregor had called death down upon himself not as the work of another's blind will but as a crowning absurdity. He wanted to laugh again, to proclaim his joy and his glory. With a single word or gesture he could have torn down the barriers and reversed the whole situation. But he would not pronounce this word or make this gesture. He would not move, and no one would know that he was the master of his death.

It was then that Clara decided to intervene. The game had been carried too far. Standing near the door, as if she were pushing back the shadows of night with her frail shoulders, she raised her head. Although she did it inconspicuously the others noticed. All eyes traveled in her direction, and Gregor's followed. From her emanated an unsuspected power; with the least of her movements, she imposed silence.

"He's lying," she said softly. "It's all a joke. And you fell for it. You don't know yet that a man can laugh while he suffers."

These words, coming from the shadows, caused Gregor to shudder. Suddenly he became aware of how dark it had grown in the bunker.

"You stop at words," Clara went on, and there was a strange resonance in her voice. "You must learn to see through them, to hear that which is unspoken."

Gregor felt the ground giving way beneath him. In his dismay he wanted to rush toward Clara and shout in her face, Be quiet. I can take care of myself. I don't need you or your help. And he would have added: Our love was just a joke too, wasn't it? Yes, it was just a joke, but a bad one. But he was too moved and too surprised to open his mouth. Once more he beheld himself stepping back from the abyss. He was alone, but his solitude was not the same. He felt joy, but it was not the joy he had felt before. He knew that he would survive, alive, but conquered.

Briefly Clara set forth the facts and proved Gregor's innocence. There was a great explosion of shouts and gestures, a state of general excitement. The partisans crowded around Gregor and congratulated him. Even if the mission had been unsuccessful, no one could any longer doubt his courage and self-sacrifice. They shook his hand, clapped him on the back,

174

smiled, and begged his pardon. Haimi was bursting with happiness. He went over to Gregor and said, simply, "Thank you." Then he turned around and started to go away. When Gregor moved after him the hunchback seized his arm and forced him to look into his eyes.

"I knew that you were acting, that you weren't a traitor. Not for a single instant did I doubt your innocence."

His voice was grave and deep and moving. Yehuda was his name, and he was not at all ugly. Twenty years old, a former Yeshiva student, he was incapable of doubt or hate. For him, a Jew could never be on the side of the executioner: the one, he explained, stops time, while the other prolongs it to infinity. He did not hate the executioner, for to hate him would mean playing his game, accepting an exchange on his terms. But he didn't love him either; he observed him.

Gregor and Yehuda became friends.

Only Yehuda had guessed the nature of the love which Gregor had felt and repressed for Clara. Gregor was on sentry duty when Yehuda came to keep him company. It was nearly dark. Gregor was listening to the sounds of the forest which mingled with those of his childhood.

"Am I bothering you?" asked Yehuda.

"Yes," replied Gregor with a start.

"Shall I go away?"

"Yes. You don't mind, do you?"

"Not at all. Only I'm going to stay." Then, after a pause, "You really don't mind, do you?"

"I mind terribly," said Gregor, breaking into a smile.

"Good!" said Yehuda.

Yehuda was eaten by anxiety. He walked lightly; he walked through life the same. On tiptoes.

"According to the Talmud," he said, "A *Talmid Hacham,* a wise-man should never go out alone at night. Now, thanks to you, I understand why. It's so he should never forget the way back."

"I'm not exactly what you'd call a *Talmid Hacham,*" said Gregor.

"But you like to go out at night alone."

Yehuda spoke more slowly than usual. He would shortly die and he knew it.

"I like to walk at night—no, with the night," said Gregor. "Don't worry; I always come back."

"Good. But every time you bring back a fragment of the night with you. That's what makes you a wise man."

"And what about you, Yehuda?"

"I'm beyond the point of return."

"What do you mean?" asked Gregor with a start. "Tell me!"

"I'd rather talk about you," said Yehuda, changing the subject.

"I'm listening."

"It's not a matter of your past or mine. It's a matter of your future." He paused and then went on in a soft voice: "It's about Clara. I'd like to talk to you about her."

Gregor stiffened.

"Are you sure I'm ready to listen?"

"No. Are you?"

"You know that I'm not. It's to Clara that you should speak about Clara. Not to me."

"I'm going to, anyway."

Something about Yehuda, perhaps his serenity, made Gregor shudder. They were in the midst of a war but Yehuda considered himself already beyond the war. He looked hard, as if studying, at the hospitable landscape of the sky.

"You love Clara," he stated simply.

Gregor did not answer, but his grip tightened on the stock of the rifle which pointed toward the enemy valley below. There, people were being murdered and here Yehuda speaks of love.

"You don't dare admit it to yourself," he said in the same calm voice, "but it's true. If you see love as a compromise, a defeat, you're mistaken. It's a victory. Above all in time of war, when men are filled with death. This is the time to love. This is the time to choose. An act of love may tip the balance."

"Be quiet, Yehuda, I beg of you. You're hurting me."

Yehuda gave him a look which shone with a strange warm light.

"I'll tell you a secret," he said. "I'm going to die. Soon. I know it. I feel it. My premonitions never deceive me; neither do my dreams. For three nights now I've had the same dream: a woman in black takes me by the hand and leads me to the edge of a flaming sea. 'Enter it' she says, 'the fire will let you pass.' I turn and ask her, 'Who are you?' 'Your wife,' she answers. 'Why are you dressed in black?' I ask. 'I mourn.' 'Who is dead?' 'My husband. I mourn because I'm a widow.' Then she starts to walk through the flames, without looking back because she knows I'm behind her. And so I am, following in her footsteps. If she weren't, I would never enter; but she does and so do I. When I awake my body is burning."

Gregor was about to say that dreams are related to the past rather than to the future, but Yehuda gestured to stop him.

"Don't speak. There's nothing you can do. I told you my dream so that you'd understand why I've talked to you about something that's none of my business. Apparently they don't concern me, but actually they are my business, as my dreams and premonitions are yours. Zeide says that we're alone, but we are capable of communicating to one another both our loneliness and our desire to break through it. You say, 'I'm alone.' Someone answers, 'I'm alone too.' There's a shift in the scale of power. A bridge is thrown between the two abysses."

He breathed deeply to free himself of a pain which almost prevented him from speaking. Grasping the rifle with a strength approaching violence, although nothing stirred in the valley and no suspicious sound broke the silence of the night, he longed to shoot, to shoot the woman in mourning, to slay the widow, to kill death.

"You love Clara," Yehuda continued, "and I am going to die. There's no apparent connection. Apparent, I say, because there *is* a connection between your love and my death, between your refusal of love and my acceptance of death. The proof is that I'm here and talking to you about it."

"Be quiet, Yehuda!" shouted Gregor. "Be quiet, I beg of you."

How had Yehuda guessed? Ever since the trial Gregor had

sought to avoid Clara. He had tried never to see her except in the company of Haimi or Yehuda. Once, when he was on sentry duty, she had brought him his meal of bread and cheese and he had refused it.

"Don't you want something to eat?"

"I'm not hungry now. Perhaps later."

Clara looked at him tenderly. "You're so young, and you like to suffer."

Gregor remained silent. It was always dangerous to talk. A man says yes, a man says no, and finally he ends up saying almost anything to fill up the silence and stop the beating of his heart.

"You're so young," Clara repeated, "and you like games. Who's your adversary?"

She stepped closer. He felt her breath and saw her breasts rise and fall under the man's shirt she was wearing.

"Go away," he said, between clenched teeth.

She started to reach out to touch his arm, then changed her mind and said wearily, "Do you really want me to go away?"

"Yes."

She gave a half smile.

"As you like," she said, and disappeared.

For some time Gregor remained motionless, hardly breathing. He got away with it. But how had Yehuda guessed all this?

"You love Clara. From this point in my life I can see everything. I have a right to say what I please. You mustn't be ashamed of your love; you should be proud of it. In an inhuman world like this one love is the great reward and the greatest of victories." Yehuda had spoken as if leaving him a testament.

"No more, Yehuda. What you have said is enough."

"No. Listen to the end. It's inhuman to wall yourself up in pain and memories as if in a prison. Suffering must open us to others. It must not cause us to reject them. The Talmud tells us that God suffers with man. Why? In order to strengthen the bonds between creation and the creator; God chooses to suffer in order to better understand man and be better understood by him. But you, you insist upon suffering alone. Such suffering shrinks you, diminishes you. Friend, that is almost cruel."

The night rolled on slowly and peacefully, an unrippled river, far from the storm. Yehuda was silent. The obsessive murmur of a breeze blew up from the valley. Gregor's fingers were cramped from holding the rifle. How could he stop Yehuda from following the widow into mourning? Once more he knew that he would be alone.

"Yehuda," he said.

"Yes?"

"You're right. I love Clara."

And Yehuda threw back his head as if with his eyes he wished to tear stars from the sky.

4

The peasant who stabbed Yehuda to death did not long survive him. Haimi, who was on watch outside, had heard it all.
Yehuda's insistent voice, the obsequiousness with which
the peasant bowed before his armed presence. "You want food
for the partisans? With pleasure, my boy. I can give you bread,
cheese, smoked meat, milk. Fresh bread, fatty cheese, and the
best meat between the Tissa and the Danube."

"Good, but quick."

The peasant obeyed, but never stopped talking. "Are you
hungry? Don't you want to have a bite before you leave?"

"No, I'm in a hurry, I tell you."

"I know, I know. I'm on your side. I admire your courage.
You're the real heroes of the war."

"Come on, hurry!"

"Are you tired? You're pale. Why don't you sit down? No?
You don't trust me? I'm only trying to help you. You must
come to see me again." He moved about, shifting objects and
utensils, noisily opening and shutting drawers. "You've come
to wake the right man. The others, my neighbors, they're all
fascists and informers, and the police are nearby. They'd have
tipped them off, for sure. With me you have nothing to fear.
I'm a friend of the partisans. I am . . ."

Then, with an unexpected movement, he seized the kitchen knife, hidden beneath a loaf of bread, and lunged at Yehuda. Haimi heard the thud of a falling body and a stifled groan. The peasant pulled himself up, panting, and went on talking: ". . . a friend of the partisans, yes . . . I'll teach you how to steal honest people's bread and meat."

Behind Haimi, the partisans walked with haste toward the scene of the murder. Half of their group had volunteered for the expedition of revenge. The village was asleep. Not a window was opened as they went by.

Zeide sent a scout ahead to make sure that all was quiet on the farm. No doubt the peasant realized that they would try to take revenge and had warned the police that they might be coming. Nevertheless the scout reported that all was calm. A trap? Possible, but unlikely. Probably the peasant hadn't imagined they would come so soon.

In a low voice Zeide outlined the plan of operation. He gave each one his assignment. Hersh and Avron, with a log that lay in the courtyard, were to break through the door. Yossel and Shmiel were to cover the windows. Tibi, Motel, Nussen, and Itzu were to form a security cordon around the farm, and watch for the police. Clara was to serve as runner, while Haimi, Zeide, and Gregor took care of the murderer.

"Clear?"

They all nodded.

"No questions?"

No questions.

"Don't shoot except in an emergency. If the police come, we disperse; we'll meet again at the bunker."

The plan was executed to the last detail and without error. In a flash the wooden door was shattered. The peasant had no time even to jump from bed and pick up Yehuda's revolver which lay nearby. Already he was caught in the beam of Zeide's flashlight.

"Who are you?" he called out dully.

He must have drunk heavily before going to bed. The smell of alcohol was about him.

"Get up," ordered Zeide.

The peasant obeyed. Haimi lit the kerosene lamp hanging from the ceiling.

"What do you want?" the man stammered, blinking his eyes. He was a well-fed, stout man, and his inoffensive naked torso exuded boredom rather than fear. This was the second night that he had been awakened from a sound sleep, but the idea of death had never crossed his mind.

"I know what you want," he said, grimacing. "You want food. Well, you've come to the right place. I have everything you need: bread, cheese, and smoked meat."

He still hadn't understood. Perhaps he was thinking that this time they were three to one and he'd have to hand the food over. It would cost him twenty pounds of cheese and all the fresh bread he had in the house. What bad luck! Shrugging his shoulders he started toward the cupboard. Let them take what they wanted and leave him to sleep in peace. But he stopped short when he saw the look in Zeide's eyes. He was beginning to understand. He broke: on his face there appeared an expression of malevolent stupidity and his body drooped. Gregor looked in vain for the mark of murder upon him, and was tempted to ask him how he had spent the day. Perhaps, since he was a respectable citizen, he had walked through the village and stroked the head of a child.

"I have bread," the peasant repeated, "fresh bread and fatty cheese. There is even some *tzuika*, and I'll throw that in as a gift. I have wine, too, and smoked meat, the best between the Tissa and the Danube."

He spoke mechanically and without conviction, aware that the partisans had not come for supplies.

"Is that all right?" he asked, raising his voice.

He was visibly paling. His body was becoming numb and heavy and his legs could no longer support it.

"What do you want?" he asked in a choked whisper.

"The body," said Zeide.

"What body? I don't understand. What are you talking about? I know nothing. You're wrong in suspecting me. Search the place, and you'll see. There's no body here. Look around if you don't believe me."

It was a useless game and he knew it. He was trying now to gain time, without being at all sure what good it would do him. Why had he put off going to the police until the next day? Now, when it was too late, he understood his mistake. Suddenly a voice tore the silence. A woman's voice came from the direction of the furnace. The voice said simply and with hate, "He's lying!"

"Shut up, you bitch!" he shouted, rage flaming in his eyes. "Keep out of it, or I'll fix you!" And he added turning to Zeide: "Don't listen to her! She's crazy. She doesn't know what she's saying."

Zeide called the woman over.

"Who are you?" he asked.

She was a miserable, ageless little creature, clad in a dirty nightgown that came down to the floor. Her black hair fell over her shoulders, her face was creased with wrinkles; she had a strident voice and a somber, pitiless glow in her eyes.

"I'm his wife," she said.

"She's crazy, I tell you," said the peasant, brandishing his fist. "I hate her. All she wants is for me to die. You bitch, you bitch."

"I'm his wife," she repeated imperturbably. "I saw the whole thing. He's lying."

"If you go on, I'll break your neck. I swear it, by the Virgin. I'll kill you."

She stared at him without emotion and her voice cracked like a whip. "I'm not afraid of you any longer. You'd kill me one day, I know that. You're just a killer, anyhow, and a liar, too. If you had your way, you'd kill the entire world just to show that you're strong and unafraid. More than once you'd have killed me, and your other women as well. . . . You, too," she added, turning to the silent partisans. "If he weren't scared, he'd kill you in cold blood with the knife there on the kitchen table. That's the truth, I tell you."

She spoke in a detached manner, without passion or calculation. Gregor was troubled. Once upon a time, he said to himself, she had loved this man.

"You're looking for your comrade," she said. "I know where he's buried."

The peasant groaned, as if he were an animal being led to the slaughter. She stared at him without fear; this was the finest moment of her life.

It was growing late. The partisans had to return before dawn. Zeide began to hurry.

"Show us the place," he said to the woman.

With a glance at her husband she went out, and Gregor followed. After no more than a minute she came to a halt near an apple tree and pointed down a slope.

"There," she said.

Gregor looked around. To the right there was a field of corn, to the left a farm; behind them a winding road that led to the village. There was no moon in the sky above, and yet a diffuse light came through the clouds. The next day it would rain.

"It's going to rain tomorrow," said Gregor. And he added, in Yiddish, "Do you like the rain?"

The old woman, with her hands in the broad sleeves of her dress, was silently weeping. She knew that she would weep for many years to come.

"I'm ashamed," she said, looking at the ground; "I'm ashamed to have lived with him so long."

"Did our comrade say anything before he died?" asked Gregor.

"Nothing."

She seemed to be expecting other questions, but Gregor had no more to ask.

"Your friend . . ." she said with a sigh. "He died with a smile. And his smile has remained alive. I helped my husband dig the grave. I was there until the very end, and your comrade was still smiling. I wept, but he smiled; he smiled even at my husband. Once I began to shout: 'Don't smile at him; he deserves your curse!' But your comrade didn't listen. And so I prayed for his soul. And his smile."

Gregor closed his eyes and felt the sky on his eyelids. He prayed: Yehuda! Intercede for us. Send us back the light! There was a long pause. Suddenly the old woman gave a piercing shriek. Someone had fired a gun nearby. She began to run and Gregor followed her.

"We must go," said Zeide, from the door.

The old woman was down on her knees, lamenting over the body.

"Forgive me, forgive me, forgive me," she moaned and her face was twisted with pain. "I beg your forgiveness. It's all my fault. It's all my fault."

Gregor wanted to touch her shoulder, to whisper a word of comfort. But she got up and stared dumbly at him, with a look of madness on her face. Then she burst out, "Go away, you murderers! You've killed my man, the man who loved me. Nobody will ever love me again."

Gregor would never have moved if Zeide hadn't pushed him out. Before leaving, the partisans gathered around the grave of Yehuda. Haimi said the Kaddish. From the farm they could still hear the old woman's lament. On the way back Gregor walked at Clara's side. All of a sudden, without touching her, without even looking at her, he told her that he loved her.

winter

1

The celebration was at its height. It seemed as if it would never come to an end. The *hasidim* were dancing, vertically, as if not moving from their place, but forcing the rhythm down into the earth. What did it matter if the walls gave way except to show that no enclosure was large enough to contain their fervor? They sang; and the song gave them life and caused the sap to well up in them and bind them together. Ten times, fifty times, they repeated the same phrase, taken from the Psalms or some other portion of Scripture, and every time the fire would be renewed again with primordial passion: yes, once God and man were one, then their unity was broken; ever since they have sought each other, pursued each other, and before each other have proclaimed themselves invincible. As long as the song and dance go on, they are.

The *hasidim* sang. The song burst their chests and lit a thousand flames in their eyes. "If I could sing," said the famous Rebbe Pinchas of Koritz," I'd force God to leave his throne and to come down among us to be at our side." The hall was stifling as if God filled it; he was the interval that separated the words and then brought them together into prayer or melody; he was the *hasid* listening with closed eyes or his companion who was clapping his hands as if to applaud a victory. He was there, let that suffice; he is there and that surely sufficed. Let the Angel of Death arrive if he chose and he would be disposed of forever. But he did not dare to come; he hid himself, awaiting his hour, for the angel of death is patient and knows that his hour will come.

At the far end of the room, facing the door, the Rebbe surrounded by his court, presided over the table of honor. A royal person of the line of David the Conqueror, he joined past glory with future promise. All those present feared and admired him and pledged him fidelity without limit, limning the forces which converged in his person and which he alone could put to use. With a single look he could destroy buildings and raise them up again. With a word he could deny the power of fate and substitute his own for it. *Hatzadik gozer vehakadosh baruch hu mekayem,* says the Talmud. The righteous decree and the Holy One, blessed be He, obeys. If the Rebbe had willed it, he could alter the course of history. But the Rebbe sat silent. His disciples sang louder and louder as if to provoke him to action, but he remained unprovoked. The hand of the Lord must not be forced; let him act when he will, choosing the hour and the instrument. We offer him only his freedom. If he exacts of his people a million children, it is because, in truth, he requires them to exalt his name (may it be blessed) and his power, for he is all of life as he is all of death. If he needs rivers of blood, let him be pitied for it is only that he lacks imagination. For man the infinite is God; for God the infinite is man.

"Open yourself and sing," said the *hasid,* nudging Gregor with his elbow.

Gregor did not answer. He had not come to sing but to say goodbye. The next day he would not be there. He was going away, anywhere, leaving the city and the country, his name, his home, and his job. "Will you be back?"

"No."

"Why are you silent? Sing. Come, sing with the rest of us! Don't hang back. The solitary are Satan's favorites."

Gregor could not take his eyes off the Rebbe. The Rebbe's person gave off a pure, almost feminine melancholy, coupled with an irresistible power which first troubled men's souls and then, with a single word or gesture, calmed them. With him combat could only be solitary. Burdens he set upon himself, while ease and comfort he desired and obtained for others. He seemed to pursue his soul to mountain tops which he insisted be high and inaccessible. The *hasidim* followed him with radiant confidence. For in his footsteps they were sure of reaching a serenity stripped of pride, where cause and effect would be joined not in death but in eternity, where the sum of defects would be transformed into plenitude. Let him walk first; liberation was at hand! And so they danced with joy, their heads almost touching the vaults of the universe.

"You aren't singing," said the *hasid*. "Why did you come?"

Gregor was about to answer: I'm going away; I came to say goodbye. But he changed his mind and said, "I'm looking for someone."

"For whom?"

"A Rebbe."

"There he is!"

"That's not the one."

Before the *hasid's* perplexity he felt he must explain: "As a child I hoped to become a Rebbe myself and to work miracles. But God was afraid and did everything to interfere. He set Europe on fire; everything was changed. But I know that somewhere in time, or else in the dreams of my dead mother, this Rebbe exists and is waiting for me."

"Why here?"

"Here and everywhere."

The *hasid's* face darkened, and he leaned toward Gregor.

"Have you been drinking?"

"No."

"You should drink. Sometimes drink is better than prayer."

"No. I'm going away. Tomorrow."

The *hasid* stared at him for a second and then said, "Very good, my friend. Follow the Rebbe. He knows all the paths and where they lead. Thanks to him, you'll find what you're seeking."

Near Gregor a man raised up his child and whispered into his ear, "Look, my child, look at him hard. Remember his face for the future." And so the child's eyes absorbed the fire that one day would consume him.

Gregor stared at the Rebbe and listened to the *hasidim's* singing. He murmured to himself: "Don't think of yesterday, or of tomorrow. Don't think at all." But he was powerless against his imagination. Where was he going? He did not know. He knew only that he must leave. Money, papers, his pen, these were what he had. The first plane or bus or train. Montreal, San Francisco, Paris. It didn't matter. And what about her? She would wait, then stop waiting. She would suffer, then stop suffering. The only solution: to go away.

He tried to remember the exact moment at which he had made the decision. While he was staring at the Rebbe? While listening to the explosion of the *hasidim's* joy? No, earlier. While walking through the deserted, snowy streets? He didn't know. In the dining room of his apartment, when he had told his wife he was going to Brooklyn, to Williamsburg for a hasidic celebration. He had not yet realized that he was setting out upon a journey without return. "Will you be back?" "Of course I'll be back." She looked at him heavily, as if through a haze. She was sitting at the table with her hands spread out before her, already prepared for his absence, already waiting. "Of course," she said several times. He realized that she had known even before he had. And she had let him go.

The *hasid* shook him.

"Your thoughts are far away," he said. "Return. Stay with us and open yourself!"

Gregor wanted to smile, but he couldn't. His face remained stubbornly closed. He mustn't think of her. Later, yes, but not now. Did she love him? One day she wouldn't love him any more. Like himself. He had loved her once, but now he didn't love her. Sometimes he even thought his love would change into hate. That he feared. He must go away first, go somewhere where silence was not an admission of guilt.

"You look worried," said the *hasid*. "What's wrong?"

For an instant Gregor felt him as a friend. I could talk to this man, I could tell him. I've always wanted to attain simplicity, but I've followed complicated ways. Now it's too late to go back; the harm is done. A woman is waiting for me and I've abandoned her."

"Well, friend, is there something bothering you? Speak, and it will be lifted."

Gregor thought, If I can manage to smile, then I'll speak. But his lips were sealed. Disappointedly the *hasid* turned away and joined again in the song.

The Rebbe sat as if there were heavy weights on his shoulders. Raising then lowering his bushy eyebrows he regulated the volume of the singing. At intervals he pounded the table with his fist. Ferocious and irresistible, he demanded greater enthusiasm and abandon. Don't caress your soul as if it were a body, feeding on kisses. Beat it without humiliating it; whip it without diminishing it; drive it out of your self in order that it may rejoin its source and become one with it in the *Heichal Hanegina,* the sanctuary of melody—it's there I await you in a secret promise. Delirious, the crowd obeyed, dancing with a vigor that might have seemed desperate. We are alone, yes, but inside this solitude we are brothers, helping one another to go forward without stumbling. Shortly the solitary self will vanish; so forcefully will we invoke God that the shell of time will be shattered, its laws abolished, and God himself will cease to exist as a stranger.

Outside it was still snowing. The pitiless winter had made the city into a ghost. The few passers-by hurried along with lowered heads, fleeing before an enemy who had cut off escape. But in this room no one was thinking of the snow.

Just then the door opened and a man, wrapped up to the ears, came into the room. He took off his fur-collared coat, threw it into a corner and was soon lost in the rejoicing crowd.

Gregor touched his neighbor's arm and asked him the meaning of the celebration. The anniversary of the death of the *Zaddik,* the righteous man, was the answer. Every year they met to celebrate and pass on the story of his miracles and wonders; they besought him to return to earth, to rejoin the living, to drink with them and enrich their memory and hope. To weep for his loss would give the Angel of Death too much satisfaction, a *Zaddik* is never really lost; even from above, he protects those who have faith in him.

The *hasid* spoke with as much fervor as if he had known the holy man in person, although he had been dead a hundred and fifty years. With a lump in his throat Gregor remembered the Saturday evenings of his childhood, when surrounded by old people and children, Kalman softly had extolled the powers of his own teachers. To tell a hasidic story, he used to say, was as worthy as learning a page of the Talmud.

When he first met the Rebbe, Gregor had said, "Has nothing changed?"

"Nothing."

"What about me?"

"You haven't changed either."

"And Auschwitz? What do you make of Auschwitz?"

"Auschwitz proves that nothing has changed, that the primeval war goes on. Man is capable of love and hate, murder and sacrifice. He is Abraham and Isaac together. God himself hasn't changed.

Gregor was angry. "After what happened to us, how can you believe in God?"

With an understanding smile on his lips the Rebbe answered, "How can you *not* believe in God after what has happened?"

They argued passionately; Gregor believed he had won. But now he was ashamed of his victory, as if it were an offense, not to the Rebbe, but to this assembly to which he meant everything.

Mendel was the one who had told him to go and see the Rebbe.

"What for?" Gregor asked him.

"For no particular reason. Just to see him and have him see you."

And Gregor had let himself be persuaded. Mendel was his friend; they shared an office at the Jewish newspaper where they both worked. He was a taciturn man, walled up in a sorrow which he tried to hide if not to subdue. Everyone knew that his only son was afflicted with an incurable disease and fighting a slow death. Mendel never spoke of him, and his colleagues at the newspaper respected his silence, pretending that they didn't know. At the same hour every afternoon he picked up the telephone and called his wife, who never left the child's hospital bedside. In an infinitely gentle voice he asked a few harmless questions: Did he eat? Is he asleep? What do the doctors say? Then he resumed his work. One day Gregor saw him start to make the usual gesture of picking up the telephone receiver, then, after a minute, put it down without dialing a number. There was not a flicker of expression on his face except for an almost imperceptible tremor of his pale lips. Thus it was that Gregor learned the news. It was at this time that he tried to make friends with Mendel who, like himself, was at first confident of being able to endure it alone.

"No one can fight the night by himself and conquer it, Mendel. Victory would be meaningless even if he won. For two persons together victory is possible."

"I have no wish to conquer the night."

For some men night is the beast which man liberates by closing his eyes. To keep the beast shut up they refuse to sleep. To Mendel night was the soul of the earth and the song of his soul. In order that the song be heard the noise of the world had to cease.

"I stay away from friendship. It's too noisy," he said.

But eventually he gave way. They lived on the same street and soon they fell into the habit of going home together. On the way Gregor talked of himself and of his childhood; he called up the memory of the hasidic world, generous and full of love, that he had known. Mendel listened and let himself succumb. He, too, had wanted to go far, to outdo himself without injuring those whom he loved; he, too, was in need of fervor, a source of enthusiasm. Soon after this he began to frequent the *hasidim* of Brooklyn and came to know them better than Gregor, who had, as a matter of fact, avoided them. He was received in private audience by the Rebbe and came away a new man. "Go see him," he said to Gregor.

The conversation between Gregor and the Rebbe opened in an atmosphere of hostility. Gregor saw in the Rebbe a stronghold inviting comfort and repose, while the Rebbe saw in him a deserter. The Rebbe preached gratitude, while Gregor preached anger.

Gregor: "Man's fall is an accusation against the Creator, who bears his share of responsibility for the betrayal."

Rebbe: "All the more reason to choose faith and devotion. Be pure, and God will be purified in you."

Gregor: "Why? I owe God nothing. Quite the contrary."

Rebbe: "That's not the question. He owes you nothing, either. You don't live his life and he doesn't live yours. You owe yourself something. What exactly, that's the question."

Their attitudes seemed irreconcilable. Suddenly the Rebbe fell silent, thrust his head forward and spoke more harshly.

"What do you expect of me?" he asked.

"Nothing," said Gregor, "absolutely nothing. And nothing from God either."

The Rebbe was motionless and continued to stare at him without saying a word.

"Yes," said Gregor. "I expect you to leave your chair and sit down on the floor, your forehead covered with ashes. To you everything seems simple and this simplicity hurts me. To you every word transmits a spark of eternal truth, every gesture corresponds to a well-defined inner conviction, and the total of these words, these gestures you attach to God, depositary of all conviction and of all truth. What I expect of you is that you raise your arms to heaven and cry out, "No, I'll have no more! I won't accept it! That's what I'm expecting."

The Rebbe received the force of his attack without flinching. His darkened eyes pierced Gregor so sharply that he felt a pain in his hands, his legs, his head.

"And what do you expect of yourself?" the Rabbi asked him.

"Very little. Almost nothing. I have only one purpose: not to cause others to suffer. My dream is a modest one, my ideal is limited and commonplace. I'm no longer intent upon measuring myself against fate and saving humanity. I'm content with little; to help a single human being is enough for me."

"Do you call that so little? Doesn't helping a human being mean rescuing him from despair? Doesn't it mean subordinating destiny to your idea of man?"

He smiled, and Gregor felt more distraught than ever. He would have preferred to see the Rebbe angry.

"Most of the people who come to see me want me to obtain riches, happiness, or good health for them," said the Rebbe after a long silence.

"I ask nothing of the kind."

"I know, I know. Your voice tells me that you are proud, and also that you have suffered. The trouble is that suffering has made you proud rather than humble."

He enveloped Gregor in his kindly smile and provoked his resentment. The Rebbe was eluding him; he would have preferred to be insulted.

"I'll tell you a story," said Gregor, trembling. "It's short and simple. In a concentration camp, one evening after work, a rabbi called together three of his colleagues and convoked a special court. Standing with his head held high before them, he spoke as follows: 'I intend to convict God of murder, for he is destroying his people and the Law he gave them from Mount Sinai. I have irrefutable proof in my hands. Judge without fear or sorrow or prejudice. Whatever you have to lose has long since been taken away.' The trial proceeded in due legal form, with witnesses for both sides with pleas and deliberations. The unanimous verdict: 'Guilty.' "

Involuntarily, the hands of the Rebbe wound and unwound nervously. His face, suffering, lost its delicate transparency and became bare and brutal. He was no longer smiling.

"Wait," said Gregor. "I haven't finished."

"I know. I know."

"Wait for the end. After all, *He* had the last word. On the day after the trial, He turned the sentence against his judges and accusers. They, too, were taken off to the slaughter. And I tell you this: if their death has no meaning, then it's an insult, and if it does have a meaning, it's even more so."

The Rebbe aged before him: years piled upon his shoulders. He was a hundred, a thousand years old; an invisible hand traced a death mask on his face, in which the colors and sorrows of the rainbow mingled and faded out together. He breathed heavily through clenched teeth, without speaking. He lowered his eyelids and when he raised them again there was such sorrow in his dry eyes that Gregor trembled and wanted to throw himself on the floor and ask his forgiveness. Then he heard the Rebbe say almost inaudibly:

"What do you expect of me? Confirmation of your victory? But what victory? Confession of my defeat? But what defeat? For those who battle at the highest, these words have no meaning, for there is no victor. So what can I give you? . . . Don't answer," he continued, at the sight of Gregor's dismay. "I can read your thoughts; they're as open as a bleeding wound. Do you want me to stop praying and start shouting? Is that what you're after?"

"Yes," whispered Gregor.

Then the mask of death shattered. The Rebbe made a gesture of revolt; he threw back his head and spoke in a grave, hoarse voice, weighing every word and pausing after every sentence.

"Who says that power comes from a shout, an outcry rather than from a prayer? From anger rather than compassion? Where do you find certainties when you claim to have denied them? The man who goes singing to death is the brother of the man who goes to death fighting. A song on the lips is worth a dagger in the hand. I take this song and make it mine. Do you know what the song hides? A dagger, an outcry. Appearances have a depth of their own which has nothing to do with the depth. When you come to our celebrations you'll see how we dance and sing and rejoice. There is joy as well as fury in the *hasid's* dancing. It's his way of proclaiming. 'You don't want me to dance; too bad, I'll dance anyhow. You've taken away every reason for singing, but I shall sing. I shall sing of the deceit that walks by day and the truth that walks by night, yes, and of the silence of dusk as well. You didn't expect my joy, but here it is; yes, my joy will rise up; it will submerge you.' "

He stopped short in exhaustion, and Gregor felt a sudden outpouring of pity and love. How difficult a thing is happiness! I shouldn't have come, he thought. I have no right to try to destroy this man, to force him to lower his head and say: Oh God, you have set yourself on the side of the torturer, you are guilty; you are the ruler of the universe, but you are guilty. Now Gregor no longer wanted to hear these words, to win the argument. Victory was no longer possible, because it had ceased to be desirable. The Rebbe must have guessed at his thoughts, for his face hardened. He clenched his fist and there was a strangely cold light in his eyes.

"So be it!" he shouted. "He's guilty; do you think I don't know it? That I have no eyes to see, no ears to hear? That my heart doesn't revolt? That I have no desire to beat my head against the wall and shout like a madman, to give rein to my sorrow and disappointment? Yes, he is guilty. He has become the ally of evil, of death, of murder, but the problem is still not solved. I ask you a question and dare you answer: "What is there left for us to do?"

Gregor could not escape from the spell of the Rebbe's eyes and voice. His heart pounded, his shoulders crumbled; he wanted to kneel down or to run away, to push thought from the room. But the Rebbe held him captive, as he went on:

"We can't stop there, that would be too easy, too cowardly. If you say A, you have to say B. And if you have followed the wrong path you must turn back and try another, knock at another door. In what direction are we to go? Where is salvation, or at least hope, to be found?"

Heavy with shame and remorse, Gregor lowered his head, bowed over.

"Straighten up," said the Rabbi

Gregor obeyed with difficulty. It was plain that his questioner judged him severely. Gregor was about to ask him to impose a penance upon him when the Rebbe's face softened. The hint of the Rebbe's frail, supremely gentle smile caused his eyes to cloud over. If only I could cry! he reflected.

Over the years, for no apparent reason, tears had collected in his chest; all day he was aware of them. They weighed on his heart. Sometimes he stopped in the middle of the street and breathed deeply in order not to break into unreasonable sobbing. Under the cold spring sun he looked at the passers-by: he felt a lump in his throat. A woman talking to her child, a widow to her dog, an old man to himself. He would wring his hands and say: Not here, not now. Some other time, in a moment of silence or happiness the tears will come, and I will cry for a whole day, a week, a year.

"Rabbi," he said, "you asked me what I expected of you, and I said I expected nothing. I was mistaken. Make me able to cry."

In a flash he felt that he was once more a child. In the house alone. His parents were working late, as always before holidays and Maria had gone to market. Someone knocked at the door, a stranger with a stick in his hand and a bag slung over his shoulder. Despite his appearance he was not a beggar. Without holding out his hand he said, "Give me something." "What do you want? Bread? Water?" "No, little one, I have bread in my bag and I like to be thirsty." "Money, then?" I have no use for money." "Then what can I give you?" "How should I know? I don't know what you have to give." The child began to cry and said, "I can give you my tears, that's all." The stranger laid his arm reassuringly on the boy's shoulder and said, "I accept, but remember, giving isn't so simple." Then, slowly and majestically he turned on his heels and went his way.

"Make me able to cry," Gregor repeated.

The Rebbe shook his head.

"That's not enough. I shall teach you to sing."

"Grown people don't cry; beggars don't cry." The Rebbe added, "Crying is for children. Are you still a child, and is your life a child's dream? No, crying's no use. You must sing."

"And you, Rebbe? What do you expect of me?"

"Everything."

And when Gregor started to protest, the Rebbe added, "Jacob wrestled with the angel all night and overcame him. But the angel implored him: Let me go, dawn is approaching. Jacob let him go; to show his gratitude the angel brought him a ladder. Bring me this ladder."

"Which one of us is Jacob?" asked Gregor. "And which the angel?"

"I don't know," said the Rebbe with a friendly wink. "Do you?"

Gregor got up and the Rebbe took him to the door.

"Promise to come back," he said, holding out his hand.

"I'll come back."

"Will you come to our celebrations?"

"Yes."

Clara was haggard with waiting when he got home. "You look upset," she said. "Where did you spend the night?"

"I walked, Clara."

Joy continued to roll in great waves over the hall; the *hasidim* shouted out their happiness, climbed invisible ladders, discarded them when they ceased to be of use. Gregor saw Mendel staring vacantly into space not far behind the Rebbe. His heart rejoiced: Mendel, my friend! He repeated the name several times, but Mendel did not hear him. Gregor was alone once more, alone among a crowd of strangers who were clenching their fists in ecstasy.

Suddenly the song was interrupted. The Rebbe raised his head, and a warm, generous light broke from his dark eyes. Silence hung over the assembly, as the Rebbe prepared to speak. Instinctively everyone leaned forward and held his breath.

In a slightly hoarse voice, but grave and melodious, the Rebbe began to talk about suffering. A man who is put to the trial, he said must give triple thanks to the Almighty: first for giving him strength to endure the trial, second for bringing the trial to an end, third for the trial itself. For suffering contains the secret of creation and its dimension of eternity; it can be pierced only from the inside. Suffering betters some people and transfigures others. At the end of suffering, of mystery, God awaits us. And at the beginning? It depends on man whether or not God is present at the beginning as well.

The *hasidim* followed the imperceptible movement of the Rebbe's lips. They were not content to hear the words; they had to see them. A word misunderstood or misinterpreted would throw the scales off balance. Gregor felt that the Rebbe was speaking to him alone, and his face flushed. Each one of the *hasidim* must have had the same impression, for all the faces around him were crimson. The Rebbe talked rapidly, his Yiddish and Hebrew filled with obscure and inaccessible allusions; he quoted the *Midrash* and the *Zohar,* told stories both marvelous and disturbing in their apparent simplicity, without bothering to furnish a key to their real meaning. His audience listened with a fervid passion. What did it matter if they understood, if they pursued the master's thought to its ultimate significance: they were purified by his voice, by his secret. It had to suffice; it sufficed.

After midnight something unexpected occurred. The Rebbe stopped in the middle of a sentence, left it suspended in the air, and began to tremble; his face drained, his look emptied, but his eyes seemed to fasten beyond sight. Petrified, no one moved, for fear of shattering the silence. What was happening? The earth seemed to stop turning; blood froze. A return to the moment before creation, when God and man were inseparable and all was possible. Where had the Rebbe gone? To do battle? On what heights? A shudder ran through the room when he brought his heavy fist down on the table.

"Who can sing in Hungarian?"

Speechless with fright the assembly made no reply. How could they? Did he really expect an answer at all?

"I want to hear a Hungarian song," the Rebbe shouted.

They drew their heads back between their shoulders as if to protect themselves from a threat unknown. The Rebbe was angry. Who knows what he saw, what dangers he strove to repel?

"I order one of you to sing me a Hungarian song," he cried furiously. "Is there no one here who will do as I ask?"

From behind him came a timid, quavering voice, that of a bent, shrunken old man.

"I'll sing for the Rebbe."

"Then sing!"

"Yes, but . . ."

"But what?" asked the Rebbe impatiently.

"I know only one song. I learned it a long time ago when I was in the army . . ."

"Never mind. Sing!"

"But . . ."

"But what?"

"The song is . . . impure."

"What of it? Since when are we to be afraid of a song? You, sing. The rest remains to me."

Fearfully, the old man began to sing the only song he remembered, a barracks-room drinking song, vulgar, obscene, and blasphemous.

202

"Good, good!" the Rebbe encouraged him. "Go on! Don't stop. Above all, don't stop! There's nothing to fear."

The singer's voice became firmer. At first he had stumbled over every impure expression, over every shady word. Now, encouraged by the Rebbe he sang with abandon. Once more he became a soldier of the Austro-Hungarian army, going to die for His Imperial Majesty. Soon other *hasidim* joined him and then others, and more, until at the end all the multitude took up the song. An army on the march. They sang the music without words. The words didn't matter. The soul has no need of words to sing. The Rebbe glowed with pride and happiness. He had accomplished a miracle.

Gregor ceased to struggle. He looked on, listened, and opened himself. The song went through him and transported him far away, to the place where he, who had been killed by the god of war, was awaiting him. So miracles existed.

The crowd was possessed by joy, a pure joy that every moment made richer, dense and bright. The voices had long ceased to sing; the song was carried now on its own wings, raising breasts, lighting faces, summoning ecstasy, and giving hearts faith. Gregor's lips moved, wishing to sing, to taste joy, to declare that it is man's ally and not his mirage. He was about to give himself over completely to the delirium, to cross the threshold, when he heard a laugh, alien, yet familiar. He paled. Cautiously he turned his head and scrutinized the perspiring faces. It was then that he saw him.

He was a man of indeterminate age, tall, thin, and bearded, with a mocking smile beneath his mustache. Gregor said to himself: No, it's impossible; my memory's tricking me. Then he worked his way through the crowd to a place where he could examine him more closely. Yes, it was he. Gregor felt the darkness descending upon him. He shut his eyes and did not open them for a long time; he dared not move his legs or awaken his thoughts for fear of breaking an invisible balance. The moment was too full. It reopened wounds he thought were now no more than scars, even if time had not healed them. All the surprises and anxieties of his childhood and of recent years welled up and took his breath away.

His body was dripping with perspiration, but he didn't notice. Suddenly he seemed to hear a thousand beasts shrieking in the middle of a forest. The song melted and was lost, the Rebbe went away; perhaps he, too, was pursuing an image, an echo which called out to him across time. The crowd was reduced to a single man, and the words to a single laugh, which floated in the air like a dying bird.

The Rebbe was right; he must come back. A chance meeting can change the whole world and bring all things into question. Nothing exists purely on its own; past and future can be conceived only as a function of the present, a present which constantly expands and exceeds itself. The simple look of man in a crowd is enough to force a new beginning. The Rebbe was right; he had to come back.

"Gavriel," Gregor murmured painfully, still staring.

The man did not see or hear him. He was observing the Rebbe, who seemed exhausted by victory. And he was observing him with a defiant air.

"You're alive!" said Gregor, fighting back his tears. "I won't ask how you managed to survive; I don't really want to know, at least not until later. I only want to know if you're Gavriel and if you've kept my name."

Nothing that Gregor said had any effect. The man seemed to be beyond him. But he continued hopefully, "I'm your friend, Gregor! Have you forgotten? You saved my life at the risk of your own; you taught me the value of silence, of laughter. Don't you remember?"

The last question, asked with increasing insistence, received no more answer than the rest. Gregor began to think that he was mistaken. Gavriel was still dead, and the stranger only looked like him, that was all. But he kept on speaking to him as if he were his friend. Perhaps he couldn't hear him, for the words never really left Gregor's lips. I think I'm speaking, but perhaps I'm not. Perhaps all this time it's been an error: I've been moving my lips but saying nothing.

"Gavriel, are you listening?"

The man had eyes only for the Rebbe, who sat with his elbows on the table, waiting with a mixture of hope and regret for the end of the night. Panic-stricken, Gregor threw himself upon the stranger and assaulted him with questions. He must answer. But he doesn't hear me. Gregor felt dizzy. Perhaps his tongue has been cut out. That would explain everything. To his surprise the idea pleased him. I'm glad his tongue has been cut out. The celebration will soon be over and I'll be alone with him. I'll tell him the sequel to our adventure; how *I* managed to survive. I'll talk about Leib and Yehuda and Maria. And Clara. To him I can speak without constraint or deception. And he won't pass judgment upon me. Fortunately, Gregor thought, the power of speech has been taken from him. All friends should be such friends as to have their tongues cut out. Save the world by killing the word. That's the solution! But then we are afraid of silence.

"Gavriel, listen! You are mute, I ask you only to listen. Listen to what I've learned. It was all a mistake. We thought the tragedy was that the possible was impossible. The impossible is possible. That's the tragedy."

Mockingly, the stranger continued to stare at the Rebbe, who had just given the signal that the gathering was to end. The crowd awakened out of song into a tired silence. The *hasidim* had a haggard look, as if they were oscillating between two realities. Now they must return to the monotonous everyday; the festivities were over. The Rebbe went toward the door, while they pressed back to clear the way. He walked lithely, looking neither to the right nor to the left, greeting no one. An invisible shield protected him from the crowd's curiosity. A few long steps, and he was outside. The faithful closed ranks and rushed after him, so as not be left without his presence. In a moment the empty room took on a lugubrious air. Of the joy which an hour before seemed great enough to move mountains, nothing remained. Where was Mendel? Gone. Gregor should have followed him and said, "Between you and Gavriel it is you whom I have chosen. You listen."

As after a night of debauchery, his tongue was thick and bitter, his body heavy and uncomfortable. Now he was alone with the stranger, who was still staring, with an enigmatic smile, at the place where the Rebbe had sat.

"Gavriel," Gregor said painfully, "give me back what I gave you. I'm alone and leading a false life. I want to change, to become again what I was. Give me back my name."

205

At last the stranger was aware of his presence. But it was impossible to say whether or not he recognized him. He seemed irritated, and Gregor wanted to ask him whether he liked surprises or whether he considered himself above them. Gavriel scowled and his expression grew hard.

"Who are you?" he asked.

"I'm called Gregor."

"That's not a Jewish name."

"I know. I had a Jewish name once, but I gave it to a friend. He hasn't returned it yet."

"This friend didn't have a name of his own?"

"No."

There was a shadow of cruelty in the stranger's smile. "That's an extraordinary story."

"My friend was an extraordinary person."

"Haven't you been drinking? Aren't you drunk?"

"I haven't been drinking."

"You didn't say *Lehaim* to the Rebbe?"

"No."

"And he didn't say *Lehaim* to you?"

"No."

"So you're drunk without drinking and the Rebbe has been drinking without becoming drunk."

"I'm not drunk."

"Then why not? By what right didn't you get drunk? For whose sake and for what reason have you kept aloof? In order to spy on the Rebbe and his disciples?"

"You're wrong. I didn't come here for that."

The man scrutinized him in silence and decided to put him to a test. "Never mind. There's something else I want to know. You're the only one who saw the Rebbe as he is and not as the idol which these blind men have made of him. Tell me, whom is he imitating?"

"Wise men say that man has power to imitate anyone under the sun: a shoemaker, a king, a clown but not a Rebbe. Whoever imitates him becomes him."

"And you? Whom are you imitating?"

Gregor gave way. The game was unfair; Gavriel was too strong. How could he find the right word, the right tone of voice? "Gavriel, Gavriel," he murmured. At the same time a small voice inside him whispered: Be careful! If you faint, you're done for. He'll go away, and you with him; you'll disappear without leaving a trace. Beware! If you cry, you won't be able to stop, and neither will he. Gavriel, Gavriel! The stranger maintained a rigid posture, like that of a judge.

"You won't answer?" he said.

Gregor dropped his arms in exhaustion: Gavriel, Gavriel.

"You're pale and tired," the stranger said more softly. "Go home and go to bed."

"No, no!" Gregor protested. "First I want to speak and have you listen and judge me. I was looking not for a friend, but for a judge, a judge who can listen."

Gregor let himself fall onto a bench, his head dropping to his chest wearily. Then the stranger began to question him. Where had he come from? From what country? From what town? From what past? He probed into every detail: what he feared? what obsessed him? what made him feel guilty? and what had he done to atone? Did he believe in God? Did he consider his body an enemy to be served or to be overcome? Docile, Gregor replied in monosyllables, in short sentences. When a friend denies you, the separation's worse than that caused by the death of your father. If a friend abandons you, it means that you are dead in him as he is dead in you. No more Gavriel. No more Gregor. The stranger's voice became more and more persistent, leaving him no way of escape. Gregor was caught in the wheels; he could neither hide nor withdraw; he had no choice but to explain, to justify himself as if he were responsible for what had happened and for what had not happened to him.

Doubts overcame him, and he felt himself to be on uncertain ground. Yes, he had been mistaken. The true Gavriel would have been glad to see him, would have fallen on his shoulder and wept with joy. Gavriel was harsh not toward others but toward himself. Gregor ceased to understand anything. He should have gotten up and said: Forgive me, sir, I have nothing to say; I mistook you for someone who would reject change; pardon my error. Come, Gregor, get up and go. Get up and say a polite goodbye and let the night finish by itself. Clara is waiting, she has not gone to bed or even moved from the table; she is waiting for the door to open. But neither his will nor his legs would obey. The stranger had taken over both his strength and his weakness; he had made Gregor into his slave, victim, memory. He compelled him not only to reply, but to want to reply as well. Gregor's head spun, spun, spun, in the opposite direction from that of the earth, which was spinning, spinning, spinning as well. Suddenly he thought of his father, who never made fun of anyone, and of Clara, who must surely be worried; she had been for weeks past. Yes, he had been mistaken. This man who resembled Gavriel and now strangely recalled his father was neither. He was nobody, and for this very reason Gregor had to justify himself for being alive instead of buried beneath the ruins.

A few late shadows dispelled by the sun, as it rose from the misty horizon of the city, stole up uneasily beside a window, looking for some place to hide from the enemy light. They remained there, fragile and innocent, then fell with infinite grace, one after the other, onto the snowy ground.

"I don't know what you want with me," said Gavriel, half teasing, half cruel. "I understand nothing of all your stories."

"Then why do you listen?"

"I like stories."

"You've changed. You used to live them, by giving them your breath, your solitude, out of which they made love and prayer. Now you are content to listen."

"Doesn't listening to a story mean living it as well?"

"So you are Gavriel?" said Gregor before this hint of a confession.

"I?" said the stranger.

"Yes, you."

"How can I be Gavriel, when you say that name is yours? To hear you, it seems as if you wanted to give the name of Gavriel to everyone on earth. That's going a bit too far."

Gregor was disconcerted. Yet there was in this man's voice an echo, a familiar vibration which bore common memories. How could he make sure?

"I have a favor to ask you," he said. "Will you grant it?"

"A favor? What?

"I'd want to hear you laugh."

"What?"

"You heard me. I'm asking you to laugh."

"You must be mad."

"That's possible."

"Then laugh yourself."

"I don't know how."

The stranger ran his fingers through his beard and stroked his chin uncertainly. "What you ask troubles me," he said at last. "What have you said that's funny? How do you know that I like to laugh? And that I can be heard laughing?"

"Do you refuse, then?"

"Of course! How can you expect me to laugh, for no good reason. It's ridiculous, after hasidic song, that I should laugh for someone who tells me insane stories."

"All right," said Gregor, with a discouraged sigh. "You win. I'll be quiet. I have nothing more to say."

"Oh!" the stranger protested. "I told you that I like stories."

Gregor knew that he had no choice but to obey. He continued the story of his life where he had broken off.

"You had just come out of the cave," the stranger reminded him. "What happened next?"

The adventures in Maria's village, the encounter with Petruskanu, the miraculous escape, Gregor described in detail his meetings with Janos, the interrogation by his comrades in the forest, the unexpected intervention of Clara, and the death of Yehuda. Gavriel seemed to take a particular interest in the last.

"You like Yehuda?" Gregor asked him.

"He died as a conqueror; that's why I love him."

"If you love him, then you are Gavriel."

"I love Gavriel, too. Doesn't that prove that I'm not he?" The stranger lowered his voice. "Who knows? I might be Yehuda, mightn't I?"

Gregor glowered at him. He wanted to be angry at this man, even to hate him. Yehuda was dead. He hadn't played games. And Gavriel? Was he alive or not? One certainty, one alone, no matter which, would be enough.

"You're not Yehuda," he said.

"How do you know?"

"Yehuda is dead. We said the *Kaddish* for him."

"That proves that he's dead for you, in you, that's all."

"We killed on his behalf," said Gregor throwing his head back. "We avenged him."

"That still proves nothing. How do you know that you did the right thing? Did Yehuda say so?"

"Since he was dead." Gregor was choking. He knew that the stranger was wrong, but how was he to purge him of his error? At the same time he knew that the stranger wasn't wrong, either. But what exactly was his error and his truth?

"It's not a question of Yehuda," he said. "It's a question of Gavriel. If you're he, I know what I have to do."

"You're tiresome with this Gavriel of yours," said the stranger impatiently. What's this obsession of yours? Are you sure that he really existed?"

Gregor was no longer sure of anything. He didn't even know whether the stranger was irritated or not. Probably he was just pretending. The stranger knew his weaknesses and where to strike.

"You may be right," he said. "Perhaps Gavriel never did exist. Or I myself either. And you? Yes, you exist; you've existed forever."

The stranger crossed his arms on his chest; he didn't laugh, but it was clear that he wanted to.

"In that case," he said ironically, "go on! I'm listening."

"I have no more to say," said Gregor with a feeling of humiliation. "Let me go away."

But he knew that the battle was lost; the judge wouldn't release him.

"Go away? Nonsense! You stay," he ordered him. "To the very end. And you must go on with your story."

"But why? Why?" Gavriel asked with a sudden burst of energy.

"You don't understand. It's so simple. Your uncertainties are what interest me. So . . . where were we? I'm listening."

Gregor began to tell him about Clara.

2

Clara's sickly pallor, her poignant, distant smile. I was talking but she wasn't listening. She was listening to someone, but not to me. I, too, heard the person to whom she was listening. I was able to keep him quiet; she wasn't.

"You're mad," Clara murmured, "completely mad. Be good and go away. Leave me alone. We'd do better not to see each other, ever."

"I'm mad," I said, "and I love you. I'll never leave you again."

It was a beautiful day, and I was aware of it. I saw everything that was going on around me, and yet I saw only the young girl walking aimlessly, as if in a dream, at my side. Passers-by were greeting one another and smiling; everything was for sale and everything could be bought. The city was opening up in the sunshine of the first post-war spring. Here and there a couple stopped to embrace, and I envied their joy; farther on others embraced without stopping and I envied their carefree ability to walk on and not to stumble.

We had been walking for hours. Borne by the vast human tide that was sweeping over Paris we had met, by sheer chance, in the Latin Quarter. We had both been living there for months, neither of us aware of the presence of the other. Like myself, Clara had refused to go back to the country of her birth, peopled with ghosts and murderers. Like myself, she wanted to go as far away as possible, under a different sky, a different name, a different skin, to become somebody new. Europe was an insatiable and corrupt monster, which for centuries had fed its pretensions upon innocent blood, and we wanted none of it.

"Leib will be happy to see you," she said, biting her lip.

I stifled a cry of horror. I knew that Leib hadn't come back.

"I know what you're thinking," she added. "You think he's dead. He is dead to the rest of the world, but for me he is alive and I love him."

She told me she thought of him throughout the day, and especially at night. She saw him in flesh and blood, more alive than the living. What was I to do? She loved him. More than ever.

"If you like, we can be friends," she proposed dreamily. You can tell me your adventures, real or imaginary, and I can tell you about my life with Leib. We're adults and free, aren't we?"

"No, Clara, we aren't."

Feverishly I began to talk, talk, talk, making alternate threats and supplications, but she would not give in.

"You risk destroying everything. Isn't it better to hold on to the little we have? You're mad, Gregor; you don't know to what you're exposing yourself. If we married, the day after next day, no, the very same night, I'd betray you with Leib."

"Leib is dead."

"I'd betray you with a dead man. If you come between us and take me away from him, he'll hate you. You don't want him to be your enemy, do you?"

"I'm not afraid of the dead."

"And me, aren't you afraid of me? I'd hate you, too. I'd consider you guilty of his death. Because if he weren't dead, you wouldn't be with me."

A silence followed. Another crossroad. Afterwards things wouldn't be the same. There was no turning back; I must choose a path, good or bad, and move forward.

"Listen," I said. "I'm not going to say that I'd die without you, that without you I'd never know happiness or joy; I would say only that without you my life would be empty and my desires unfulfilled. The difference between us is this: you are content to call the weakness of man human; I go further and say, true, but we can never succumb to it. My ambition isn't to define myself by victory or defeat, but by my determination to return to the source. Often I feel pain just as you do. But I work to tame and disarm my suffering, whereas you give in to yours and often summon it. Both attitudes are human, but one is a link to strength and life, the other the resignation, to death."

I waited for her reaction, but there was none. Neither yes nor no, neither joy nor refusal. Nothing. Were my efforts wasted? Perhaps, but I had to go on.

"Let's leave the graveyard, Clara. Let's try to walk together. I know how to sing, and listen, and wait. I offer you my song and silence and my hand."

I paused. Tears were streaming down her face. She shook herself and said, "Forgive me. I took you for Leib. We used to go for long walks, and with him I discovered the world: the sun setting over the mountains, the desolation of an old drunken woman sitting on the curbstone, the calm demeanor of a pious Jew on his way to synagogue. You were talking, and I heard Leib. I thought I was dead, and with him again, that we were ghosts walking and remembering."

She took a handkerchief out of a pocket and dried her tears before going on.

"I could marry you, love you, live with you, for you. On one condition; that you become Leib. You want that?"

This time I couldn't control myself.

"No!" I said loudly. "I refuse."

"I'm sorry," she said, a note of sadness in her voice.

It had begun to rain out of the sunshine, but we went on walking. Before long, like a luminous cloud, twilight detached itself from the horizon and descended upon the city. The future, impatient, seemed to be coming to meet us. I felt overpowered by fatigue, and for a long time we said nothing. Time slipped through us, passed us. The streets emptied, and a clock rang out first eleven and then twelve times. Two police-

men on bicycles came around a corner, pretending not to no-
tice us. The city slept, calm and serene. Somewhere a man
was telling his wife that life is worth living. Somewhere a man
looked at his wife and told her that their hell would endure
forever. I glanced at Clara. Was everything over?

"I'm sorry," she said, continuing where she had stopped
hours before. "I'm sorry you're so stubborn. I could teach
you to smile his smile, to look at me the way he did. I'd
show you everything. At night, before you took me, you could
tell me a story, and in the morning I wouldn't let you go.
Why do you say no?"

I knew I had lost, and I was sorry to have spoken, or even
to have come to Paris. A buzzing sound spread through my
whole body. We have rediscovered each other only in order to
part. Perhaps, I've been too hasty. I should have waited a few
days, a few weeks to prepare her. Too late.

"I refuse because I'm alive," I shouted. "And because I love
you. Because I want to save you!"

"I'm sorry."

I wanted to take her by the shoulders and shake her, even if
it meant that I'd never see her again. Sadness and anger over-
whelmed me. What was I to do? Give her up? Leave her to
go on alone with Leib?

"Leib is dead and he was my friend," I said gently. "That
doesn't make me love death. You must know this, Clara: death
deceives, it lies. It takes everything and gives nothing; it keeps
none of its promises. And you must know this as well: there is
more of eternity in the instant which unites two people than in
the memory of God, more peace in a gaze into a beloved's
heart than in the kingdom of heaven. How to discover this
instant, to recognize this gaze, that's the problem, I agree. It
requires patience, much abandon. I wish you such abandon,
such patience."

I talked for another hour, two hours, as we walked along.
The exhausted city barely breathed as it lowered its eyelids for
the last time before opening them upon a new day. Some-
where a man looked at his sleeping wife and smiled: rest,
love, peace, close the door on all demons so that we may live;
wake up, I want you. Two embracing bodies; mystery dwells in

their union; it is enough that a man and woman give themselves to each other for God to confer his powers upon them and for the world to be brought once more out of chaos. Somewhere a man is looking with hatred and bitterness at his wife's tormented face; another night without sleep, without oblivion. God, my God, why have you forsaken me?

Soon after, they were married. It was a rainy day, and the Rabbi said, "That's a good sign."

3

The first nights together, the first troubled awakenings, the efforts to fill empty moments, dragging hours, and heavy, hostile silences. They were playing a game: I love you, you love me; we'll have children who will not be killed either by love or by hate; they will conquer the desert and not be humiliated by their conquest. They had no child.

Gregor lived in a state of anguish or the fear of anguish. When Clara spoke to him, he never knew exactly to whom she was speaking, and neither did she. He took her in his arms, held her tight, and told her that all would be well, that love would shield them. But in the midst of a passionate embrace she was transfigured, her eyes wandered and she became another woman; she had rejoined her lover. "Come back!" cried her husband despairingly; "I'm here." But she was elsewhere, too far away.

Months went by and there was no change. One day was like another and every night like the night before. Gregor was physically mortified, but he did not show it. Will she ever love me? She did love him, but only when she took him for Leib. Eventually this name froze him. "I'm not Leib," he said, freeing himself from her embrace; "Leib is dead." "I know that, my love, Leib is dead and I'm making love to a dead man." But determined to win the battle, Gregor held fast. To cure his wife and free her; nothing else mattered.

"How do you manage to hold out?" she would ask him.

"The secret is patience. Most men exclude waiting from their lives, and that's their misfortune. In their hurry to set out, to arrive, to succeed, they run too fast, reach their destination too soon, and either abandon their dream or are abandoned by it. In the East they will tell you that the man who can control his breathing and his will forges a key to the kingdom. Immortality is the prize of those who are long-winded."

Gregor got a job with a newspaper. They went abroad, to North Africa, the Far East, and finally to the United States, where they settled indefinitely. The sages claim that a change of place means a change of star, but Clara proved the contrary. Her condition worsened; she cried in her sleep and perpetually sought to seduce her lover. As if whipped by fever, she raved and called to him. In the morning she sobbed disconsolately, and when he went out, solitude weighed upon her. She opened her eyes upon her husband and failed to recognize him. No longer was she the beautiful and fresh young girl whom Gregor had known in the forest.

"You're leaving her?" Gavriel asked. "She needs you and you've decided to go away; is that it?"

Yes, that was it. He could no longer live a lie. He didn't have his former strength, his former power of resistance.

"I don't want to hate her," he said. "It would be better to die, better to lose my memory."

"No solution. You've forgotten your eyes. Clara would read the truth in them. You must get rid of them, too. And your hands; Clara understands gestures."

Gregor gave way, defeated.

"You're making fun of me. You saved my life only to turn it to ridicule. You called yourself my friend only to show me that friendship doesn't exist, that it can't survive the years. You spoke of the Messiah only to extinguish the light of his face."

There were tears in his voice as he continued, "Why did you do it? Tell me Gavriel, why are you so set against me, against us? What are you getting at, what do you want to prove?"

There was a look of amusement on Gavriel's face. Now I

could hate her, Gregor said to himself. He started to leave, but Gavriel restrained him.

"Let me go," said Gregor.

"Not yet. You haven't finished."

"What more do you want to hear?"

"Everything."

"I've told you everything, the beginning and the end."

"The list of your defeats, is that it?"

Gregor did not reply.

"Never mind," said Gavriel, "Go on. I don't like victories."

Gregor realized that he no longer loved Clara the day when his eyes met those of a young woman sitting across from him on a subway train. Their glance lasted only a minute. He did not notice the shape of her neck or the color of her hair. He saw only her look, the depth of which made him dizzy; he entered and lost himself, but only for an instant. Then he took her hand and told her to follow him and lose her fear of the night. In the course of that irrevocable second, so physically real that it was painful, they decided to join their hopes and regrets, forget all about them, suffer from them; then, at the approach of death they swore to forego eternity if it meant separation. The train stopped at a station, and although the woman remained seated, lost in her own dream, Gregor turned his head away. He breathed deeply and as hard as he could, in order to recover his balance, to throw off the enormous weight that was crushing his heart.

He never saw her again, but her look haunted him, day and night, like the mirage of a fire that deludes the traveler searching for a woodland cabin. He did not know her name and would never learn it; he did not know whether she was beautiful, serene, or haughty; whether she was capable of choosing to be free, of throwing everything into the balance and starting out on an untried path. Of all these things he had no idea, but he knew that he could have loved her. And that somewhere a crucial error had been committed. He had opened a door which perhaps was not his.

He knew as well that in two persons' common existence a rigid situation can only degenerate. Their love can increase or decrease, but it cannot stand still. When love ceases to grow it changes direction and sooner or later it enters the magnetic field of hate, for anything is better than the dryness of the desert. Gregor felt all this coming upon him and could not sleep. Man is not an angel; his paradise and his hell are mingled, like the roads that lead to them. It is not by doing something else that he can obtain access to either one. He cannot do anything else.

He can do nothing, and Gregor knew it. He dreaded the day when, submitting to lies and constraint, he would regard the girl he had tried to save as an enemy. Knowing that now he was open to all the appeals which cross and compose the adventure of a soul, of a hope, he would have given anything to stay faithful to his image of himself; better to explode than to resign himself. Anything and everything rather than give in to decrepitude. Everything? Yes, everything. But everything is only a word, and words are no dam. Hate strikes a man dumb.

He had already thought several times of breaking with Clara and going away, of leaving before the final test, the certainty, of making off with his secret doubt. In the morning, when he set out for the newspaper and in the evening, just before he put the key in the lock, this thought recurred to him and made his heart pound. A practical and necessary solution, a clean break, a preventive blood-letting, an infliction of pain before the pain grew. The silences between them were increasing. You feel well? Yes, thanks; and you? Are you hungry, thirsty? I'm tired. So am I. Did you have a good sleep? I did too. They avoided looking at each other in order not to see themselves as the giver and recipient of suffering. What had happened? Nothing? How, then, had things come to this? Outwardly nothing had changed and yet everything was different. Whatever had made Clara beautiful before now made her ugly. Her gestures, which had once aroused wonder, now brought irritation. When would the wounded begin to scream? He must leave first. Clara would understand; Clara was intelligent; Clara was generous. If he had said: I must disappear, I don't know where or for how long, she would have smiled courageously and given her approval: Go, and take my blessing with you; come back whenever you feel the need; I'll be waiting. That's what's always said. Then one day she would stop waiting and suffering and even remembering. She would love another man and tell him: I only thought I was in love before; don't hold it against me. I found out afterwards that it wasn't real.

But Gregor stayed on, in order to spare her from suffering that evening, the next morning, the following day. So that she wouldn't stay sitting at the table with her empty, reddened eyes staring at the door that did not open, that would never open again. To say that all wounds are healed by time is to evade the question: man cannot substitute himself for time. He cannot substitute himself for anything. Guilt is defined in relation to the immediate present, not as a function to eternity.

He would stay. And just as he did not know why he had decided the previous evening to go away, so now he did not know why he was reversing his decision. Gavriel could explain, but he was silent and would not even laugh. Where was he?

"Speak, Gavriel! Laugh! I want to hear your voice, to have it trace the boundary between you and me, to confirm the fact that I didn't imagine your past or betray my own."

Gavriel showed no emotion; he merely listened, and Gregor felt sad. He knew that once again he was going home, where he would find Clara uneasily staring at the door, her face hollowed by waiting. Where were you? I have been walking.

Outside it was no longer snowing and dawn had come. Men changed kingdoms and kings. Gregor wanted to detain Gavriel, but he knew that this could not be, he wanted to make him speak, but to no avail. Never again would he hear Gavriel's voice, his laugh, his questions. The judge would leave before pronouncing sentence. Gregor wanted to protest. Against whom, against what? A judge can't be judged.

I've grown, Gregor thought, I'm older. Gavriel, do you remember the cave, the forest, the war? Are you troubled by the same nostalgia as I am? You look at me and I don't know whether or not you understand. I don't know whether you're even looking, much less whether you're looking at me.

It was different in the forest, Gavriel. The forest meditates;

it listens to voices instead of stifling them. The forest has ears, a heart, and a soul. In the forest simplicity is possible; simplicity belongs there. And unity, too. There liberty isn't forced on you like a straitjacket. I am what I choose to be; I am in my choice, in my will to choose. There is no divorce between self and its image, between being and acting. I am the act, the image, one and indivisible. Outside, things are too complicated; too many roads are open, too many voices call and your own is so easily lost. The self crumbles. To choose one direction means to refuse and condemn others. They had an easy task, those righteous, just men who took refuge in the forest and learned the language of trees, birds, clouds. Nothing is easier than to live in a cloistered universe where I am alone with God alone, against God. They paid with blood and tears for their right to solitude and peace, but at least the blood and tears were their own. We aren't so lucky. The man that chooses solitude and its riches is on the side of those who are against man, who pay with the blood and tears of others. Anyone who describes the future as virgin is mistaken; for it is mortgaged from the first day, from the first cry.

4

Gregor fell silent, with the feeling that someone was watching him. He rubbed his eyes. He had talked too much: His throat and chest ached and his head was heavy with echoes. From far away he heard an unknown or forgotten voice. He saw a child standing in front of him. A pupil of the Yeshiva, with black earlocks and clipped hair framing his pale but luminous face. He was observing Gregor with a slightly mocking air.

"What makes you laugh?"

"You," said the boy nonchalantly.

"Explain."

"Looking at you I say to myself: there's a foolish man. He has the luck to pass a whole night under the Rabbi's roof, and how does he use it? To sleep, to dream, to waste it. In the Yeshiva we spend our sleepless nights in study and prayer and meditation. That's why you make me laugh. You're not offended, are you?"

"Not at all. When I was young I did the same as you."

Gregor looked about the empty, disorderly hall. Where was Gavriel? Gone.

"Who are you?" he asked the boy. "What are you doing here so early in the morning?"

"I already told you," said the boy, shrugging his shoulders. "I belong to the Yeshiva, upstairs."

What about Gavriel? The boy had not seen anyone go away. He must have disappeared into the morning air.

"Have you been down here long?"

"That depends. What do you mean by long?"

"A couple of hours."

"Well, what is long for you may not be long for me. For me a minute is long."

Gregor studied the boy and asked, "Have you seen anyone but myself in this room?"

"When?"

"This morning."

"No. There was a whole crowd last night, though."

"I know that."

To whom had he been talking? To a stranger who had borrowed the features of Gavriel?

"We need a tenth man for the *Minyan,* the morning prayer," said the boy. "Someone has a *Yahrzeit* today. Come with me."

Gregor got up with difficulty; he was stiff.

"I'll come," he said.

As they left the room he thought of his father. The anniversary of his death: when was it? Not today. He had learned that it had been the eighteenth of the month of *Shevat.* Buchenwald. At three o'clock in the morning of that day he died. On the wooden bed, where he had agonized his last, calling on the name of God, perhaps even to bless it there lay a body of sorts, but it had no likeness to what he had been. The ravaged face, covered with ashes, was no longer his own. There was a time, in Europe, when Jews were forbidden to possess a body.

Usually Gregor kept this anniversary by taking refuge in memory. He went to synagogue, lit two candles, and prayed that the soul of his father might rise higher and higher in order to tell its story to Abraham, Isaac, and Jacob: Here is what happened and how; you must reveal to me why. As a good son, he studied alone, or in the company of a congregation, a chapter of the *Mishnah,* then recited the *Kaddish,* by which he proclaimed to anyone willing to hear that great and terrible is the God of the Jews, that his ways are righteous and impenetrable, that he has the right to hide himself, to change face and sides, that he who gives life and light may also take them away.

"Are you coming?" said the boy impatiently.

For the last time Gregor tried to tear himself free. No, he wouldn't go away, far away to a place where the dead are silent and no longer think of vengeance. In his thoughts he was already there. But someone—it could have been his father, or Gavriel, or Leib, or the boy from the Yeshiva—was bringing him back. And this someone was saying: "Do you know why God demands that you love him? He doesn't need your love, he can do without it, but you can't." "So God doesn't love us?" "Yes and no, it doesn't matter." "It's not a question of him but of yourself. Your love, rather than his, can save you."

"Are you coming? You move like a sleepwalker."

"So be it," said Gregor to himself. "Let's pretend that today is the anniversary of the death of my father, who will never die. I shall pray. Thy will be done. I shall proclaim your glory. You always win and I'm sorry for you."

The boy led him to the synagogue, a small overheated room on the second floor. It seemed to Gregor as if every step took him back to the past; soon he would enter the synagogue of the Borsher Rebbe and find waiting for him the child that he had once been. He shook himself to get rid of the sensation of cold that clung to his skin. The Borsher Rebbe was dead and the old synagogue and his childhood buried under its ashes. He would pray for the soul of his father and for that of the Borsher Rebbe and for his lost childhood. And for the soul of God.

"What's your name?" asked the boy.

"Gregor." He blushed and corrected himself: "Gavriel. Gavriel's my name. Gregor isn't a Jewish name, you know that."

The boy asked if he had his phylacteries with him. No, he didn't. He did not say that he hadn't carried them for years.

"Don't worry; I'll give you another pair." And as if guessing Gregor's thoughts, he added: "You can take them with you if you want."

"I want to."

Clara will be astonished. "What?" she'll say. "You're going back to religion?"

Clara, Gregor said to himself, and his heart leaped up. She must be saying: He's gone; he'll never be back. No, Clara; I'm not going; I've decided not to go. Wait for me; I'll be back. After prayers, after the *Kaddish*. Let's resume the struggle. What I hoped to achieve with you, I must achieve with myself. It's better to sleep on the trodden ground, if the ground is real, than to chase mirages. It's up to us to see to it that the earth itself is not a mirage.

He prayed in a low voice. The *Tefillin* were wound around his left arm. As soon as the prayers were over he would take the road home, the road of solid ground. He would say to his wife, "Sit down; I want to talk to you." He would not spare her. "Know then that all of us have our ghosts," he would say. "They come and go at will, breaking open doors, never shutting them tight; they bear different names. We mustn't let ourselves be seduced by their promises." He would tell her about meeting Gavriel. "Yes, Clara," he would say, "they'll continue to haunt us, but we must fight them. It will be a bitter, austere, obstinate battle. The struggle to survive will begin here, in this room, where we are sitting. Whether or not the Messiah comes doesn't matter; we'll manage without him. It is because it is too late that we are commanded to hope. We shall be honest and humble and strong, and then he will come, he will come every day, thousands of times every day. He will have no face, because he will have a thousand faces. The Messiah isn't one man, Clara, he's all men. As long as there are men there will be a Messiah. One day you'll sing, and he will sing in you. Then for the last time, I'll want to cry. I shall cry. Without shame."

At the appropriate moments Gregor recited the *Kaddish,* that solemn affirmation, filled with grandeur and serenity, by which man returns God his crown and his scepter. He recited it slowly, concentrating on every sentence, every word, every syllable of praise. His voice trembled, timid, like that of the orphan suddenly made aware of the relationship between death and eternity, between eternity and the word.

He prayed for the soul of his father and also for that of God. He prayed for the soul of his childhood and, above all, for the soul of his old comrade, Leib the Lion, who, during his life, had incarnated what is immortal in man. The last *Kaddish* would be for him, to ask that the warrior find peace; that the angels, jealous of his strength and, above all, of his purity, cease to persecute him, that he himself cease to cause suffering to those who once loved him and still love him. Yes, the last *Kaddish* would be for him, our messenger to heaven.